AN EYE FOR AN EYE

"Where is the rest of the gang?" Guthrie asked, leaning over the dying man. "Tell us where they are, an' I'll let you have this pistol to put yourself outta your misery." He turned his attention to Smoke. "Smoke, you're a mountain man, what do you think will get him first, the buzzards or the wolves?"

Smoke scratched his chin. "With that much blood around, I'd bet on the wolves. Course," he added, "the buzzards'll finish up what the wolves leave."

"All right, damn you," the dying man said. "They're holed up at a ranch 'bout ten miles south of here."

Smoke looked up, judging the distance and direction. "That must be the Sanders ranch." He leaned over and stared into the man's pain-filled eyes. "What happened to Mr. and Mrs. Sanders?" he asked.

"Whatta you think? "Now, give me that pistol."

As Guthrie started to hand the gun to the man, Smoke reached out and took it from him. He squatted down, holding the gun just out of the man's reach. "Joel and Bertha Sanders were sixty years old, you scum. They were worth more than all of you bastards put together." Smoke pitched the pistol off to the side. "When you get to hell, mister, tell the devil to keep the door open, 'cause your friends are gonna be coming soon."

The dying man's eyes opened wide when he saw Smoke throw the gun away. "But, you promised . . ."

"So sue me," Smoke said and stood up. "Come on. I know a short cut to the Sanders's place. Maybe we can catch them while they're still there."

"What about these bodies?" Jed asked, looking around at the dead men scattered everywhere. "Shouldn't we bury them or something?"

"To hell with them," Smoke said. "Wolves got to eat, same as worms."

BOOK YOUR PLACE ON OUR WEBSITE AND MAKE THE READING CONNECTION!

We've created a customized website just for our very special readers, where you can get the inside scoop on everything that's going on with Zebra, Pinnacle and Kensington books.

When you come online, you'll have the exciting opportunity to:

- View covers of upcoming books

- Read sample chapters

- Learn about our future publishing schedule (listed by publication month *and author*)

- Find out when your favorite authors will be visiting a city near you

- Search for and order backlist books from our online catalog

- Check out author bios and background information

- Send e-mail to your favorite authors

- Meet the Kensington staff online

- Join us in weekly chats with authors, readers and other guests

- Get writing guidelines

- AND MUCH MORE!

**Visit our website at
http://www.pinnaclebooks.com**

VALOR OF THE
MOUNTAIN MAN

William W. Johnstone

PINNACLE BOOKS
Kensington Publishing Corp.

http://www.pinnaclebooks.com

PINNACLE BOOKS are published by

Kensington Publishing Corp.
850 Third Avenue
New York, NY 10022

All Kensington Titles, Imprints, and Distributed Lines are available at special quantity discounts for bulk purchases for sales promotions, premiums, fund-raising, and educational or institutional use. Special book excerpts or customized printings can also be created to fit specific needs. For details, write or phone the office of the Kensington special sales manager: Kensington Publishing Corp., 850 Third Avenue, New York, NY 10022, attn: Special Sales Department, Phone: 1-800-221-2647.

Pinnacle and the P logo Reg. U.S. Pat. & TM Off.

First Printing: July 2001
10 9 8 7 6 5 4 3 2 1

Printed in the United States of America

One

The territorial prison was an adobe brick building that stood in the middle of 180 acres between 14th East and 21st South in the town of Sugar House in the Utah Territory. Though built to house less than two hundred men, it was already crammed to the breaking point with some of the meanest men west of the Mississippi—from footpads to rapists to bank robbers to murderers, sooner or later they all ended up here.

In Cellhouse No. 1, over thirty men slept on cots in corridors between the cells, eating their meals in three shifts and using buckets for privies since the toilet facilities were so primitive.

The place was barely tolerable in the heat of summer, but now that the fall was upon the region and the nighttime temperatures often fell into the twenties, the situation was almost unbearable.

One of the hardest men in the group of very hard men indeed, Ozark Jack Berlin, leaned over the bucket full of piss and shit and spat out his food. He was a big man, standing three inches over six feet, with muscular shoulders as broad as an ax handle. His face was rough-featured, set under a full head of unruly black hair, with a nose that'd been broken more than once and lips that were thin and cruel.

"This stuff ain't fit for man nor beast!" he groused to the half-breed Modoc Indian sitting on a cot next to his. The Indian had long black hair hanging down over his ears to his collar, and his reddish-bronze skin framed a hooked nose over full lips that he was constantly licking.

Blue Owl looked up from his plate, which was empty except for a small piece of biscuit he was using to sop up the gravy from the maggot-riddled horse meat. "If you no want yours, shove it over here," he growled. "It's better'n buffalo meat any day."

Berlin handed Blue Owl his plate. "I tell ya', Blue Owl, I think it's 'bout time to bust outta this joint."

Blue Owl didn't answer, being busy shoving Berlin's food into his mouth, but he cut his eyes to the side and nodded his agreement.

"I got me an idea how we can do it," said Berlin.

Blue Owl grunted, his eyebrows raised.

"Today's payday for the guards. I figger they'll all head for town soon's they get their money to spend it on whores an' whiskey."

Blue Owl nodded again, his Adam's apple bobbing as he swallowed.

"That'll only leave one man in Cellhouse No. 1, an' a couple more in the other parts of the building. If'n we can get our hands on the guard's gun, we can break into the armory an' steal us some more weapons an' take over the rest of the prison."

Blue Owl burped loudly, wiping his lips with the back of his hand. "Then what, Jack?" he asked. "We gonna walk all the way to Salt Lake City?"

Berlin smiled, shaking his head. "Naw. We'll take the guards' hosses an' the supply wagons they keep around back, and head toward Colorado. They's plenty of sodbusters an' farmers 'tween here an there. We'll just take what we need along the way."

Blue Owl shrugged, flipping his hair out of his face with a thick, meaty finger. "Sounds all right to me. Anyway, it'll beat sittin' here an' waitin' to be hung."

* * *

After the evening meal, prison guard Joe Johnson moved through the cell block, picking up plates and tin cups from the inmates. Following protocol set up by the warden, he wore no weapon while in the company of the criminals he was working with. He was watched by guard Billy Thornton, who was standing outside the bars of the cell block, a .44 Colt in a holster on his hip and an American Arms 12-gauge shotgun cradled in his arms.

It was a ritual they'd played out countless times, and Thornton was bored. He leaned against a wall and covered his mouth with a hand as he yawned. He'd been up most of the night playing poker after his shift the night before, and hadn't slept well when he'd finally crawled into his bed in the morning. As Joe Johnson leaned down to take Berlin's plate from him, Berlin glanced over his shoulder and saw Thornton leaning back against the wall with his eyes closed.

Quick as a flash, Berlin grabbed the back of Johnson's head and hit him in the throat with his closed fist.

Johnson's eyes bulged and his mouth opened as he gulped for air like a fish out of water. As the skin of his face turned blue and he dropped to his knees, his hands at his throat, Berlin turned and called to Thornton.

"Hey, Billy. Somethin's wrong with Joe. He's choking!"

Thornton came to attention, looked into the cell block, and saw his friend Joe on his knees, his face blue and his mouth open and gasping as he jerked wide eyes back and forth.

Thornton quickly grabbed the keys to the cell door off his belt and shoved the bars open. He ran to Joe's side and went down on one knee to see if he could help.

Blue Owl stepped up behind Thornton, put his hands together, and swung them like a club into the back of Thornton's neck.

The guard dropped as if he'd been poleaxed.

Berlin grabbed the shotgun before it could hit the dirt floor of the cell, and Blue Owl slipped the .44 Colt from Thornton's holster as he fell facedown on the ground.

Berlin ran toward the cell door, shouting over his shoulder to one of the men standing there as Johnson finally gasped his last breath, "Grab them keys, boys. We're gettin' outta here!"

Sam Cook, in prison for raping and killing two women, took the keys off the unconscious Thornton's belt and followed Berlin and Blue Owl through the door. Behind him, the other thirty men in the cell block scrambled to their feet and rushed after them.

Berlin slowed to a walk as he rounded the corner in the corridor leading from Cellhouse No. 1. He eared back the hammers on the shotgun and pointed it ahead of him as he walked toward a desk at the end of the corridor.

Bob Colton, head guard, was sitting behind the desk, finishing his supper of fried chicken and mashed potatoes. He looked up, and almost choked on his chicken leg when he saw Ozark Jack Berlin stalking toward him with the double-barreled shotgun aimed at his gullet.

"Howdy, Bob," Berlin said amiably. "How 'bout you take that hogleg outta your holster and put it on the desk there?"

Colton swallowed, and gingerly pulled his pistol out of his holster and placed it on the desk in front of him.

"Don't do nothing stupid, Ozark," he croaked through a suddenly dry throat.

"Stupid would be stayin' here to be hanged, Bob. Now, get to your feet and walk on back into the cell back there, or I'll spread your guts all over the wall."

As Colton walked down the corridor, Berlin called, "Sam, put him in the cell with the others and lock the doors."

Less than thirty minutes later, Berlin, Blue Owl, and the other thirty men were in the prison armory, where they had armed themselves with pistols, shotguns, and rifles, and were stuffing their pockets with boxes of ammunition.

Two other guards who happened upon the group were stripped of their weapons and placed in the cell house with the others.

The prisoners then made their way to the stables, saddled up ten horses, hitched up a couple of teams to two supply wagons, and raced out of the prison gates. The dayshift guards continued to sleep in their barracks, unaware of the prison break.

As the escapees rode down the trail away from the town of Sugar House toward the mountains in the distance, Blue Owl inclined his head toward the men riding in the wagons. "We ain't gonna make much time with them wagons, Ozark. What're we gonna do?"

Berlin shrugged. "There's plenty of farms 'tween here and the high country. We'll just stop along the way and take what horses and supplies we need." He grinned, exposing blackened teeth. "After all, who's gonna stop us?"

Two

Warden Joshua M. Stevens came out of a sound sleep with his heart hammering as someone pounded on his door.

His wife, Sofie, blinked her eyes and stared at him in fear at the harsh sound.

"Josh, what's that noise?" she asked sleepily, rubbing her eyes.

"Go back to bed, dear," he said, climbing out of bed and pulling on a robe. "It's just someone at the door. I'll take care of it."

On the way to answer the door, Stevens paused to pick up a Colt off a dining room sideboard. Being the warden of a prison that housed hundreds of desperados made a man cautious—especially when awakened in the middle of the night.

"Who is it?" Stevens called from behind the closed and locked door, earing back the hammer on his pistol. Over the years, he'd made plenty of enemies, some of whom had vowed revenge when they got released.

"It's Brock Jackson, Warden," the answer came.

Brock was the assistant warden, Stevens's second in command at the prison.

Stevens eased the hammer down on the Colt and opened the door.

"What the hell are you doing here at this ungodly hour?" Stevens asked irritably as he showed the man in.

Jackson twirled his hat in his hand nervously as he entered the warden's drawing room.

"There's been a prison break, Josh," he said without preamble.

Stevens's heart began to pound again at the news. "Anyone injured?" he asked.

Jackson nodded, his eyes grim. "One of the guards, Joe Johnson, was killed. Another, Billy Thornton, was knocked unconscious, but he's recovering."

"Tell me what happened while I boil some coffee," Stevens said curtly, walking toward the kitchen.

After a fire was lit in the stove, Stevens took a cigar out of a box and lit it, sitting at the kitchen table.

"Ozark Jack Berlin and that breed Blue Owl killed Johnson, and when Thornton went in to help, they knocked him out and took his weapons." Jackson shrugged. "After that, they got the drop on the other night-shift guards, broke into the armory, and stole some weapons and ammunition, then took horses and wagons out of the stables and hightailed it toward the mountains."

"How many got out?"

"Over thirty . . . all from Cellhouse No. 1," Jackson answered.

"Damn! Those are the worst men we've got," Stevens said, a worried look on his face.

"You're right about that, Josh. There ain't a one of 'em that wouldn't cut the throat of a baby if it meant they'd go free."

Stevens sighed. "Anybody told Mrs. Johnson about Joe yet?" he asked.

"I sent one of the guards who's a good friend over to break the news to her."

As the coffee began to boil, Stevens got to his feet and poured them each a cup.

"Well, I'll get dressed and head on over to the telegraph office. I've got to notify the governor as soon as it's light."

"What do you want me to do?"

"We don't have enough men to go chasing them, not

and still guard the prison. You'd better get on over to the Army post and see if they'll send a patrol out after them."

"Yes, sir."

"And Brock . . ."

"Yes?"

"Tell the captain over there to send plenty of good men. Let him know what kind of galoots they'll be going up against."

"Yes, sir."

Ten miles east of Salt Lake City, Ozark Jack Berlin held up his hand as his men crested a small ridge looking down on a valley below. The sun was just peeking over the horizon, sending bright orange and red rays over the farm below.

There was a main house, a large barn, and off to one side a bunkhouse. In a corral next to the barn, about fifteen horses could be seen.

Berlin nodded. "Looks like just what we need, boys," he growled.

His men pulled out their weapons and leaned over their horses as Berlin led the charge down the side of the hill.

As they galloped down the slope, a man and a woman appeared on the porch of the house. The man gave a yell and the woman disappeared back inside. Men began to boil out of the bunkhouse, some still in their long underwear and pulling their boots on.

The battle was over quickly, the seven hands and the ranch owner no match for thirty hardened gunmen. Within minutes, eight men lay dead on the ground, along with one of Berlin's men.

Berlin, breathing heavily, pointed to the corral and barn. "Get them hosses saddled an' see what else you can find in the barn and bunkhouse," he called. "We need some clothes an' supplies, an' don't forget to get their guns and ammunition 'fore we leave."

Blue Owl cut his eyes toward the house, where the woman had disappeared. "You go ahead, Boss. I got me some business in the house."

Berlin grinned. "Save a little for the rest of us, Blue Owl. Don't cut her up till we get our turn."

Blue Owl stared at him. "But Ozark, that's half the fun."

"You can cut her when the rest of us are done, but it's been a long time since most of us have had a woman, so take it easy."

Blue Owl nodded as he turned his horse's head toward the house.

Later, Berlin took stock of what they'd found. Most of the men were able to get out of their prison coveralls and into jeans and shirts, though some were too big to fit into the clothes of the farmer and his hands. They also found enough horses in the corral and barn to get all of the men on horseback and off the wagons, along with more guns, rifles, shotguns, and even some dynamite the farmer used to bust up tree stumps.

All of the food was taken from the house. Then, with the farmer's wife's body still lying on the bed in their bedroom, Berlin put a torch to the house.

As they walked their horses toward the distant mountains, Berlin said, "A couple'a more farms like this, an' we should have enough supplies and horses to get us through the mountains an' into Colorado."

Blue Owl glanced at the snow-covered peaks. "It'll be hard goin' if the snows come early," he observed.

Berlin laughed. "Not as hard as goin' the other way. I suspect the Army'll be on our trail by now."

Blue Owl smiled. "If they try to follow us up into the high country, it will be easy to ambush them."

"That's what I figured. If we can kill enough of 'em, they'll soon tire of chasin' us," Berlin said, spurring his horse into a canter toward the mountains ahead.

* * *

Army Captain Wallace Bickford looked across his desk at Brock Jackson. "Are you telling me thirty of the worst criminals in your prison just walked out last night?"

Jackson nodded grimly. "Yeah, Captain. Only, they didn't just walk out. They killed one guard and smashed another's head in. Like I told you, these men are all killers—about as bad as men can be. If we don't do something soon, they're gonna leave a trail of blood behind them that'll make newspapers all over the country."

Captain Bickford looked out the window for a moment. "Mr. Jackson, I want to be honest with you. I just got a batch of fresh recruits here. Not only have these boys not seen any action yet, I'm just not sure they're up to a job like this."

Jackson leaned forward, his hands on the desk. "Captain, ready or not, the Army took them in and made them soldiers. Now, they got a job to do and I'm afraid there isn't anyone else available to do it."

Bickford pursed his lips. "Maybe it'll be all right if I send them out with a couple of sergeants who've been around for a while."

Jackson stood up, a tight smile on his face. "Good. But Captain, be sure and send plenty of men. If I'm right, there are gonna be quite a few who don't come back."

"That's what I'm afraid of, Mr. Jackson," Bickford said.

Jackson put his hat on. "I'll be sure and tell the governor how cooperative you've been."

Bickford smiled ruefully. "Yeah. Maybe he'll be so grateful he'll write the letters to the families of the boys who don't come back."

Three

Smoke Jensen pushed the batwings to Louis Longmont's Saloon open and stepped inside. Out of long habit, he stood to the side of the door, his back to the wall, until his eyes had adjusted to the relative gloom of the establishment.

Cal and Pearlie followed him inside and did the same on the other side of the door, hands near their Colts until they were sure there was no danger waiting inside. Such were the actions that years of standing by the side of one of the most famous gunfighters in the West had taught them.

Louis Longmont, owner of the saloon, looked up from his usual table in a far corner and smiled over his coffee, smoke from the long black cigar in his hand swirling around his head, stirred by a gentle breeze from the open windows in the walls.

"Smoke, boys, come on in," he called, waving them to his table.

As they approached, Longmont's eyes drifted to Smoke's waist. Then his eyebrows raised in surprise. He'd noted Smoke wasn't wearing his usual brace of pistols on his belt.

He looked up at his friend walking toward him, noticing again his imposing stature. Standing a couple of inches over six feet, with wide, muscular shoulders and a narrow waist, wearing his trademark buckskins, Smoke still looked dangerous, even though he was unarmed.

Louis, an ex-gunfighter himself, couldn't imagine what had made Smoke leave his ranch at the Sugarloaf, a few miles north of the town of Big Rock, without wearing his pistols.

Louis was a lean, hawk-faced man, with strong, slender hands and long fingers, nails carefully manicured, hands clean. He had jet-black hair and a black pencil-thin mustache. He was, as usual, dressed in a black suit, with white shirt and dark ascot—something he'd picked up on a trip to England some years back. He wore low-heeled boots, and a pistol hung in tied-down leather on his right side. It was not for show, for Louis was snake-quick with a short gun and was a feared, deadly gunhand when pushed.

Louis was not an evil man. He had never hired his gun out for money. And while he could make a deck of cards do almost anything, he did not cheat at poker. He did not have to cheat. He was possessed of a phenomenal memory and could tell you the odds of filling any type of poker hand, and was one of the first to use the new method of card counting.

He was just past forty years of age. He had come to the West as a very small boy, with his parents, arriving from Louisiana. His parents had died in a shantytown fire, leaving the boy to cope as best he could.

He had coped quite well, plying his innate intelligence and willingness to take a chance into a fortune. In addition to the saloon in Big Rock, he owned a large ranch up in Wyoming Territory, several businesses in San Francisco, and a hefty chunk of a railroad.

Though it was a mystery to many why Longmont stayed with the hard life he had chosen, Smoke thought he understood. Once, Louis had said to him, "Smoke, I would miss my life every bit as much as you would miss the dry-mouthed moment before the draw, the challenge of facing and besting those miscreants who would kill you or others, and the so-called loneliness of the owlhoot trail."

Sometimes Louis joked that he would like to draw against Smoke someday, just to see who was faster. Smoke allowed as how it would be close, but that he would win. "You see, Louis, you're just too civilized," he had told him on many occasions. "Your mind is distracted by visions of operas, fine foods and wines, and the odds of your winning the match. Also, your fatal flaw is that you can almost always see the good in the lowest creatures God ever made, and you refuse to believe that anyone is pure evil and without hope of redemption."

When Louis laughed at this description of himself, Smoke would continue. "Me, on the other hand, when some snake-scum draws down on me and wants to dance, the only thing I have on my mind is teaching him that when you dance, someone has to pay the band. My mind is clear and focused on only one problem, how to put that stump-sucker across his horse toes-down."

As Smoke and Cal and Pearlie took their seats at his table, Louis asked, "You gents want some breakfast?"

Pearlie, who never turned down food, grinned and said, "I thought you'd never ask. Eggs, bacon, pancakes, and some of those fried potatoes Andre is famous for."

Cal just shook his head. "Dang, Pearlie, we ate once this mornin' already."

Pearlie assumed a hurt expression. "But that was hours ago, Cal, an' it was a long ride in from the Sugarloaf."

Smoke smiled. "All right, boys." He glanced at Louis. "Would you ask Andre to bring us all some eggs and bacon and coffee?"

Louis called out toward a window in a back wall leading to the kitchen. "Andre, we got some hungry cowboys out here. Fix them something special."

Andre, Louis's French chef and friend of many years, stuck his head out the small window, saw Smoke and the boys, grinned, and nodded. He loved cooking for them, especially Pearlie, who was lavish in his praise of the chef's cuisine.

The waiter brought cups and a fresh pot of coffee, and poured it all around. Once the men were drinking, Louis stared at Smoke and inclined his head toward his friend.

"I notice you are only half-dressed this morning. Any particular reason?"

Smoke looked down at his naked waist, grinning ruefully. "Well, after that last little fracas, when Sally had to dig two bullets out of my hide, she sat me down for a long talk."

"And?" Louis asked, knowing Smoke loved Sally enough to do almost anything she asked.

"The upshot of it was, I'm not getting any younger. She thinks I'm too old to go traipsing around fighting every saddle tramp and would-be famous gunslinger who wants to make a name for himself by shooting Smoke Jensen."

Louis, who was a couple of years older than Smoke, frowned. "And her solution for this deplorable situation?"

Smoke shrugged. "She said if I quit wearing my guns, there would be less chance of my getting shot."

Louis shook his head. "Typical woman's thinking. And what if by chance some gunny braces you anyway?"

Smoke glanced at Cal and Pearlie sitting next to him. "I'm supposed to let Cal and Pearlie . . . show them the error of their ways while I stay out of it."

Louis leaned forward, his eyes earnest. "Smoke, old friend, you know I respect Sally more than any other woman I've ever met, but she's dead wrong this time. Taking your guns away from you is like taking the fangs off a rattlesnake and thinking he'll lie down with the rabbits."

Smoke laughed. "I agree with you, Louis. In fact, I'm gonna take you out to the Sugarloaf and have you tell that to Sally."

Louis leaned back, a look of terror on his face. He held up his hands in front of him. "Oh, no, Smoke. I'd facedown a gang of cutthroats for you, stand with you against a band of bloodthirsty Indians, but I wouldn't have the nerve to face up to Sally when she's in her 'protect my man' stance. She'd tear me apart."

Cal and Pearlie laughed at Louis's description, remembering the times Sally had saddled up her horse, packed her Winchester and snub-nosed .36-caliber handgun, and gone riding to protect Smoke's back. They knew Louis was right.

The conversation was halted when Andre and the waiter appeared bearing platters heaped with scrambled eggs, layers of steaming bacon, fresh-cut tomatoes, and fried potatoes.

Smoke looked at the red, ripe tomatoes on the platter. "Andre, where did you get fresh tomatoes at this time of the year?"

Andre grinned, puffing up a little at the compliment. "Monsieur Smoke, I have constructed myself a greenhouse out behind the saloon. There I can grow the tomatoes, and other vegetables, almost year-round."

"You'd better not tell Sally," Smoke said, spearing a few slices off the platter. "Otherwise, she'll be down here raiding your crop. She hates the taste of the tinned ones we eat in the winter."

"Madame Sally may have all she wants," Andre said, "and be sure to tell her I have a new recipe she asked about, the one with the duck à l'orange."

Pearlie glanced up from the prodigious pile of food on his plate. "Duck? I ain't never ate duck fit to swallow."

"That is because you have never eaten duck prepared by Andre," Andre said haughtily as he turned on his heel and went back into the kitchen.

"I hope I didn't hurt his feelin's," Pearlie said, a worried look on his face.

"Don't worry, Pearlie," Louis said. "Andre's ego is impervious to insult."

"Whatever that means," Pearlie muttered, lowering his head and resuming the stuffing of food into his mouth.

The men had finished their meal and were enjoying after-breakfast coffee and cigarettes when the batwings swung open and four men walked in.

They stood in the doorway, brushing trail dust off their clothes for a moment before proceeding toward the bar.

Smoke's eyes took in their garb. Two of the men were dressed mostly in black, with shiny boots, vests adorned with silver conchos, and pistols worn low on their right hips. They appeared to be related, bearing a strong resemblance to each other, and both looked to be in their early twenties. The men with them were more nondescript, wearing flannel shirts, trail coats, and chaps, but they also wore their pistols in the manner of gunmen rather than trail hands.

When the men bellied up to the bar and ordered whiskey, Louis whispered, "Uh-oh, looks like trouble."

Smoke glanced at the Regulator clock on the wall, which showed it to be ten o'clock in the morning. "Yeah, it's awfully early to be drinking liquor."

As the men downed their shots, one glanced over and noticed Louis and Smoke looking at them. He frowned, put his glass down, and sauntered over toward them.

He stopped a few feet from the table and stared at Smoke. "Hey, mister," he said belligerently, "you look familiar, like I seen you someplace before."

Smoke shrugged, his face flat. "I've been someplace before."

The man's face looked puzzled as he tried to figure out if Smoke was making fun of him for a moment. Then he scowled.

"I got it, you're Smoke Jensen."

"Congratulations," Smoke said evenly.

The man glanced over his shoulder, as if to see if his friends were watching.

"My friends an' me traveled a long way to find you."

"And just who might you be?" Smoke asked.

Louis slid his chair back a little and straightened his right leg, letting his hand rest on his thigh next to his pistol, ready for trouble.

"My name's Tucson," the man said.

"You must be from Arizona," Louis said.

Tucson's eyes flitted to Louis. "How'd you know that?" he asked.

Louis shook his head, grinning. "A lucky guess."

Smoke turned his back. "I'm afraid you're out of luck, Tucson. I'm not hiring anyone at the ranch just now."

Tucson scowled again. "I didn't come lookin' for work, Jensen."

Smoke looked back at him. "Then why did you come?"

"I came to kill you."

Smoke's expression didn't change. "Any particular reason?"

"Yeah. A few years back, you killed my cousin."

"What was your cousin's name?"

"Billy Walker."

"And where did this happen?"

"He came up here from Texas. Billy rode with a man named Lazarus Cain."

"Now I remember," Smoke said, smiling. "Cain was a crazy Bible-thumper who thought God was protecting him. Turned out he was wrong."*

"Billy weren't crazy," Tucson said angrily. "You gut-shot him an' left him to die."

"If he rode with Cain, he deserved to die," Smoke said simply, and turned back to his coffee.

Tucson let his hand drop next to his pistol. "Stand up and face me like a man, Jensen!"

Pearlie and Cal got to their feet. Pearlie took the rawhide hammer-thong off his Colt and stood off to the side, as did Cal.

"Settle down, mister," Pearlie said slowly. "As you can see, Mr. Jensen ain't wearin' no guns."

Tucson glanced at Smoke's waist. "Why ain't he heeled? He afraid to die?"

Pearlie shook his head. "Nope. It's just that Smoke's a mite tired of killin' scum like you, fellow. You see, he's done killed a couple of hundred or more an' he's gettin' sick of it. Now me, I ain't killed near that many, so it don't bother me none if you want to try your hand."

* *Guns of the Mountain Man*

As Pearlie spoke, Tucson's friends edged away from the bar to stand next to him, their hands near their weapons.

Cal grinned cockily. "Four to two, Pearlie. That ought'a make it about fair."

Louis stood up, sweeping his black coat behind his back, exposing his pistol. "Four to three, Cal," he said, smiling around the cigar stuck in his mouth.

"Hold on just a minute," Smoke said, standing up. "I'm not used to letting other people fight my battles for me."

He stepped over to stand just inches from Tucson. "You think you're pretty fast with that hogleg, son?"

"Fast enough to beat you, old man," Tucson said.

Smoke squared around. "Then go for it! If you can get it out and fire before I take it away from you and stick it up your ass, then you'll have your revenge."

"But . . . but you ain't got no gun," Tucson said.

"I don't need a gun to beat a pup like you, Tucson. Grab leather!"

Tucson's hand went for his gun. Before he had it half out of his holster, Smoke's left hand moved quicker than the eye could follow.

He grabbed Tucson's right hand where it was holding the handle of his pistol, and squeezed.

The sound of Tucson's fingers breaking was like dry twigs snapping, and he yelled in pain and let go of his gun, doubling over and holding his broken, mangled hand against his chest.

At the sound of their friend's screams, the men behind him went for their guns.

Three shots rang out almost simultaneously and the three men were blown backward to land spread-eagled on their backs.

Tucson stopped moaning long enough to glance in horror over his shoulder. "Goddamn!" he muttered at the speed with which his friends had been killed.

Smoke shook his head. "That could be you lying there, spilling your guts all over the floor, boy. Now get on your horse and ride off, while you still can."

Without another word, Tucson ran out of the door, and a few moments later they could hear his horse's hoofbeats as he hightailed it out of town.

Smoke looked at the dead bodies lying on the floor.

"What a waste," he said, shaking his head.

Meanwhile, Louis stared at Cal and Pearlie. "I'd never have believed it," he said.

"Believed what?" Cal asked, holstering his pistol.

"Yeah, what?" Pearlie asked, sitting back down and calmly finishing his coffee.

"You boys almost beat me to the draw," Louis said.

"What do you mean, almost?" Cal said with a grin.

Four

Ozark Jack Berlin and his men slowed their horses as they approached the outskirts of the small mining town named Lode in the mountains east of Salt Lake City.

Berlin glanced at Blue Owl, riding next to him. "Tell the men to ride with their guns loose," he said.

Blue Owl smiled grimly. "You expecting trouble from these desert-rat miners?" he asked scornfully.

Berlin stared at him for a moment. "You never know, Blue Owl. These men have been workin' for years to pull silver outta those mountains, an' they're liable to not take kindly to anybody who tries to take it away from 'em."

Blue Owl nodded and jerked the head of his horse around to pass the word among the men riding behind them.

As they rode down the muddy center of the town, the men looked around. The town consisted mainly of tent-buildings, some with wooden storefronts and tents on the rear. The businesses consisted mostly of brothels and saloons, with a couple of small general stores selling food and mining equipment. There didn't seem to be a jail or sheriff's office, which caused Berlin to feel a little better about the town.

Several of the men whistled and yelled at some of the prostitutes, many of whom were standing at the doors to their brothels, waving and showing lots of leg and chest to the men as they rode by.

When they came abreast of what appeared to be the

largest saloon, Berlin pulled his horse to a stop. He dismounted and tied the animal to a rail. As his men gathered around, he said, "We're gonna go in here and have a few drinks to clear the trail dust outta our throats."

The men grinned and laughed, until Berlin held up a hand. "But," he warned, "I'll shoot the first man who causes any trouble or brings attention to us. Understand?"

The men sobered and nodded and followed Berlin into the saloon. The room was a very large tent with what appeared to be handmade tables and chairs scattered around a dirt floor. The bar consisted of two twelve-inch-wide boards placed across a couple of sawhorses in front of a wooden wall holding hundreds of bottles of whiskey, most without labels on them.

It being early in the day, about ten in the morning, the place was largely unoccupied, with only ten or twelve men sitting at various tables.

Berlin walked to the bar, took a couple of boiled eggs out of a large jar, and slid the jar down the wooden planks toward the men with him.

The bartender glanced around at the thirty men crowding into the space near the bar, smiling in anticipation of a very profitable morning trade.

"What'll it be, gents?" he asked.

Berlin pointed to several bottles of amber-colored liquid on the wall. "Give us four bottles of your best whiskey an' some glasses," he said.

The barman raised his eyebrows. "But them bottles are twenty dollars apiece," he said, his eyes looking at Berlin's not-too-prosperous-appearing clothing.

Berlin reached in his pocket and pulled out a handful of gold coins, tossing them negligently on the bar.

"Yes, sir!" the barman said, and put the bottles and a tray of small shot glasses on the bar.

"Let's find some tables," Berlin said, taking one of the bottles and a glass and walking to a table at the rear of the saloon.

Once he was seated, at a table with Blue Owl and Sam

Cook, Berlin leaned forward, speaking in a low tone of voice.

"Have you thought about what we're gonna do next?" he asked.

Cook upended his glass and swallowed the whiskey in one long draught, coughed, and shook his head.

Blue Owl let his eyes roam over their men sitting at nearby tables. "We got to make a choice, Ozark," he said.

"Yeah?"

"Once word gets out about the jailbreak, there are gonna be lawmen all over the state looking for us. Traveling with thirty men makes us stand out like a sore thumb."

"And just what do you think we ought'a do about it?" Berlin asked, sipping his whiskey.

Blue Owl stared back at him. "If we want to disappear, get away clean, it'd be better if we took off on our own."

Berlin leaned back in his chair, shaking his head. "And then what, Blue Owl? Get us a job punchin' cattle, or digging holes in the ground lookin' for ore?"

Blue Owl let his eyes drop. "We could rob us some banks, or hold up some stages," he said in a low voice.

"Penny-ante stuff," Berlin said. "Look at what we got here, Blue Owl." He looked around at the men sitting nearby, slowly getting drunk on the whiskey he'd bought.

"We got us a ready-made gang here. Thirty of the meanest, most bloodthirsty men in Utah. Ain't nobody can stand against us. We can ride into towns, take what we want, an' nobody can do nothin' about it."

"You're forgetting about the Army, Ozark. I figure it won't be long before they're on our trail."

Berlin grinned. "That's where we got the real advantage, Blue Owl. The Army has to wait for orders 'fore they do anything. If we keep movin', crossin' state an' territorial lines, the Army ain't never gonna catch up to us."

"What if they do?" Blue Owl asked.

Berlin shrugged. "Then we blow 'em outta their saddles, just like we do anybody else who tries to cross us."

"If we're gonna go up against the bluecoats, Ozark, we're going to need more guns."

Berlin leaned forward again. "That brings us to my next plan. . . ."

After they finished off the whiskey, Berlin and his men got on their horses and rode down the street until they came to the livery stable.

Berlin and Blue Owl went inside. An old man with a gray beard was using a pitchfork to throw hay into stalls for the animals inside.

"You the owner?" Berlin called.

The man stopped, leaned on the handle of the pitchfork, and nodded. "Yep."

"Got any mules?"

"I got four, but they ain't for sale. I can rent 'em to you for a day or two though."

"That ain't good enough, old-timer," Berlin said, stepping forward. He pulled a long-bladed knife from a scabbard on his belt and in a quick motion, slashed the blade across the man's throat.

As the owner groaned and fell to the ground, Berlin motioned for Blue Owl to gather up the mules and lead them outside.

They took the mules and rode back down the street toward a large general store in the middle of town.

Berlin and Blue Owl, followed by the rest of the men, went inside. They began to pile up supplies, beans, bacon, flour, sugar, and jerked meat on the counter, waiting until the other customers had finished and left the building.

Berlin nodded at Blue Owl, who walked to the door, pulled the shade, and turned the sign on the door around until it said CLOSED.

"Hey, what the hell do you think you're doing?" the owner asked, coming around from behind his counter.

Sam Cook, without saying a word, drew his pistol and

slammed the barrel down on the man's head, knocking him out cold.

As Cook dragged him by his boots back behind the counter, the rest of the men proceeded to load all the supplies on the mules, taking additional clothing and stuffing it in their saddlebags.

Berlin and Blue Owl walked to the back wall of the store. There were over twenty rifles, assorted handguns, and boxes of ammunition stacked there. Berlin began to hand the guns out to the men, along with the ammunition.

"Blue Owl," he said, "take some of those boxes of dynamite and fuses along too. We might need 'em if the Army gets too close."

In less than half an hour, the mules were loaded down with boxes and canvas bags of supplies, including several boxes of dynamite and two cans of gunpowder. Meanwhile, Berlin had gone to have a talk with the local assayer. Then he returned to the store.

He was the last to leave. He shut the door, leaving the sign on it saying the store was closed for the day.

He mounted up and waved his hand. "Let's ride, men," he called. "We're burnin' daylight."

"What about the whores?" an eighteen-year-old boy named Billy Bartlett asked.

"There'll be other towns, Billy," Berlin said.

Lieutenant Jonathan Pike held up his hand to the forty troops riding behind him. They were in the main street of Lode, and he could see a crowd of miners and prostitutes gathered around the general store.

Sergeant Bob Guthrie leaned to the side and spat a stream of brown tobacco juice onto the mud of the street. "What do you make of it, Lieutenant?" he asked.

"I don't know," Pike answered. "Keep the men here and I'll ride up and see what all the commotion is about."

Guthrie wiped his mouth with the back of his hand.

"Do you think we could let the men get a drink or two in that saloon over there, sir?" he asked. "It's been a long, dusty ride."

Pike grinned. "Yeah, Sarge, but beer only. No whiskey. If we happen to run into those escaped prisoners, I don't want any drunk men doing my fighting for me."

"Yes, sir!" Guthrie said with enthusiasm.

While Guthrie got the men organized and into the saloon, Pike walked his horse toward the crowd up ahead.

He dismounted and approached a man who seemed to be in control.

"Excuse me, sir," he said. "I'm Lieutenant Pike with the Army. May I ask what's going on here?"

The man turned, frowning. "Howdy, Lieutenant. My name's Wilson Smith, an' I guess you could say I'm the mayor of this here town." He paused and glanced at the door to the general store they were standing in front of. " 'Bout four hours ago we had a group of twenty or thirty men ride through here. They killed the livery owner . . . slit his throat clear through, an' they knocked out the owner of this general store. Doc's in there stitching up his head now."

"Why'd they kill the livery owner?" Pike asked.

"To get his mules, I guess. That's 'bout the only thing we can find that's missin' down there."

"Mules? Why would they need mules?"

"Why, to haul off the stuff they took from the store, I guess."

"Excuse me, Mayor. I'm gonna go inside and talk to the owner."

"Best be careful, Lieutenant. He ain't in too good a mood."

Pike nodded and stepped through the door.

He found an elderly man in a black coat and white shirt leaning over the counter, upon which lay another man with blood on his face and shirt.

Pike walked up and introduced himself, then said, "Could you tell me what they took?"

The owner of the store glanced at him, an angry look on his face. "Damned near everything that wasn't nailed down, Lieutenant, that's what. Clothes, food, rifles and pistols, ammunition, and even some dynamite and gunpowder."

"Damn!" Pike exclaimed. He knew having the escaped prisoners thus armed was going to make his job that much harder.

"About how long ago did they leave?"

"How the hell do I know?" the man asked angrily. "I was stretched out dead to the world."

The doctor glanced over his shoulder at Pike. "Best we can tell, it was about four hours ago."

Pike glanced at his watch. It was now almost three-thirty in the afternoon. It would be dark long before they could catch up to the escapees, and he didn't relish coming upon them in the dark.

"Is there anyplace in town I can billet my men until tomorrow?" he asked.

"You going after those bastards?" the store owner asked.

"Yes, sir," Pike answered. "But I want to track them in daylight, not at night."

As the doctor leaned back, finished with his sewing, the owner sat up. "I'm Josh Collins. I own one of the houses down the street. It's got a sign on the front that reads Pleasure Palace. Now, it ain't really no palace, but it's got enough beds and couches in it so's your men can get outta the weather."

Pike nodded. "Thank you, Mr. Collins. I'll give you a voucher so you can send your bill to the Army."

"Don't need no voucher," Collins said. "Long as you get the sons of bitches that did this to me, I'll call it square."

"That's what the Army's paying us to do, Mr. Collins," Pike said, though he knew it wasn't going to be easy, not now when the men were as heavily armed as his own troops.

Five

Cal glanced at Pearlie as they rode back with Smoke toward the Sugarloaf. He raised his eyebrows, wondering if he should say anything. Smoke had been uncharacteristically quiet on the return trip, not laughing and joking as he usually did on these excursions to town.

Pearlie returned Cal's look, shrugging. He too was unused to Smoke's quiet mood.

Cal considered his options. He'd been more than an employee of Smoke's for several years—in fact, both Smoke and his wife Sally looked upon Cal as more a son than a hired hand. Cal had come to work at the Sugarloaf while just a boy in his teens. He'd been on his own, penniless and starving, and had actually tried to hold up Sally one morning while she was on her way into town to buy supplies.

After he drew down on Sally and asked her for some food, she got the drop on him with the snub-nosed .36-caliber pistol she carried in her purse. Cal laughed and showed her that the ancient pistol he was pointing at her was unloaded anyway.

Realizing the boy was starving, Sally took him to the Sugarloaf and offered him a job. He'd been part of the family ever since.

"Smoke," Cal said hesitantly.

"Yeah?" Smoke answered, his eyes fixed on the trail ahead and his jaw clenched.

"You been awfully quiet this trip. Anything wrong?"

Smoke glanced at Cal, and his eyes softened. "So, you noticed?"

Both Cal and Pearlie laughed. "Hell, yes," Cal said.

Smoke took a deep breath. "It's just that I'm not used to relying on someone else to pull my fat outta the fire."

"What do you mean?" Pearlie asked.

Smoke patted his hip where his pistols usually lay. "I feel naked without my Colts. After more years than I care to remember with them at my sides, it just doesn't feel right not to be wearing them."

Cal nodded. "Why don't you try talkin' to Sally about it, Smoke? She's usually reasonable about these things."

Smoke looked at Cal, a small grin on his face. "You ever try talking a woman outta something when she's got her mind set on it, Cal?"

Cal shook his head. "No. Matter of fact, I ain't had a whole lot of experience with women at all, Smoke."

"Keep it that way, Cal, and you'll have a whole lot less gray hair when you get to be my age," Smoke observed.

"You could just put the guns back on and tell Sally that's the way it's gonna be," Pearlie observed.

Smoke nodded. "I could, but the problem with that is it would make Sally very unhappy. And since I love her, her unhappiness would make me unhappy too."

Pearlie shook his head. "Love is a bitch, ain't it?" he said to no one in particular.

"It sure can be sometimes," Smoke said. "Other times, it's the greatest feeling in the world."

Sally Jensen walked out on the porch of their cabin when she heard Smoke's and the boys' horses arrive.

As he dismounted, Smoke said in a low tone, "Not a word about what happened in town."

"Are you men hungry?" Sally asked, wiping flour off her hands onto her apron.

Pearlie grinned. "Now, Miss Sally, what kind of a question is that?" he asked.

"You ever know Pearlie to admit he wasn't hungry?" asked Cal. "The man's stomach is a bottomless pit."

"We had breakfast at Louis's," Smoke said as he stepped up on the porch and gave her a hug and a kiss.

"Then I guess you didn't leave room for any bear sign," Sally said, smiling.

"Bear sign?" Pearlie asked, licking his lips.

Bear sign, the sugary doughnuts that men were known to ride dozens of miles to sample, were one of his favorite foods.

"I made a couple of dozen, but since you've already eaten . . ." Sally began.

Pearlie took a few quick steps toward the porch. "Outta my way, Smoke. I can hear them bear sign callin' my name," he said as he pushed by Smoke and Sally.

Cal, slightly more deliberate, tipped his hat at Sally. "If you don't mind, Miss Sally, I'd kind'a like a few of them too. That is, if Pearlie ain't already eaten 'em all 'fore I get through the door."

"I might have room for one or two also," Smoke said, walking into the kitchen with his arm around Sally.

As the boys sat down to eat, Sally poured them all mugs of rich, dark coffee. When she leaned down to put the mugs on the table, she sniffed loudly.

"You boys smell like gunpowder," she observed, standing back from the table with her hands on her hips. "Anything happen in town I ought to know about?" she asked.

Cal and Pearlie glanced at each other, then at Smoke, waiting for him to answer.

Smoke paused, a bear sign halfway to his mouth. He pursed his lips, as if considering how he should respond.

Sally nodded, looking in turn at each of the men sitting at her table. "Uh-huh, I know when all of you get lockjaw at the same time that something must have happened while you were in town."

Smoke laid the bear sign down, took a sip of his coffee,

and leaned back in his chair, staring at Sally. "You're right, as usual, dear."

"Come on," she said impatiently, "give."

"While we were eating breakfast at Louis's, we were braced by three young gunnies looking to make a reputation for themselves," Smoke said evenly.

"Didn't they see you weren't wearing any weapons?" Sally asked, a look of alarm on her face.

"Didn't make no difference to that kind'a men, Miss Sally," Pearlie said. "Once they knew who Smoke was, they was bound and determined to egg him into a gunfight."

Sally arched an eyebrow. "And what did you do, Smoke?" she asked.

Smoke shrugged. "What could I do, Sally? I wasn't wearing any guns, at your request."

"So why do I smell gunpowder on you all?"

Smoke's face got dark. "Because, when those gunslicks drew on me, Cal and Pearlie saved my bacon by drawing and shooting them before they could kill me."

Sally sighed and stepped over to the table, putting her hands on Cal and Pearlie's shoulders. "Thanks, boys," she said.

Smoke threw his napkin down on the table and stood up, his face angry. "And I'll tell you something else, Sally," he said. "It's gonna happen again, sooner or later, long as you insist on me not wearing any guns."

He turned and walked rapidly out of the room, calling over his shoulder, "I'm gonna ride out and take a look at the herd."

Cal and Pearlie, embarrassed to be present at this scene of domestic disturbance, kept their heads down as they ate bear sign and tried to pretend they hadn't heard anything.

Sally walked around the table and sat down at Smoke's seat. She stared at Cal and Pearlie. "You boys think I'm wrong in asking Smoke not to wear his Colts?"

Pearlie, his face flaming red, shrugged. "We know it's 'cause you love Smoke and don't want him to get shot no more, Miss Sally." He paused, glanced at Cal, then continued. "But you been out here in the West long enough to know that don't make no difference to the kind'a men who come lookin' to make a reputation by killin' the famous Smoke Jensen."

Cal looked over at Sally. "Pearlie's right, Miss Sally. Makin' Smoke go without his guns ain't gonna keep him safe . . . it's more than likely gonna get him killed."

Sally looked out the window, tears in her eyes, as she thought over what they'd said. After a few moments, she nodded to herself and got up.

"You boys finish the bear sign," she said as she walked to the door and took Smoke's gunbelt off the peg in the wall where it had hung since she'd asked him not to wear it anymore.

She hung it over her shoulder and walked out the door toward her horse, reined in at the hitching post in front of the cabin.

As she stepped into the saddle, Cal and Pearlie looked at each other. "Finally," Pearlie said, "she's showin' some sense."

Smoke was sitting on his horse, hands crossed over the pommel, looking out over the herd of cattle in the valley below, when Sally rode up, reining in beside him.

When he glanced over at her, she took the gunbelt off her shoulder and handed it to him. "Here," she said simply.

"What's this?" he asked.

"Take it, please, Smoke," she said. "The only reason I asked you not to wear it anymore was I was getting tired of either taking bullets out of you myself, or standing around while Doc Morrow did it."

Smoke took the belt and slipped it around his waist, buckling it up. "You sure this is what you want?" he asked.

She leaned over and put her hand on his where it lay

on his thigh. "Smoke, the only thing I want is for the man I love to stay alive. I don't look good in widow's black."

Smoke leaned to the side and kissed her gently on the lips. "I promise you, I'll be extra careful, Sally," he said, his voice growing husky.

She looked around at the lush green grass and the maple and birch trees that were just beginning to come alive with the colors of fall. "You suppose we might get down off these horses and sit under that maple tree over there and talk about it for a while?" she asked, a mischievous look in her eyes.

Smoke grinned. "If we get down off these horses, I have a feeling we're gonna be doing a whole lot more than talking."

Sally swung down out of the saddle, unhitched the belly-strap and let her saddle fall to the ground. She took the saddle blanket off the horse, hung it over her arm, and walked toward the nearest tree, looking back over her shoulder with an unmistakable invitation in her eyes.

Six

As the dawn sun peeked over mountain tops to the east, Lieutenant Jonathan Pike knocked on Sergeant Bob Guthrie's room at the Pleasure Palace.

Guthrie, his hair disheveled and his eyes still full of sleep, cracked the door. "Yes, sir?" he asked.

Pike glanced over Guthrie's shoulder, seeing a large thatch of red hair sticking out from under the covers and an empty bottle of whiskey lying on its side on his bedside table.

"Sun's up, Sergeant," Pike said, trying to hide a smile. "We're burning daylight."

"Yes, sir!" Guthrie said, covering a wide yawn with the back of his hand. "I'll get myself presentable and muster the men soon's I can."

"I'll wait for you in the dining room, Sergeant," Pike said. "And," he added as Guthrie started to close the door, "I'll have breakfast waiting for you, so no . . . further delays."

Guthrie grinned. "Yes, sir. I'll get right on it."

After he closed the door, the woman in the bed stuck her head out, rubbing eyes that were red from a late night. "That mean you don't have time for a mornin' pick-me-up?" she asked.

Guthrie shook his head. "I said I'd get right on it, Mary Belle," he said as he dropped his trousers to the floor. "An' that's just what I intend to do."

He laughed as he dove beneath the covers, his cold hands making Mary Belle yelp as he grabbed her.

Guthrie's breakfast was cold by the time he arrived at Lieutenant Pike's table, and his cheeks showed patches of whiskers he'd missed in his hasty attempt to shave.

"I'm afraid your eggs are cold, Sergeant," Pike said, frowning.

Guthrie bent his head and dug right in. "I been in the Army nigh on twenty years, Lieutenant," he said with his mouth full. "I'm used to bad food, long days, an' cold nights."

Pike's face relaxed in a slight smile. "I trust last night wasn't too cold for you, Bob?"

Guthrie grinned without looking up. "No, sir. Last night the temperature was right tolerable."

"Good," Pike said. " 'Cause it's liable to be the last warm night we spend for quite some time. The outlaws headed up into the high country, and I intend to follow 'em till we catch every last one of the scoundrels."

Guthrie looked up from his eggs, a frown on his face. "You think that's wise, sir?" he asked. "It's not gonna be an easy campaign, followin' those galoots up into the mountains."

"What do you mean?" Pike asked, sipping his coffee and staring at the sergeant.

"Well, number one, they're gonna know we're comin' after 'em, an' if they're at all smart, they're gonna have someone watchin' their back trail. Once they find out we're on their trail, it'll be an easy matter for 'em to set an ambush along the trail where they'll have the high ground."

Pike leaned back in his chair, his gaze stern. "So, you think we should just let them go on their way after all they've done?"

Guthrie shrugged. "Not exactly, sir. But they ain't gonna

do no one any harm up in those mountains, especially with winter just around the corner. It's my guess they'll soon get tired of wanderin' around up to their asses in snow and freezin' their butts off an' come down to civilization. If we check the map, we can find out where they're liable to come down and have someone waitin' for 'em when they do."

Pike looked out the window, his lips pursed as he considered what Guthrie had said. After a moment, he shook his head. "No, Sergeant, I don't relish just giving up the hunt. Captain Bickford assigned me to track these criminals down and bring them to justice, and I intend to follow my orders."

"Even if it means gettin' half our men killed?" Guthrie asked, his eggs ignored on the plate in front of him.

Pike nodded. "My men didn't sign up in the Army for easy duty, Sergeant, and I think you overestimate the fighting ability of our foes. After all," Pike said, spreading his arms, "these men we're tracking are ordinary killers, not military geniuses. I think when they see the number of men after them, they'll more than likely give up without a fight."

Guthrie clenched his jaw and went back to his breakfast, knowing it was no use arguing with an officer who had his head up his butt. He knew the men from the prison wouldn't just give up, and he also knew that before this campaign was over, there was going to be blood on the snow of the high lonesome. . . .

Ozark Jack Berlin crawled out of his sleeping bag and stood up, checking the weather. The wind was blowing out of the north, carrying with it small particles of ice and snow and chilling him to the bone.

The night before, he'd made camp for his men in the shelter of a group of boulders piled against the steep side of a mountain ledge. The fire they'd built was nothing but coals now, and was giving off little heat to combat the frigid cold of the north wind.

Berlin stepped over to Blue Owl's sleeping bag and nudged the sleeping figure of the Indian with his foot.

"Blue Owl," he growled, "get your ass outta bed an' get the men movin'. We need a fire an' some coffee 'fore we freeze to death."

As Blue Owl stirred, trying to come awake, Berlin made the rounds of the other men, kicking them awake and telling them to get up and get ready to travel. By the time he'd finished, Blue Owl had the fire going and several pots of coffee cooking on the coals.

Billy Bartlett and Moses Johnson, a black man who'd killed a farmer and his family when they'd refused him work, were filling skillets with eggs and slabs of fatback bacon, while kettles of pinto beans bubbled and boiled on iron trestles over the flames.

Soon, thirty men were gathered as close to the warmth of the fire as they could get, drinking steaming coffee from tin mugs and wolfing down eggs, bacon, and beans as if they hadn't eaten in weeks.

Blue Owl, his shoulders hunched inside a buffalo robe he'd taken from town, held his coffee mug in both hands to keep them warm and glanced up at Berlin, who was standing next to him smoking a cigarette and staring at the mountains to the east.

"Yo, Boss," he said, "what are your plans for today?"

Several of the gunmen who were sitting nearby looked up, waiting for what Berlin had to say.

"We ain't got no choice but to head eastward," Berlin said. "We got a town full of angry miners and half the goddamned Army behind us, so I guess we'll just keep on movin' east."

Blue Owl shook his head, staring at the flames of the campfire. "If we keep goin' east, that means we gotta climb higher up in those mountains, an' it's gonna get colder'n a well-digger's asshole up there."

He looked up at the clouds overhead. "We got us a big

norther blowin' in, an' this is just the beginnin' of the bad weather we're gonna face if we go any higher up into the mountains."

Berlin took a last drag off his cigarette and flipped the butt into the fire. "I'm open to suggestions, Blue Owl. If'n you got any better ideas, now's the time to give 'em."

"I think we ought'a head on back down the mountain. We got more'n enough men an' guns to fight off the Army."

Berlin nodded. "And then what?"

"Then we could head south, skirtin' the mountains, till we come to a pass somewhere's where we don't have to go up into snow country."

"Uh-huh," Berlin said, a sneer on his face.

"Well?" Blue Owl asked. "What's wrong with that plan?"

Berlin shook his head. "Just about everything. First off, you want to engage the Army in a fight on level ground with these men." He indicated the group of murderers and rapists and robbers sitting around the fire listening to them with a wave of his hand. "Men who might be brave enough, but they aren't exactly trained in fightin' on horseback against men who are."

He paused to bend down, grab the coffeepot, and pour himself another cup of coffee. After he took a drink, he continued. "Secondly, assuming we could win against the Army, and the miners from the town we just passed through, by the time we'd traveled fifty miles, someone would have telegraphed ahead an' there'd be another group of Army men, or lawmen, or bounty hunters waitin' for us."

"So, what's different about your plan?" Blue Owl asked.

Berlin put his coffee cup down and built himself a cigarette, turning his back to the wind so he could get it lit.

"First off, while we make our way up into the mountains, we're gonna station some men on our back trail to warn us if the Army tries to come after us. If they do, then we'll fix up a nice little surprise for 'em that'll take them out without gettin' half our men killed."

"What about the telegraph you're so worried about?" Blue Owl asked. "The miners in the town back yonder can still telegraph ahead an' have people waitin' for us."

Berlin shook his head. "No, they can't," he said. "By the time they figure out the Army's failed, they won't know which way we're headed. Once we reach the pass at the top of the mountains, we can go north, east, or south, an' nobody's gonna know which way we've gone."

"What about the weather?" Billy Bartlett asked, holding his arms around himself and shivering in the cold.

Berlin nodded. "I'll admit it's gonna get a mite cold, but we got plenty of supplies, an' we'll be able to get more from the soldiers we kill if'n they come after us. With any luck, we'll only be up here for a week or so. Then we can head back down the other side of the mountains to warmer weather."

A large, barrel-chested man with a thick beard stood up from the other side of the fire.

"You got a question, Mack?" Berlin asked.

"Yeah," Mack replied, squaring his shoulders and letting his hand hover near the pistol on his belt. "I want to know who made you the boss. I don't recall no election."

Berlin's eyes narrowed. "You got an objection to me callin' the shots, Mack?" Berlin asked, shifting his coffee mug from his right hand to his left as he talked.

"Yeah, you ain't got no right to—"

Before Mack could finish, Berlin drew in a lightning-fast movement and fired through the flames. His slug took Mack in the chest, knocking him backward to land spread-eagled on his back in the gathering snow on the ground. Blood pumped out of his chest to mix with the ice and snow in a scarlet pool, steam rising from the liquid as it cooled.

Berlin looked around at the men gathered around him, his smoking pistol still in his hand. "Now, you men got to make a choice. This ain't the Army, an' it ain't prison. Any of you who wants to can go your own way, an' there'll be no hard feelin's."

Blue Owl glanced over at the body of Mack on the ground and laughed. "Yeah, Boss, I can see that," he said as other men in the group joined in with nervous laughter.

"No, I mean it," Berlin said. "Any of you who want to can leave, but those of you who stay have got to know who's runnin' things around here. If you stay, you're gonna do things my way, or you can do like Mack and take your chances that you're faster with a gun than I am. Any questions?"

The men all shook their heads and went back to eating their breakfast and drinking their coffee, some glancing nervously at Mack's body lying nearby.

Seven

Lieutenant Jonathan Pike sat on his horse at the head of his column of men as they prepared to ride out of Lode, Utah, on the trail of the escaped prisoners.

Mayor Wilson Smith stood nearby, watching as the men readied their mounts.

"Mayor," Pike said.

"Yes, sir, Lieutenant?"

"I need you to do me a favor," Pike said.

"Whatever you need, Lieutenant."

"Would you send some telegraphs for me?"

"Sure, where to?" the mayor asked.

"I'd like you to notify Fort Collins and Denver in Colorado, and the sheriff's office in Cheyenne, Wyoming, of what's happened here the past couple of days. If for some reason those criminals get by us in the mountains, they've got to either turn north to Wyoming, or south toward Colorado. I'd like the authorities to be aware that they may have to take action, if we fail to stop them."

Mayor Smith nodded. "I'll take care of it, Lieutenant, you got my word."

Sergeant Guthrie walked his horse up next to Pike's. "There's one other thing, Mayor," he said, cutting a corner off a square of chewing tobacco and sticking it in his mouth.

"What's that, Sergeant?" Smith asked.

"If worse comes to worst an' we lose this battle, there's a small chance those men may head back down this way.

If I were you, I'd make sure the town was ready for 'em if they decide to backtrack down here."

Smith smiled grimly. "Oh, we'll be ready for 'em, Sergeant. They won't get another chance to raid this town."

Guthrie nodded, glanced at Pike, and waved his hand to the men in the column behind him. "Forward, ho!" he growled, and began walking his horse toward the mountain peaks in the distance.

Jesus Santiago squatted next to a small fire on a bluff overlooking a winding trail up the mountainside. The fire was set back from the edge of the cliff among stunted pines, its smoke whipped into nothingness by the strong winds coming from the north.

Santiago slapped his hands on his arms, then held his hands in front of the flames, trying to get some warmth from the fire. "God almighty!" he exclaimed. "I'm freezing my ass off up here."

Wiley Gottlieb walked from the ledge, where he'd been looking along the path through binoculars, and took a small bottle of whiskey from his saddlebags. He pulled the cork and took a long drink, wiping his mouth with the back of his hand. "Ozark Jack Berlin is crazy if he thinks the Army is gonna be fool enough to follow us up here in this blizzard," he growled.

Santiago glanced up at heavy, dark clouds through swirls of snow and particles of ice slanting with the wind. "You think this is a blizzard, Wiley?" he asked. "Hell, this is nothing but a little fall storm. Just wait till we get to the high country; then you'll see what a real blizzard looks like."

"It gets any colder'n this an' I may just take Ozark up on his offer to hightail my ass back down the mountain," Gottlieb said, putting his whiskey bottle back in his saddlebag and walking back over to the edge of the overlook.

He put the glasses to his eyes and pointed them back down the trail.

Santiago had begun to stir the coals, trying to coax more heat from the fire, when Gottlieb yelled, "Jesus, I'll be goddamned!"

Santiago jumped up and ran to stand next to Gottlieb, staring in the direction of his binoculars. He could see, through the mist and snow and sleet, a line of shadowy figures on horseback winding their way up the trail in the distance, their blue and gold uniforms clearly visible through the gloom.

"How many you make it?" he asked Gottlieb, who was still staring through the binoculars.

Gottlieb shook his head, "I can't tell for sure, but it looks to be fifty or more."

"Damn, Ozark was right," Santiago said, rushing back to the fire and scattering the wood, kicking snow and ice over it to put out the fire. "We got to get going and warn the others."

They caught up with Ozark Jack Berlin and the rest of the escapees an hour later. It was only midafternoon, but the storm made the light low and gloomy and cut visibility to less than two hundred yards.

Berlin nodded when they told him of what they'd seen. "I figured the Army wouldn't give up," he said, looking around at the land surrounding them.

Up ahead, the trail they were riding could be seen passing between two walls of stone as it traversed through a small valley.

Berlin began to point at different men as he gave his orders. "Billy, you and Moses and Wiley and Jesus take another ten men and head off to the right. Get your horses up that hillock and out of sight, then get the dynamite and gunpowder and plant some charges along the top of that cliff, under boulders and such." He reached into his saddlebags and handed Billy Bartlett a handful of cigars. "Get these goin' so you won't have to worry 'bout gettin' the fuses lit when the time comes. On my signal, light the fuses and get under cover. After the charges blow, step up to the ledge and use your rifles to pick off any survivors."

As Billy and the other men spurred their horses up the hill, Ozark Jack told the remaining men to do the same on the other side of the trail. "We'll box the bastards in and then pick 'em off one at a time," he said, grinning around his cigar as he followed his men up the trail.

Sergeant Guthrie was riding point, hunched over his saddle, trying to keep his mustache from icing over. It was no use. Even the bandanna he had over his face was becoming coated with a layer of ice and slush from the frigid wind in his face.

"I knowed I should'a quit when I had my twenty in," he muttered to himself, grabbing his saddle horn with both hands as his mount's hooves slipped on icy rock on the trail.

He glanced back over his shoulder. His men were riding two by two along the winding trail, all hunched over as *he* was. He knew they were in dangerous territory, riding without being able to scout out the area ahead of the troops, but Lieutenant Pike was adamant that they make good time. He'd refused Guthrie's request to send a small party of men ahead to make sure it was safe to proceed.

"Damned fool's gonna get us all killed," Guthrie muttered to himself, watching the fog of his breath torn away by gusty winds.

When the trail turned around a corner and seemed to disappear into a valley between two rock walls ahead, Guthrie reined his horse's head around and trotted back down the line of troops to where Pike was riding.

"Sir," Guthrie said, "I don't like the looks of that valley up ahead. It's a natural place for an ambush."

Pike raised his head and stood up in his stirrups to get a better look. He stared at the valley, then at the cliffs overlooking the trail.

"I don't see anything, Sergeant," he said after a moment.

You damn fool, Guthrie thought, you expect 'em to stand up and wave at us if they're waiting to bushwhack us?

"That's the point, Lieutenant," Guthrie persisted. "We can't see nothin' in this weather. Let me stop the men an' send a patrol ahead to check it out."

"You want me to stop the men out here in the open and let them freeze while you go traipsing up ahead to see if anyone's waiting to fire on us?" the lieutenant asked sarcastically.

"But sir," Guthrie began.

"No, carry on, Sergeant," Pike said. "I think it'd be better to get the men into that valley where we have some cover and let them take a break there. We can build some fires and warm up the horses and men and have some coffee before we move on."

Guthrie shook his head as he jerked his horse around. He hoped the outlaws were as dumb as his leader, or there was going to be hell to pay.

Guthrie was well into the valley when he heard the first explosion. He looked up in time to see sheets of flame explode from both sides of the cliffs on either side of the men, sending boulders, dirt, debris, and tons of snow cascading down toward them.

Without thinking, Guthrie dove sideways off his horse to land sprawled on his face in ankle-deep snow. He scrambled on hands and knees to get as close to the side of the cliff as he could, hunkering down between two large stone formations there.

Seconds later he was buried under an avalanche of dirt and snow as blackness opened up and swallowed him.

* * *

As soon as their dynamite and gunpowder exploded, Berlin's men moved to the edges of the cliffs ringing the small valley below.

Putting rifles to shoulders, they waited for the dust to clear. Below them was a scene of unbelievable carnage . . . men and horses were half-buried under tons of rocks, dirt, and snow. Horses and men were screaming in pain and terror, trying to escape the falling boulders.

As the dust settled, blown away by rushing north winds, Berlin's men began to fire their weapons into the milling mass of humanity below.

One after another, both men and horses were felled by hundreds of bullets raining down upon them. A few gallant soldiers managed to draw weapons, and fired blindly into the night sky, unable to even see their targets.

Within moments all movement in the valley had ceased, though eerie sounds of moans and muted cries for help still came from some of the men who were wounded but still somehow alive.

Berlin and his allies climbed on their mounts and descended to the valley of death below, holding their guns at the ready. They lit torches and held them aloft as they walked their broncs among the dead horses and men scattered along the valley floor. Occasionally, they would come upon someone still alive, moving slightly or raising a hand pleading for mercy.

The outlaws were relentless, stopping momentarily to gaze down upon helpless soldiers before slowly taking aim and putting them out of their misery with a single gunshot to the head or chest. . . .

Guthrie came awake, choking and gagging as he tried to breathe dirt. He managed to get his hands up to his face and clear a small opening so he could breathe.

He shook his head, trying to remember where he was and what had happened to him. It felt like his horse was lying on top of him, and he could barely move his arms.

When he realized what had happened, he slowly began to dig his way out of the dirt and snow covering him. He managed to get his face clear and wipe his eyes after about ten minutes. It was full dark now, with no sign of any light from stars or moon.

He was lying between two boulders under a pile of small boulders and dirt, hidden from view in the darkness. His body was still covered, and he couldn't get his hand down to his pistol when he saw several men riding around with torches in their hands. He put his facedown on the dirt so they wouldn't see the whites of his eyes, and listened.

He could hear men moaning and screaming in pain, some crying out for help or begging for mercy. Then he heard several shots ring out as other men laughed and yelled curses at the wounded men.

"Sons of bitches are slaughtering my men," he said to himself as he struggled to free his lower body and get to his weapon.

Still unable to reach his gun, he lay still when two horses rode within six feet of him. He could hear the men talking as they walked their mounts up the trail.

"We got all the guns and ammunition we can carry, Ozark," one of the dark figures on horseback said.

"Good. Hurry up and kill anyone left alive and let's make tracks. Colorado's waitin' for us, Blue Owl."

They rode on out of sight, swallowed by the night, as Guthrie struggled to free himself from a half ton of dirt and rocks.

By the time he was able to scramble out from between the rocks, all of the outlaws were gone, leaving behind forty-five men lying dead in the snow, some still on horseback, their dead mounts beneath them.

Guthrie walked among his men, tears stinging his eyes and freezing on his cheeks as he looked up the trail after the outlaws.

"I swear to God, I'm gonna come after you and see every one of you bastards in the ground for what you done here tonight," he vowed, shaking his fist in the air.

Finally, he turned to the grisly task of searching each and every body lying on the ground to see if anyone had survived the ambush.

He found Lieutenant Pike sitting with his back to a boulder, over fifteen gunshot wounds in his body, his right leg twisted at an unnatural angle beneath him.

Guthrie stood over him, shaking his head. "You were a damn fool, Lieutenant, but nobody deserves to die like that, not even you."

After he made sure there were no survivors, having to shoot several horses that were too badly injured to survive, Guthrie hunted down a horse among the few that had managed to survive and were scattered in the surrounding area, got in the saddle, and headed up the trail.

Before he left, he made the rounds again of his fallen comrades, taking several extra rifles, a couple of extra pistols, and as much ammunition as he could stuff in his saddlebags. He also took as much food as he could carry, knowing it was going to be a long, hard ride through the high country and food was going to be scarce.

He loaded the extra rations and weapons on the back of another horse, and tied a dally rope to its saddle, using it as a packhorse.

He intended to go after the outlaws until he had a chance to avenge his men. Sergeant Bob Guthrie was going to war, and he didn't intend to stop until he had killed every one of the men who'd slaughtered his friends.

He'd heard the leader of the band mention Colorado as their final destination, and he was going to ride hard and fast and see if he could be there waiting for them when they arrived.

Eight

Smoke and Sally Jensen were sitting on the porch of their cabin, enjoying the first cup of coffee in the morning, when a rider approached.

"Yo, the cabin!" called the voice of Monte Carson, sheriff of Big Rock.

Smoke stood up. "Howdy, Monte. Come on in."

Monte dismounted, tied his horse to the hitching rail near the porch, and ambled up the steps.

He tipped his hat. "Mornin', Sally," he said.

"Good morning, Monte," she answered, getting to her feet. "Would you like some breakfast, or coffee? Smoke and I were just fixing to have some eggs and bacon."

He nodded, a grin appearing on his face. Sally's cooking was known far and wide as the best in the area. "That'd sure hit the spot, Sally."

After she'd gotten him a mug of coffee, Sally went back into the kitchen to fix breakfast while Monte and Smoke stayed on the porch.

Monte built himself a cigarette and leaned back, crossing his legs with the mug on his knee.

"What brings you way out here to the Sugarloaf so early in the day, Monte?" Smoke asked.

Monte took a drag on his cigarette and let the smoke trickle from his nostrils as he answered. "I got a wire from the mayor of a little town in Utah called Lode yesterday."

"Lode? I don't think I know it," Smoke said.

"It's a small mining camp a few hundred miles from Salt Lake City. It's just up in the mountains there."

Smoke nodded. "And what did this wire say that was so important you had to ride out here?"

Monte took a sip of his coffee. "It seems there was a prison break at the Utah Territorial Prison a few days ago. Evidently more than thirty of the most dangerous felons in the place managed to break out and make their getaway."

"Uh-huh."

"They proceeded to steal some horses and guns and made their way up to this little town. When they got there, they stole more guns and horses, and lots of supplies, and headed up into the mountains after killing the livery owner."

Smoke frowned. "What's that got to do with us here in Colorado?"

"The Army sent men after them, and the man in charge asked the mayor of Lode to wire all the towns near the border in Wyoming and Colorado that the escapees might just head on down our way if they made it through the mountains."

Smoke smiled, shaking his head. "That won't be an easy task, with the winter storms starting in the high country."

Monte nodded. "I know it's a long shot, an' we'll probably never see hide nor hair of 'em, but I thought I'd use the wire as an excuse to ride around the area and warn all the outlying ranchers to be on the lookout."

"Well, I'm glad you did, Monte. It's been far too long since you've paid us a visit out here. Sally was just asking the other day about how you and Mary were doing."

"My wife's fine, Smoke, though her cookin' don't compare to Sally's."

"I heard that, Monte," Sally said from the doorway, "and I intend to tell Mary what you said next time I see her."

Monte assumed a look of horror and held up his hands.

"Don't you dare, Sally. She'd have my hide if she heard that."

Sally laughed. "Come on in, you two. Breakfast is on the table and it's getting cold."

While they ate, Smoke told Sally what Monte had said about the escaped criminals.

"Do you really believe there's any chance they'll come all the way down here before they're caught?" she asked.

Monte shook his head and spoke around a mouthful of scrambled hens' eggs and bacon. "No, I don't really think so, Sally. I imagine the Army will catch up with them before they get too far. In my experience, men in prison aren't smart enough to escape the Army for long."

"I hope you're right, Monte," Smoke said. "There are lots of folk living up in the high lonesome that wouldn't stand a chance against those kind of odds."

Monte grinned. "Don't tell me you're worried about all your old mountain-men friends who still winter up in the mountains."

Smoke shook his head. "No, not at all. If they try to bother any of those old beavers, they'll find out they've bitten off more than they can chew," Smoke said. "But, since gold has been discovered up in the Rockies, a lot of miners have moved up there with their families, and most of them are pilgrims that don't know how to take care of themselves against a crew like these prisoners."

Monte finished off his eggs and bacon and took a final drink of his coffee before standing up. "Well, it most probably won't come to that anyhow. Thanks again for the food, Sally. It was wonderful, as usual."

As he walked out the door, Sally called, "Give my regards to Mary."

"I'll do it," Monte answered, climbing on his horse.

"And let us know if you hear any more news about those men," Smoke added.

"Will do. Adios," Monte called as he waved good-bye and spurred his horse down the road toward the next ranch.

Smoke reached inside the door and got his hat and gunbelt off the peg next to the door.

"What are you doing?" Sally asked.

"I'm gonna ride on up to the north pasture where Cal and Pearlie and some of the boys are mending fences. Might as well let them know to be on the lookout for any strangers."

"Just a minute," Sally said, walking into the kitchen. She took a platter of fresh biscuits, put them in a paper sack, and handed it to Smoke.

"Take these with you. It's been a couple of hours since Pearlie has eaten, so I know he'll be hungry."

Smoke laughed. "Pearlie's always hungry, but I'll take the sinkers. It'll give him an excuse to quit working for a while and eat."

Nine

The early winter storm was clearing, and a bright sun filled azure skies without giving out much heat as Ozark Jack Berlin and his men rode a trail down Blue Mountain toward the banks of the White River.

Berlin held up his hand to stop his men as he pulled a map taken from the general store in Lode out of his saddlebag.

He lit a cigar and puffed as he used his finger to follow the line on the map that was labeled "White River." He glanced up, peering into the distance to where he could see a scattering of buildings near the riverbank where a smaller creek branched off.

Blue Owl walked his horse up next to Berlin. "You figure out where the hell we are yet, Boss?" he asked.

Berlin nodded. "That looks like the White River, an' that there smaller branch seems to be Douglas Creek. If that's so, then that town must be Rangely, Colorado."

"Don't look like much of a town to me," Blue Owl said.

"It ain't. Probably just a bunch of miners an' such tryin' to scrape a livin' outta the rocks up here."

Blue Owl pulled a pair of binoculars out of his saddlebag and put them to his eyes. They were marked U.S. ARMY, and he'd taken them off a soldier just after he put a bullet through his head.

"I don't see no telegraph lines nor poles," he said, grinning. "That means they ain't heard about us yet."

Berlin returned the smile. "Yeah, an' this time of the

mornin', most of the men are gonna be up in the mountains diggin' in their mines. Won't hardly be anyone left in town to give us any trouble."

Blue Owl nodded. "I hope they's some womenfolk in town. It's been too long since I had me a woman."

"Well," Berlin said, putting his map away and drawing his pistol, "ain't but one way to find out, is there?"

He spurred his horse and took off at a gallop, his men riding hard behind him.

They raced across the wooden bridge over the White River, their hoofbeats beating a hollow tattoo of sound as they entered the town's limits.

The town consisted primarily of faded clapboard buildings and wooden cabins arrayed in a straight line on either side of the main street. There was an assay office, a general store, three saloons, a two-story hotel and boardinghouse, a livery stable, and fifteen or twenty smaller houses on the outskirts of the town.

As the thirty outlaws raced down the main street, several older men and a few women ran for doorways, ducking into buildings to get out of the way of the running horses.

Two middle-aged men stayed in the street, both reaching for pistols, to be gunned down before they could clear leather.

Berlin jerked his horse to a stop in the center of town. "Fan out!" he hollered to his men, waving his arm in a circle. "Make sure there ain't nobody left armed until we can see the lay of the land."

In less than an hour, every living soul in the town was rounded up and gathered together in the largest saloon, called the Nugget. There were twenty-two men, ranging in age from thirteen years old to more than seventy. There were also fifteen women, ten of whom were obviously prostitutes or saloon girls. The other five were elderly women whose husbands were out at their mines working.

Berlin stood at the bar, a bottle of whiskey next to him, as he looked over the prisoners, who were huddled on one side of the large room.

The bartender was hurriedly pouring whiskey all around for the outlaws, while Moses Johnson and Billy Bartlett held shotguns on the prisoners.

"Jesus," Berlin said to Jesus Santiago, "you and Sam Cook get on over to the assay office and see if there's any gold there we can take."

"Yes, sir, Boss," Jesus said, gulping his whiskey down and heading for the door, followed by Sam Cook.

"Now, you people, just take it easy an' nobody has to get hurt," Berlin drawled to the townspeople. "We're gonna take some supplies an' be on our way soon, so no need gettin' all riled up and doin' somethin' stupid."

"You bastards will never get away with this," an elderly man off to one side said, drawing himself up and staring at Berlin.

"And just who's gonna stop us?" Berlin asked in a low voice.

"When the men get back from the mines they'll track you down and kill every one of you sons of bitches!" the man answered.

"Billy," Berlin said gently, "teach this man some manners."

Billy Bartlett grinned and let go with one of the barrels of his shotgun. The gun exploded, sending a charge of buckshot into the man's midsection, almost cutting him in half and spraying the people around him with blood and guts.

"Now," Berlin said loudly over the screams of the women in the room, "are there any other complaints I need to deal with?"

Several of the men managed to quiet the women while looking over their shoulders at the gunmen who were covering them.

When no one spoke up, Berlin nodded. "Good. Then that settles it." He glanced out the window at the boardinghouse and hotel across the street, then walked over to the crowd and grabbed one of the women by the arm.

"Get your friends and come with me," he said gruffly.

"Where are we going?" the woman asked, terror in her eyes.

"My men an' me been on the trail for a while now an' we're in need of some feminine companionship," Berlin answered.

As the younger women followed him out of the door, he called over his shoulder to his men, "Ten of you come on with us. The others can stay here and keep them covered. We can take turns till everybody's had their fill."

Blue Owl grabbed his bottle and started toward the door. "Not you, Blue Owl," Berlin said. "You got to go last."

"Why's that?" Blue Owl said angrily.

" 'Cause I don't want you an' that pigsticker of yours spoilin' the goods till everybody else has had a chance at 'em," Berlin answered.

Blue Owl grinned. "Oh," he said, smiling and returning to the bar.

"Moses," Berlin said, "send a couple of men to stand guard at the town limits in case some of the miners come back before dark."

"Yes, sir, Boss."

In two hours, all of the men with Berlin had their turns with the prostitutes, including Blue Owl. Only one of the girls was damaged beyond repair. Blue Owl had left his woman in pieces on a bloodstained bed in the hotel.

Berlin gathered his men, along with twelve pounds of gold dust from the assay office, assorted food and supplies from the general store, and enough ammunition to replace what they'd used on the soldiers, and they prepared to take their leave from Rangely.

"You people stay here in the saloon until after we're

gone, an' nobody'll be any the worse for wear," Berlin said, walking back and forth in front of the townsfolk.

"If you stick your heads out before then, we'll blow 'em off," he warned.

He led his men out the door and they all mounted up. "Sam, you and Moses open up the livery and scatter the hosses so they can't follow us later," he ordered.

After that was done, he trotted out of town, heading south by southeast toward the next town.

Sergeant Bob Guthrie arrived in town three hours later, just before dark. He was met by a group of men holding rifles and shotguns.

"Who the hell are you?" a tall, thin man with a full beard asked angrily.

Guthrie held his hands out where the men could see them. "I'm Sergeant Bob Guthrie, United States Army."

"What do you want here?" the man asked, lowering his rifle, but keeping his hand on the trigger.

"I'm followin' a band of outlaws that killed my men up in the mountains. There's about thirty of 'em, an' they're mean as snakes."

"Get down off your horse, Sergeant," the man said. "Your outlaws have already paid us a visit."

He stuck his hand out. "I'm Jacob Walker, sort'a the mayor of Rangely."

Guthrie took his hand. "Howdy. How long ago did they leave?"

" 'Bout three hours or so," Walker said, leading Guthrie into the saloon where the people had been held prisoner.

Guthrie sank into a chair, exhaustion evident on his face. "I been in the saddle over twenty hours now, tryin' to catch up to those bastards," he said.

"Emmett," Walker said to the bartender, "get Sergeant Guthrie some grub an' some coffee. He looks like he could use it."

While he ate, Guthrie told the townspeople the story of the prison break, the trouble in Lode, and the subsequent slaughter of his command.

Walker looked around at his fellow citizens. "I guess we got off lucky then," he said. "They only killed four here, along with stealing all our gold and some supplies."

"You folks have a telegraph here?" Guthrie asked.

Walker shook his head. "Nope. Nearest one's over at Meeker, sixty miles to the east."

"Which way did they head?" Guthrie asked.

"Southeast. That means they're either heading to Rifle or Grand Junction."

"How big are the towns?"

"Rifle's just 'bout the same size we are," Walker said. "Grand Junction has a railroad line and is quite a bit bigger."

"You say Grand Junction has a railroad?" Guthrie asked.

"Yeah. It goes over toward Crested Butte and then on down to Pueblo." He walked over to the bar, reached behind it, and pulled out an assayer's map of the territory. He unfolded it on the table and showed it to Guthrie.

Guthrie thought for a moment as he studied the map. "I'd figure they're gonna head for Rifle first, being's it's the smallest town an' probably don't have much law."

"You're probably right," Walker said.

Guthrie looked up. "If I can trade for a couple of horses, I'm gonna hightail it to Grand Junction, notify the Army by telegraph there, then take the railroad down to Crested Butte. With any luck, I'll be waitin' for 'em when they finally get there."

"If you don't mind my saying so, Mr. Guthrie," Walker said, "you don't look in any shape to make that journey tonight."

Guthrie leaned back in his chair. "You're probably right, Walker. I'm liable to fall off my horse and break my neck if I don't get some sleep."

Walker poured him another cup of coffee. "From the looks of the sky, we got another winter storm coming in soon. Those outlaws won't be able to make much time over the mountains between here and Rifle if it snows. Why don't you get some sleep and start off first thing in the morning? That'll still give you plenty of time to get to Grand Junction and get the train to Crested Butte ahead of those outlaws."

Guthrie drained his coffee and stood up. "I think I will, Mayor. I'm much obliged to you."

"You get the men who raided this town and we'll call it even, Sergeant."

Guthrie turned eyes cold and black as stone on Walker. "Oh, I intend to do that, Mr. Walker. You can count on it!"

Ten

Sergeant Bob Guthrie awoke at noon the next day, to weather that was cold but with no traces of the storm of the previous week. The mayor of Rangely provided him with two fresh horses and he took off toward Grand Junction, a trip of approximately fifty miles. He planned to use the horses in tandem and hoped, if the weather held, to make the trip in three days or less.

Ozark Jack Berlin and his gang of outlaws didn't fare so well. A blue norther, sweeping down out of Canada, hit them with the force of a freight train, dumping two feet of snow and dropping temperatures below zero on their trip toward Rifle, Colorado.

They arrived at Rifle more than ten days after they left Rangely, a journey that would usually only take four days. They were cold, saddle-weary, and dead tired when they rode into sight of the small mining town.

While on the outskirts of the town, Berlin gathered his men around him, their faces crusted with ice and snow.

"All right, men, we been through hell on the way here," he said. "We're gonna need a place to rest up and recuperate from the trip, so I want you all to be on your best behavior while we're here. No shootin' an' no killin' till we're ready to leave town. You got that?"

The men nodded wearily, all anxious to get in front of a fire somewhere and warm up. Their blood lust was for the moment dampened by their misery in the frigid air surrounding them.

As they rode slowly into Rifle, Blue Owl looked around at the clapboard buildings and tents of the town. "Hell, Boss," he said, "it don't look like there's much here for the taking anyway."

"That's true, Blue Owl, but I want you to keep a tight rein on the men while we're here. Ain't no need of gettin' the town all riled up till we've rested a mite an' got our strength back."

"You think they might've heard anything 'bout us yet?" Blue Owl asked, peering through the falling snow at the few townspeople who were foolish enough to be outside in such weather.

"Naw. I don't see no telegraph wires, so there ain't no way they know anything 'bout us so far."

The men reined in their mounts in front of the largest saloon in town, called the Mother Lode, and hurried through the batwings, standing inside the door and stamping snow and ice off their boots before taking tables in the almost empty room.

Berlin went over to the bar. "Bring my men whiskey, an' plenty of it," he growled. "We're 'bout frozen to death."

The barman raised his eyebrows. "You men been out traveling in this weather?" he asked incredulously.

"We were on our way here from up north," Berlin said, "when the storm hit. For a while, we didn't know if we were gonna make it or not."

"You're plenty lucky to have made it through the passes 'fore the snow accumulated," the barman said, bringing several bottles of whiskey out from under the bar. "Another day, an' you would've been trapped up in the mountains till the snow melted."

Billy Bartlett and Moses Johnson walked over, picked up the whiskey bottles and some glasses, and took them to the nearby tables.

Berlin inclined his head toward the large Franklin stove

in the corner. "You think you could stoke that stove a mite?" he asked, shivering. "We'd sure appreciate a little extra heat in here."

"Sure thing," the barman said. "An' if you and your men want some grub and a place to bunk down, the boardinghouse up the street sets a fine table."

Berlin nodded, pouring himself a large glass of whiskey and drinking it down. "Much obliged, mister," he said. "Soon's we get a little firewater in our gullets, we'll head on over there."

"Livery's right next door too," the man added. "With this storm, it'd be best to get your animals under cover soon's you can."

"We'll do that," Berlin said, taking his bottle and heading over to the table where Bartlett, Blue Owl, and Sam Cook were sitting.

"What's the plan, Boss?" Cook asked.

"I figure we'll hold up here a couple'a days, till the storm passes. We can use the time to get our mounts rested an' our bellies full." He looked around at his men, some of whom were still shivering from the cold. "After all, we ain't in no hurry to get anywhere since we took care of the Army."

Guthrie rode into Grand Junction three and a half days after he left Rangely. He pushed his horses, both of which were on their last legs, and rode directly to the train station on the eastern edge of town.

He dismounted and rushed to the ticket window. "I need to get to Crested Butte as soon as possible," he said.

The ticket master shook his head. "That might be a bit of a problem, mister," he said. "Had a big storm go through the area south of here last couple'a days. Some of the passes might be blocked with snow."

"When will you know?"

"We're gonna send an engine with a snowplow on the

front through this afternoon. If it makes it, the engineer will telegraph us from Crested Butte and we'll send the next train on ahead."

Guthrie bit his lip, thinking for a moment. "Any chance of me hitchin' a ride on that snowplow?"

The ticket master frowned. "What's so all-fired important about getting to Crested Butte in such a hurry?" he asked.

"There's a group of thirty outlaws headed that way," Guthrie answered. "If I don't get there first and warn the town, there's liable to be dead people lyin' all over the streets of Crested Butte by tomorrow."

"Well, since it's a kind'a emergency, I'll check with the engineer and see if he'll let you ride along." The man paused, then continued. "I gotta warn you, though. It won't be an easy ride, what with the cold and snow and everything."

"I'll take my chances," Guthrie said. "A lot of lives depend on me getting through."

The ticket man nodded, and Guthrie asked, "Where's the telegraph office?"

The man pointed toward the center of town. "Right up the street there, you can't miss it."

Guthrie walked to the telegraph office and entered. He grabbed a sheet of yellow foolscap off the table and began writing a message to the Army post at Glenwood Springs, fifteen miles east of Rifle. He hopped they could send men to the small town in time to avoid a massacre if Berlin and his men headed there. Fort Collins, a much larger post, was too far away to do anything in time. Guthrie had been stationed for a short time at Glenwood Springs and he knew it was a small post, but at least they might be able to warn the town of Rifle that Berlin was on his way.

* * *

It was a measure of the smallness of the post at Glenwood Springs that the commanding officer was a shavetail lieutenant. He was fresh from officers' training and Glenwood was his first command. His name was Riley Woodcock. He was twenty-two years old, with a lack of experience to match his young age.

Sergeant Mark Goodson was the real leader of the small command, and Goodson prayed nightly that nothing untoward would happen that would test his young commanding officer's mettle.

It was Sergeant Goodson who got the wire from Sergeant Guthrie, and he was shaking his head as he carried it into Lieutenant Woodcock's office.

Woodcock looked up from his morning coffee. "Yes, what is it, Sergeant?" he asked, not liking the worried look on Goodson's face when he'd entered the office without knocking.

"Just got this wire from Grand Junction, sir," he said, handing the paper to Woodcock.

Woodcock read the wire, then laid it on the desk, a look of anticipation on his face. As much as Goodson prayed for nothing to happen, Woodcock had waited eagerly for some trouble in which he could act heroically and make a name, and perhaps gain a promotion, for himself.

"What's the status of the men, Sergeant?" Woodcock asked, standing and striding to the corner coat rack and buckling on his sword.

Goodson sighed. He'd been afraid of something like this ever since he'd read the wire. "Ready, sir," he said fatalistically.

Deciding to try to salvage the situation, Goodson added, "It seems a small matter to occupy you, sir. Perhaps I could take a squad of men and ride over to Rifle and warn the civilian authorities there of what may be coming."

Woodcock glanced over his shoulder. "There are no civilian authorities in Rifle, Sergeant. You know that." As he settled his hat on his head, he continued. "If anyone is to save the good people of Rifle from these desperados, it's got to be the Army."

"Yes, sir," Goodson said unhappily.

"Gather the men together in front of my office, geared up and ready to ride. Full arms."

"Yes, sir," Goodson said, snapping off a salute. As he walked out the door, he hoped the outlaws had headed someplace other than Rifle. He had no desire to go up against thirty armed and dangerous men with this kid leading the way. It was a sure recipe for disaster, he thought as he rounded up his men.

Thirty minutes later, Goodson had fifteen men sitting on their horses in formation in front of Woodcock's office.

Woodcock strolled out the door, set his hat firmly on his head, and climbed into the saddle.

"Sergeant, you may lead the men by columns of two off the post."

"Yes, sir," Goodson said. "Forward, ride!" he called, waving his hand and leading the way south by southwest toward the town of Rifle.

Lieutenant Woodcock rode alongside halfway down the column, sitting straight in the saddle, sure he was on his way to finding his destiny.

Eleven

Ozark Jack Berlin was enjoying the first real rest he'd had since escaping from prison a couple of weeks before. He and his men had been constantly on the run, sleeping and eating mostly on the trail, through some of the worst weather he'd ever seen.

This was the first time he'd been able to sit back and take it easy since he'd been caught after robbing that train up at Moab, Utah, and sentenced to ten years hard labor at the territorial prison. If he could only manage to keep his men in line and out of trouble, they might just stay here until the weather warmed up a bit. He didn't relish any more mad dashes through the mountains with winter storms beating them in the face.

Still, there was always the possibility someone would be on their trail. With this thought beginning to worry him, Berlin got out of his bed at the boardinghouse and walked down the hall to the room being shared by Jack McGraw and Tony Cassidy, two of the men who'd helped him rob the train that'd gotten him prison time.

He banged on the door until a hungover and sleepy-looking Jack McGraw opened the door.

"What the hell do you . . . oh, it's you, Boss," McGraw said, opening the door all the way and stepping to the side.

"I been thinkin', Jack," Berlin said.

"Yeah?"

"We might just be gettin' a mite careless lately. There's an outside possibility somebody may be on our back trail."

McGraw nodded, rubbing his eyes and trying to staunch the massive headache a fifth of whiskey from the night before was causing.

"I think we ought'a post a couple'a men on the north side of town, just in case trouble comes lookin' for us."

"Yeah?" McGraw said again, still not following what his boss was saying.

"You and Tony are gonna take the first watch. I want you to station yourselves in that little saloon right inside the town limits to the north. If you see anybody that don't look right, you hightail it on over to the boardin'house here and give us a warnin'."

"But Boss," McGraw whined, "it's might near freezin' outside."

Berlin's face got hard. "I don't aim to make the same mistake got us caught the last time, Jack. Now you and Tony get your asses over to that saloon . . . an' go easy on the whiskey while you're on watch. Beer only, you hear me?"

McGraw rubbed his temples. "Beer's about all I can handle right now anyway, Ozark," he answered.

"Get Tony outta bed and haul your butts over there. I'll send somebody to relieve you in time for lunch."

"Yes, sir," McGraw said with poor grace as he turned to wake his friend up.

Sergeant Bob Guthrie was standing in the cab of the snowplow engine, sweating from the heat coming from the furnace as the engine slowly plowed through three feet of snow on the railway line between Grand Junction and Crested Butte. It had been slow going through the previous day and last night, with the mountain passes having accumulated snowdrifts four and five feet high, but they were getting close to breaking through to lower elevations where the snow wouldn't be so bad.

"You think we'll make it by noon?" Guthrie yelled to the engineer, trying to be heard over the roar of the steam engine as it struggled to push the plow through the snow.

The engineer leaned his head out of the window and spat a brown stream of tobacco juice into the snow alongside the tracks before he answered.

He glanced ahead of the engine, shielding his eyes from the glare of sun off the snow, then leaned back into the engine compartment. "I reckon so. This ought'a be 'bout the last of the heavy snow. From here on in, it's gonna get flatter, an' that means we can go faster."

"Good," Guthrie said.

"You never did tell me why you're in such an all-fired hurry to get to Crested Butte," the engineer said. "There ain't much there to get all excited about."

"I got a date with some outlaws," Guthrie said shortly.

The engineer laughed. "Hell, if that's all you're lookin' for, you can find them just 'bout ever'where you look in these parts. 'Bout the only kind'a men who come to the high lonesome in the winter are either miners crazy with gold fever or men on the run from someplace else."

"Well, these men are the worst of the lot," Guthrie said, his lips tight. "They need killin' in the worst way, an' I intend to oblige 'em."

When the squad of Army men crested a hill overlooking the town of Rifle, Sergeant Mark Goodson reined his horse to a stop and waited for Lieutenant Riley Woodcock to ride up next to him.

"Why are you stopping, Sergeant?" Woodcock asked.

"I was thinkin', Lieutenant," Goodson said. "If those outlaws are already in Rifle, maybe we'd better split up the men and sneak into town one or two at a time. No need to warn 'em we're comin' after 'em."

Woodcock thought for a moment, then shook his head. "I don't intend to split up my command, Sergeant. That's a mistake General Custer made against the Sioux, and it cost him the lives of all his men."

"But Lieutenant," Goodson started to protest.

"You heard me, Sergeant. Let's ride in showing the colors at full force. If those outlaws have any sense, when they see the United States Army arrive, they'll give themselves up without a fight."

Goodson started to remind the lieutenant they hadn't given themselves up the last time they faced the Army, but then figured it wouldn't make any difference. The lieutenant had his mind made up, and didn't appear ready to listen to reason.

"Yes, sir," Goodson said. He stood up in his stirrups and addressed the men. "Make ready your arms," he called. "I want every one of you ready for trouble the minute we hit the town limits."

"I'll take the point from here on in, Sergeant," Woodcock said, spurring his horse to lead his men into the town.

"Damn fool!" Goodson whispered to himself as he followed the lieutenant down the hill toward Rifle.

Tony Cassidy was sitting next to a window overlooking the main street of Rifle, nursing a beer and eating boiled eggs, when he saw the squad of Army men riding into town.

He almost choked on his eggs as he punched Jack McGraw in the shoulder. "Look at that, Jack," he whispered urgently.

McGraw turned his attention from the prostitute he'd been talking to and glanced out the window.

"Goddamn!" he uttered, pushing her off his lap and putting his beer down.

"How many you make it?" he asked.

"Looks like seventeen," Cassidy answered. "And they're loaded for bear. They all got their rifles at the ready."

"You ease out the front door and keep an eye on 'em," McGraw said. "I'll sneak out the back door and let Ozark know what's goin' on."

"You think they're comin' here after us?" Cassidy asked.

"They didn't ride through this weather to pick flowers, Tony," McGraw answered as he walked rapidly toward the back door of the saloon.

He ran as fast as he could, stumbling through the two feet of snow on the ground, until he came to the back door of the boardinghouse, where the rest of the men were staying.

He pounded up the stairs and burst into Berlin's room without knocking.

"What the . . . ?" Berlin said, jumping out of bed, his pistol in his hand.

"Soldiers, Ozark, 'bout seventeen of 'em an' they're headin' up Main Street as big as you please."

Berlin began pulling his trousers on over his longhandles. "Get the rest of the men up and ready," he ordered.

Within several minutes, the entire gang was gathered in the sitting room of the boardinghouse. Berlin began to give orders rapidly. He assigned six men to upstairs windows with rifles, and told the rest to sneak out the door and spread out in the alleys fronting Main Street.

"We'll catch the dumb bastards in a crossfire," he said, checking the loads in his pistol as he spoke.

As they walked their horses down the middle of Main Street, Goodson tried to reason with Woodcock one last time. "Let me get the men to dismount an' spread out, Lieutenant," he pleaded. "We're easy targets out in the middle of the street like this."

Lieutenant Woodcock glanced around at the town. There were only a couple of miners visible on the boardwalks, and no horses were seen reined in front of the various saloons at this early hour.

"I think we're wasting our time, Sergeant. I see no evidence of thirty men gathered in this town. Perhaps the outlaws were caught in that storm and haven't made it down out of the mountains yet."

"Just the same, sir," Goodson began, but he never got to finish his sentence.

Explosions of gunfire erupted from the upper stories of a boardinghouse to their right, knocking four soldiers out of their saddles without warning.

The soldiers' horses began to crow-hop and jump under the onslaught of the fire from above, making the soldiers unable to return fire.

Just as Goodson got his mount under control, men began to pour out of alleys and doorways on either side of them, firing and shooting as fast as they could.

Lieutenant Woodcock was hit in the left arm and stomach and blown off his horse, along with seven more of his men, in the first volley of gunfire.

Goodson leaned over the neck of his horse, pulling his Colt from its holster, as he spurred his mount forward toward the men in the street.

He got off three shots, killing two of the outlaws before a bullet hit him square in the forehead, blowing brains and hair out of the back of his skull. Goodson was dead before his body hit the ground.

The last four soldiers managed to wound only two more of the outlaws before they were killed in the assault. Main Street of Rifle, Colorado, was immersed in a heavy cloud of cordite and gun smoke when the battle ended, just three minutes after it began.

The townspeople, showing good sense, remained indoors, not wanting any part of whatever was going on in their town.

Berlin reloaded his pistol as he walked among the dead

and dying soldiers, some of whom were moaning and crying for help as they lay in the bloodstained snow of Main Street.

"Hey, Ozark," Blue Owl called. "There's an officer here who's still alive."

Berlin strolled over to where Blue Owl was standing over a man with lieutenant's bars on his uniform.

Berlin squatted in front of Woodcock, who was holding his stomach and groaning in pain.

Berlin slapped him in the face to get his attention. "Lieutenant, how'd you know we was here?" he asked.

"Go to hell," Woodcock grunted, staring at Berlin with hatred.

Berlin cocked his pistol and put it against Woodcock's right knee. "I'm gonna ask you one more time, Lieutenant. Who told you we was here?"

"You wouldn't dare!" Woodcock said, his eyes wide with fear and pain.

Berlin pulled the trigger, blowing Woodcock's right kneecap off and shattering the bones of his leg.

"Aiyeee!" screamed Woodcock, rolling to the side and retching in the snow next to where he lay.

Berlin rolled him back over and put the pistol against his left knee. "You gonna answer me?" he growled.

"All right . . . we got a wire from an Army Sergeant in Grand Junction," Woodcock rasped, barely able to speak. "He said you'd killed all his men and were headed this way."

"Son of a bitch," Blue Owl said. "We must've let one of those soldiers live back in the mountains."

Berlin stood up and holstered his pistol. "Well, this changes our plans a mite. We gotta get movin', 'fore somebody else gets on our trail."

"You gonna finish this one off?" Blue Owl asked.

Berlin looked down at Woodcock, who was watching blood pump from his shattered leg.

"Naw, the bastard'll be dead in five minutes the way

he's leakin' blood all over the ground. Let him suffer as long as he lasts."

"What are we gonna do now?" Blue Owl asked.

"Round up the men. We're headin' south."

Twelve

As soon as the snowplow engine made it to the train station at Crested Butte, Colorado, Sergeant Bob Guthrie thanked the engineer for his help and jumped to the ground. He ran as fast as he could through the several feet of accumulated snow to the office, and asked for directions to the sheriff's office in town.

"You can't hardly miss it, stranger," the laconic stationmaster drawled. He walked to the door and pointed down the main street. "Ain't but one street in Crested Butte, an' the sheriff's office is smack dab in the middle, on the left 'bout halfway down the street."

"Thanks," Guthrie said, already moving in the direction the man had pointed.

When he got to the sheriff's office, he entered, to find a long, tall man, thin as a string bean, sitting leaned back in his desk chair with his boots on the desk and a steaming mug of coffee wrapped in his hands on his chest.

"Howdy, mister," the sheriff said. He inclined his head toward a potbellied stove in a corner with a pot of coffee warming on the top. "Grab yourself some coffee to ward off the chill and have a seat."

Guthrie slapped his arms against his chest, kicked snow off his boots, and made his way toward the coffeepot.

"If you call this a chill, I'd hate to see what it's like when you say it's cold," he said.

The sheriff smiled. "Oh, this is just a little fall storm.

We won't get the real cold weather for another month or so."

Guthrie poured the coffee, which was so dark and thick he thought it could float a horseshoe, and walked over to take a chair in front of the sheriff's desk.

"I'm Wally Pepper," the sheriff said, "and if you're looking for the law in this town, I guess I'm it."

"I'm Sergeant Bob Guthrie," Guthrie said, holding his mug with both hands as he sipped, trying to stop shaking from the cold.

"Well, we're a mite far from any Army posts, Sergeant," Pepper said, putting his feet on the ground and leaning forward with his elbows on the desk.

"That's what I'm here about," Guthrie said. "About two weeks ago, thirty of the worst killers in Utah escaped from the territorial prison."

Pepper's eyes narrowed and his expression became more serious.

"Since then, the desperados have been making their way in this direction," Guthrie said. "Along the way, they've slaughtered over forty men in my command, along with an unknown number of civilians in Lode, Utah, and Rangely, Colorado."

Pepper pursed his lips as he ran a hand over a two-day growth of beard. "You say there's thirty of these killers?"

"Thereabouts," Guthrie answered. "Before I came down here, I wired the Army post at Glenwood Springs in hopes they'd send some men to Rifle to see if they could stop the bastards before they killed anyone else."

"Ain't no telegraph in Rifle," Pepper said, as if to himself, "so I guess we won't know for a while if they managed to do any good or not."

"That's what I wanted to talk to you about, Sheriff. If the Army failed to stop them, an' they keep on their same track, they'll be headed here to Crested Butte in the next few days."

"And you think we ought'a arrange a little welcome for

these killers?" the sheriff asked, a slow grin curling his lips up over blackened stubs of teeth.

Guthrie leaned back in his chair, glad to see the sheriff was getting his drift. "Yes, sir. They are all hardened criminals with nothing to lose, so they kill at the drop of a hat."

"And I guess I can assume they're well armed?"

"They've stolen all the rifles and ammunition, along with considerable amounts of dynamite and gunpowder, they need to go through this town like grain through a goose," Guthrie said.

"Well," the sheriff said, "we'll see about that. The miners in this town work hard for their money, and they ain't exactly gonna be thrilled at the idea of a bunch of prison rats trying to steal it."

"I don't mean to push, Sheriff, but we may not have much time."

Pepper held up his hand. "Hold onto your water, Sergeant. We got us a fire bell at the end of town. Come on with me and I'll ring the damned thing and before you know it, the town'll be full of men armed to the teeth, ready and willing to fight for what's theirs."

True to his word, in less than an hour, Sheriff Pepper had over a hundred men gathered in front of his office, and about thirty women who looked every bit as hard.

"Folks," the sheriff said, standing on the boardwalk in front of the crowd. "The sergeant here tells us we got us a gang of cutthroats and killers headed this way. They've managed to make a mess of a couple of towns on the way here, and the sergeant is worried they might do the same to Crested Butte."

One of the men, heavyset, with arms as big around as barrels and a full beard, held up a short-barreled shotgun. "You tell the sergeant to step back outta the way, Sheriff, an' watch us teach those bastards a lesson they won't soon forget!" the man shouted, to resounding cheers and yells from the rest of the crowd.

"Jacob, I'm glad to hear you say that," Sheriff Pepper said. "Why don't you and Billy Bob and Sammy head on up north of town and stake out the trail coming from Rifle. If you see those sons of bitches headed this way, you scamper on back here and let us know."

As the men in the crowd nodded agreement with this plan, the sheriff rubbed his hands together. "Meanwhile, I'd suggest most of you stay here in town for the next couple of days in case we need you." He hesitated, then grinned. "I'm sure Sadie and the rest of her girls can use the extra income."

"You're right about that, Sheriff," a woman with a large feather hat and painted face hollered. "And to make sure everybody has a good time, drinks are gonna be half price till the outlaws are killed."

A young man who looked to be no more than eighteen years old hollered back, "How about the rest of your merchandise, Sadie? That half price too?"

Sadie threw back her head and laughed. "I'll tell you what, Joe. You last longer'n ten minutes, an' you can have it for free!"

The crowd yelled their approval as the young man's face turned beet red, until finally he began to laugh too.

The sheriff took Guthrie to a nearby boardinghouse, and offered to buy him supper for him taking the trouble to travel through the mountain passes to bring them a warning.

Guthrie shook his head. "That's not necessary, Sheriff. Those bastards killed my men, an' my commanding officer. I intend to track 'em until either they're all dead an' buried, or I am."

Sheriff Pepper nodded. "Vengeance is a powerful motivator, Sergeant. Just be sure it don't cloud your mind enough to cause you to make fatal mistakes."

"Those *bandidos* made the mistake, Sheriff, when they killed my friends. I ain't gonna rest till they're made to pay for what they done."

As they headed out of Rifle, Ozark Jack Berlin sent a half-breed Indian named Spotted Dog ahead to check out the trail. Spotted Dog had been a scout for the Army, until the day he'd raped and killed a ten-year-old girl who'd wandered off the Army base.

Luckily for Spotted Dog, he'd managed to get away from the post before he was caught. Otherwise, he'd never have lived long enough to be sentenced to hang. The escape from the territorial prison had come one month to the day before he was due to be executed.

Spotted Dog was an excellent tracker, and headed out ahead of the gang, staying off the trail so he wouldn't be seen by anyone who might be waiting for them.

The gang was just rounding a turn in the trail when Spotted Dog came galloping toward them.

Berlin held up his hand, halting his men, and sat waiting for Spotted Dog to arrive.

"Ozark," he yelled as he reined his sweating horse to a halt in front of Berlin.

"Yeah, what'd you see, Dog?" Berlin asked, bending into the wind to light a cigar.

"There are several men ahead, waiting in ambush in rocks that look down on the trail."

"How many you talkin' 'bout?"

"I see four, but may be more in bushes," Spotted Dog answered, accepting a small bottle of whiskey Blue Owl offered and taking a long drink.

"They must've gotten word we was comin' somehow," Berlin said, almost as if to himself.

"You think it could'a been that sergeant that officer told us about in Rifle?" Blue Owl asked.

Berlin shrugged. "Don't really matter who or how; fact is, we got to change our plans now," he said. "If they got men on the trail out here, then the town's bound to be ready for us too."

Berlin sat there in his saddle, thinking and smoking for a few minutes. Finally, his gaze lit on the railroad tracks off to the left of the trail, and he nodded.

"I know what we're gonna do."

He jerked his horse's head around and began to ride out cross-country, having to go slow through the snow.

Blue Owl rode next to him, the gang following along behind.

"Where the hell you goin', Boss?" Blue Owl hollered, trying to be heard over the wind.

"We're goin' to catch a train, Blue Owl," Berlin answered.

Thirteen

Ozark Jack Berlin led his gang cross-country, keeping the small buildings of Crested Butte, Colorado, in view off to their left. He stopped occasionally to consult the map he'd taken from the general store in Lode, checking to make sure they were headed in the general direction the train tracks took when they left the town.

A little over four hours after leaving the trail, they crossed the tracks several miles from the southern limits of Crested Butte.

Berlin followed the tracks until they made a wide turn around a small hillock. He reined his horse to a stop.

"Blue Owl, take a couple of sticks of dynamite and blow that big maple tree down over there," he said, pointing to a large tree next to the tracks.

"All right," Blue Owl said, reaching into his saddlebags.

After the tree had been felled and was lying across the tracks, Berlin led his men back into a strand of trees and out of sight.

"When is the train due?" Wiley Gottlieb asked.

"How the hell should I know?" Berlin answered.

"Well, should we make a fire and cook some coffee?" Gottlieb asked. "I'm 'bout near frozen through."

"Sure," Berlin answered, "but try an' use old wood so it won't smoke so much. We don't want them to see the smoke over in Crested Butte."

* * *

The men managed to get their fill of hot coffee, laced with whiskey, before the mournful whistle of the oncoming train sounded about an hour later.

"Mount up, men," Berlin shouted. "We got us a train to catch."

When the train rounded the bend in the tracks, the engineer saw the tree blocking the rails and hit the brakes, causing the wheels to lock and send up bright red and orange sparks as the train slowed.

Berlin shouted, "Let's ride!" and led the way out of the trees and down the slight slope toward the train before it had stopped completely.

The engineer held up his hands and stepped to the doorway of the engine when he saw the gang of outlaws riding toward him with guns drawn.

He stood there until Berlin reined to a halt next to the engine.

"You gents are outta luck," the engineer said, a worried frown on his face. "We ain't carryin' no money nor gold on this trip."

Berlin grinned. "You got us wrong, mister," he said. "We ain't gonna rob you . . . we just want a ride."

While some of the gang tied ropes to the tree and pulled it off the tracks, others went car to car, confiscating weapons and what small amounts of money and jewelry the passengers had.

Once they had everyone covered, they went to the baggage cars, threw the suitcases and valises out onto the ground, placed ramps up to the cars, and led their horses onto the train.

While they were loading the horses, Berlin had Spotted Dog climb up the telegraph pole near the track and cut the wires to keep anyone in Crested Butte from warning the towns down the line that they were on their way.

While Spotted Dog was cutting the wires, Berlin took four sticks of dynamite and stuffed them under the tracks behind the train. When the dynamite exploded, the rails were left bent and curled, with twenty feet of track destroyed.

"Now, won't have to worry 'bout nobody comin' after us on this track," Berlin muttered to himself as he surveyed the damage.

When they had everything loaded, Berlin sent Billy Bartlett up to the engine to tell the engineer to start the train.

As it began to slowly move forward, Berlin put all the passengers into one car with a couple of men left to keep them covered, and told the rest of his men to spread out and get some sleep.

"Where we goin'?" Jack McGraw asked.

"I'd like to put a few hundred miles 'tween us an' the Army," Berlin said, glancing again at his map. "I figure we can ride this train down near Pueblo an' get off there. That ought'a be far enough to throw 'em off our trail."

Sergeant Bob Guthrie was having breakfast the next morning with Sheriff Waldo Pepper at the boardinghouse where he was staying while in Crested Butte.

Pepper finished his eggs and bacon, sopped up some gravy on his biscuit, and stuffed it in his mouth. As he chewed, he pulled out his pocket watch.

"It looks like your bandits ain't gonna be coming this way after all, Sergeant," he said in his husky voice. "Maybe the Army men you sent after 'em from Glenwood Springs got 'em after all."

Guthrie shook his head. "Maybe, Sheriff, but it just don't figure."

"Well, they've had plenty of time to get here by now if they was coming," the sheriff said, leaning back in his chair and sipping his coffee.

"You're right about that," Guthrie said. "Maybe we oughta take a ride out to the men you've got stationed north of town and see if they've seen or heard anything."

Pepper shrugged. "If you say so, Sergeant, but I'm beginning to think this is a waste of time."

They saddled up their horses and rode northward out of town, toward the sentries Pepper had placed there.

They hadn't traveled more than a few miles before Guthrie slowed his horse and shaded his eyes against bright sunlight.

"What's that you see?" Pepper asked, following the sergeant's gaze.

"Smoke," Guthrie answered shortly. "The damn fools you've got on sentry duty have a fire goin'."

Pepper shrugged. "So what? It's damn cold out here."

Guthrie gave him a look, his eyes flat. "If we can see the smoke, Sheriff, the outlaws can too. You think they're dumb enough to ride into an ambush?"

"I didn't think of that," the sheriff replied.

"Come on," Guthrie said, spurring his horse forward.

When they got to the small rise where the sentries were keeping watch, they found them sitting around a large fire, holding their hands out to keep them warm.

"Howdy, Sheriff," one of the men called. "We ain't seen hide nor hair of anybody all morning."

Guthrie just shook his head, muttering to himself as he turned his horse's head northward and rode up the trail toward Rifle, followed by Sheriff Pepper.

Two miles from the sentry post, they came upon a collection of horse tracks still evident in the snow on the trail. The tracks showed where the gang had stopped and milled around for a while. Then the tracks led off the trail cross-country to the southwest.

Guthrie leaned over his horse's head, his arms crossed on his saddle horn. "Looks like the outlaws saw your sentries an' decided to take out cross-country, Sheriff."

"Damn!" Sheriff Pepper growled. "There ain't nothing out there for a hundred miles, 'cept mountains. If they try and cross those on horseback in this weather, they're gonna freeze to death 'fore too long."

Guthrie shook his head. It just didn't make sense. The outlaws weren't that stupid, he thought to himself.

He walked his horse off the trail, following the outlaws' tracks. After twenty yards, he came to the railroad tracks.

"Son of a bitch," he said, slapping his thigh.

"What is it?" Pepper asked, coming up next to him.

"Which way does the railroad go when it leaves Crested Butte?" he asked.

"Why, it curves off to the southwest 'bout a mile or two out of town," Pepper answered.

Guthrie jerked his horse's head around. "Come on, Sheriff. I think the outlaws plan to stop the train after it leaves town and use it to get out of the area."

"Damn!" Pepper said. "I hope we're not too late. We had a train go through town yesterday."

When they got back to Crested Butte, a man ran out into the street, waving his arms at them.

"Who's that?" Guthrie asked as they slowed their horses.

"It's Sam Wright, the telegraph operator."

"Sheriff," Wright said when they stopped in front of him. "The telegraph line is down south of town. I ain't gettin' no signal at all."

Pepper looked over at Guthrie. "Looks like you was right, Sergeant."

"You better get some men together an' let's go see if we can fix the wire," Guthrie said. "And tell the station-master to hold the next train when it gets to town. He's gonna have another passenger."

"I'll be goddamned," Pepper said two hours later when they came upon the destroyed track.

Guthrie sighed. "How long will it take you to get the track repaired?" he asked.

Pepper shrugged. "At least a couple of days in this weather."

"Maybe we can fix the wire an' send a message on down the tracks," Wright said hopefully.

Guthrie shook his head. "The outlaws are too smart for that," he said. "They'll probably stop the train every few hours an' cut the wire in a different place. I think our only chance is to work fast to get this track repaired and go after them by train, at least until I can get to a town that has a workin' telegraph."

Pepper nodded. "I'll get every man in town working on fixing the rails. Maybe we can cut the time down to one day."

Guthrie nodded. "I'll contact the stationmaster in town and see if we can get an engine down here that might be able to catch them 'fore they get too far. If we cut all the cars loose, I can make faster time than they can."

Pepper's gaze followed the tracks as they disappeared in the distance. "I wonder what they're gonna do with all the passengers on that train they stopped."

Guthrie stared at him, his eyes haunted. "You probably don't want to know, Sheriff."

Fourteen

The train carrying the outlaws sped through mountain passes, stopping only to take on water when the boiler got low. There was plenty of food, so on the few occasions when they came to small towns, Berlin had the engineer keep the train at full speed through the stations.

Once his men were rested up from their long journey on horseback from Rifle to Crested Butte, Berlin decided to do something about the passengers.

He had the engineer stop the train on one of the mountain passes, high among the peaks of the Rockies.

He pulled his pistol from its holster and walked back to the passenger car where the civilian prisoners were being kept under watch by his men.

"All right," he called from the front of the car. "All you men, get your belongings together and get off the train."

One of the men, a drummer selling the latest in mining tools, stood up, terror in his eyes. "You aren't going to shoot us, are you, mister?" he asked, his hands trembling as they held his bowler hat in front of him.

Berlin grinned. "Nope, I'm just gonna put you off the train so's my men won't have to spend all their time watchin' you."

Another man, dressed in dungarees and a heavy buckskin coat, leaned over to glance out the window. "They won't have to shoot us, drummer," he said, pulling his coat tight around him as he straightened up. "Chances are, we're gonna freeze to death soon as the sun goes down."

"You can't do this to us," a woman traveling with a daughter in her teens cried. "We'll all die out here in the wilderness without food or water."

Berlin shook his head. "Oh, don't worry, miss," he said, his voice husky. "I ain't throwin' you women off the train, just the men."

The cowboy in the buckskin coat shook his head, took a leather valise down from the rack over the seats, and walked toward the door to the car, mumbling, "You'd be better off with us, lady."

Once the male passengers were all off the car, standing in a group next to the tracks, Berlin told one of his men to have the engineer start the train.

As the whistle blew and steam poured from the engine and the wheels began to roll slowly down the track, he put his pistol back in his holster and walked over to stand before the girl in her teens sitting next to her mother.

"You," he said, grabbing the girl by her wrist, "come with me. I got something to show you up in my car."

"Let her go!" the mother screamed, reaching for his arm.

Wiley Gottlieb stepped over and pulled her back. "Take it easy, Mama. You're gonna be busy enough back here with us so's you won't have to worry none 'bout your little girl."

The rest of the men laughed and moved forward, grabbing the other women on the train, even the seventy-year-old grandmother in the front seat.

The work crew from Crested Butte, working well into the night, managed to get the tracks repaired in sixteen hours.

After Sheriff Pepper stopped the next train through the town, Guthrie had the conductor disconnect all the passenger cars, leaving only the engine and coal car attached.

Guthrie stepped onto the engine platform, leaned down, and shook Sheriff Pepper's hand. "Thanks, Sheriff, for all you and your men done."

"You sure you don't want some of us to ride along with you?" the sheriff asked.

Guthrie shook his head. "It ain't your problem now, Sheriff, but you could do something else for me."

"What's that?"

"Have your telegraph operator wire some of the towns to the north, where the wires ain't been cut. Then, they can try to wire other towns in a circle around us until they get word to Pueblo to be on the lookout for the stolen train."

"Damn, that's a good idea," Sheriff Pepper said.

Guthrie shrugged. "It's worth a try, though with these winter storms, some of the other lines might be down too. If they manage to get through, tell the sheriff in Pueblo to try an' get the Army to send some men to help. It's too big a job for one or two men to handle alone."

"You got it, Sergeant."

"Adios, Sheriff Pepper. Try not to freeze your balls off this winter."

Pepper grinned and tipped his hat as the train pulled out of the station. "I'll sure do my best, Sergeant," he called.

The next morning, after twelve straight hours riding the engine through the mountains, Guthrie came upon the group of men Berlin had kicked off his train.

He had the engineer stop the train when he saw the group huddled around a fire next to the tracks. Two bodies lay nearby, covered with pine tree branches.

"Thank God!" the drummer hollered, running for the engine.

Soon, the men had filled Guthrie in on what Berlin had done, and how he'd kept the women on board.

"Come on up," Guthrie said. "It's gonna be crowded with all of you in the engine, so leave the dead ones where they are. We'll send someone back for 'em from the next town."

As the cowboy in the buckskin coat swung on board, he looked at Guthrie. "You goin' after those bastards all by yourself?"

Guthrie nodded.

The cowboy grinned. "If you don't mind, I might just ride along with you for a spell."

"This ain't your fight, cowboy," Guthrie said, his eyes narrow.

"It is now!" the cowboy growled. "Back in Texas, where I hail from, we don't let men treat womenfolk that way and get away with it."

"These are pretty dangerous men, Texas," Guthrie said evenly, letting his eyes fall to the empty holster on the cowboy's belt, noting it was tied down low on his hip.

"So am I, Army," the cowboy replied. "So am I."

Fifteen

Smoke Jensen and Pearlie were riding in the back of a buckboard, throwing bales of summer hay off for the cattle to eat, while Cal drove the wagon.

"I can't hardly believe we got snow coverin' the ground so early in the season," Pearlie complained, straightening up and sleeving sweat off his brow.

Smoke glanced at heavy dark clouds covering the sky. "Yeah, looks like it's gonna be a cold winter this year."

Cal laughed from the front of the wagon. "Hell, I ain't never seen a warm one up here in the high lonesome, Smoke," he said.

"I told you when I saw how fat the squirrels were getting from eating all those acorns, it was going to be a particularly bad one this year," Smoke said.

"Hold on a minute, Cal," Pearlie said. "I want to build me a smoke 'fore you take off again."

Cal stood up and climbed over the seat to join Smoke and Pearlie in the back of the buckboard. "I think I'll have one with you," he said.

"Be careful you don't set this hay to burning," Smoke said.

"Hell," Pearlie replied as he put a lucifer to his butt, "least it'd keep us warm."

Smoke had started to reply when he noticed a trio of riders coming toward them across his ranch.

"Looks like we got company coming," he observed, sitting on a bale and pulling a long, black cigar out of his pocket.

He'd just gotten it lit when Sheriff Monte Carson and two other men reined in next to the wagon.

"Howdy, Monte," Smoke called. "What brings you out here on such a cold morning?"

"Smoke, I got some bad news. This here is Sergeant Bob Guthrie, from Utah, and Jed McCulloch, from Texas."

Smoke looked at the two men Monte introduced. He liked what he saw. Guthrie was of medium height, broad-shouldered, with a square body and a face wrinkled from years under the sun. McCulloch was tall and lanky, with a wiry build, sky-blue eyes, dark, unruly hair under a large, Texas-style Stetson hat, and a grin that made him look like a kid in his teens.

Smoke smiled. "You any relation to Big Jake McCulloch down in Texas?" he asked the Texan.

Jed's lips curled in an answering grin and he nodded. "He's my uncle."

"I met Big Jake a couple of years ago when I was down at the King Ranch getting some breeding stock. Jake's ranch is only slightly smaller than King's," Smoke said.

Jed nodded. "That's right, but Jake's has got better grass, and better stock."

Smoke laughed. "So I hear."

He turned his attention back to Monte Carson. "What's the bad news, Monte?"

"You remember those escaped outlaws I told you about last week? The ones escaped from the territorial prison in Utah?"

"Uh-huh," Smoke said.

"Well, Bob and Jed here have been on their trail. Seems they stole a train up in Crested Butte a couple of days ago headed toward Pueblo."

"Stole a train?" Smoke asked. "Don't you mean robbed a train?"

"No," Guthrie replied. "They stopped the train and got on board, including their horses. After they rode it for about a hundred miles, they put the male passengers off, but kept the women."

Smoke's eyes hardened and his jaw muscles tightened. He knew what that meant. While most men of the West adhered to a code of conduct that kept women and children safe, he knew there were some so depraved they would prey on anyone that crossed their paths.

"How'd you two come to be on their trail?" Smoke asked.

Guthrie's face got somber. "It was my command sent after 'em in Utah. They ambushed us up in the mountains an' killed all my men, including the lieutenant in charge. I been doggin' their trail ever since."

Smoke's eyes drifted to Jed.

"I was one of the passengers on the train they high-jacked," he said. "When Bob here picked us up after the outlaws put us off the train, I decided to ride along. I don't much care for men who abuse women and children."

"The train carrying the outlaws roared through Big Rock without stoppin' early yesterday morning," Monte added. "Late last night, Bob and Jed came followin' 'em in their own train."

"We were dead tired after riding for almost thirty-six hours straight," Guthrie said. "We decided to take a short break for some food and much needed sleep. When we started out this morning, we found they'd dynamited the tracks behind them, evidently to keep anyone from following 'em. The sheriff here said if we wanted to track 'em on horseback, there wasn't anybody knew the country better'n you, Mr. Jensen."

Smoke looked at Monte. "You wire Pueblo to be on the lookout for the outlaws?" he asked.

Monte nodded. "I told 'em to put up a barrier on the tracks to keep 'em from blasting through town. If those bastards stay on the train till it gets to Pueblo, they're gonna be in for a surprise."

Smoke stroked his chin, thinking. "It's about thirty miles cross-country to Pueblo, more like fifty the way the tracks go."

"I don't figure they'll stay on the train all the way to Pueblo," Guthrie said. "So far, the man who's been leadin' 'em has been pretty smart. He's bound to know they'll be waitin' for him somewhere's down the road."

"Who's the man in charge of the gang?" Pearlie asked.

Guthrie looked at him. "Ozark Jack Berlin," he answered shortly, frowning as if the name left a bad taste in his mouth.

"Ozark Jack Berlin the famous train robber?" Cal asked, his eyes wide. Cal was addicted to dime novels, and followed closely the exploits of famous men of the West, both good and bad.

"Yeah," Guthrie replied. "He's hard an' mean as they come, an' he knows trains."

Smoke climbed up onto the seat of the buckboard. "Come on back to the house," he said. "We'll get some food and provisions and then we'll see what we can do about Mr. Berlin and his men."

As they started off toward Smoke's cabin, Jed said, "We might ought'a take some extra provisions along, just in case we find the women alive."

Smoke nodded. "I'll ask my wife Sally to come along. She's pretty handy at fixing people up who've been hurt."

Guthrie protested, "This ain't no job to take a woman along on, Mr. Jensen."

Monte Carson laughed. "Wait until you meet Sally," he said. "She ain't a woman to take no for an answer if she thinks somebody needs her help."

"Still . . ." Guthrie started.

"Don't worry about it being too tough a job for Sally," Smoke said. "She came up here to teach school when there wasn't hardly nothing but Indians and mountain men and a few settlers in these parts. She can handle anything thrown at her, and then some."

* * *

Sally came out on the cabin's porch when she heard the men ride up.

"Hello, Monte," she called, wiping her hands on an apron tied around her waist.

"Mornin' Sally," Monte replied, tipping his hat as he climbed down off his horse.

"Sally, this here is Jed McCulloch and Sergeant Bob Guthrie," Smoke said, introducing the two visitors.

"Pleased to meet ya, ma'am," Jed said, while Guthrie touched his hat and nodded.

"Come in, gentlemen," Sally said. "It's a little late for breakfast, but I've got a batch of bear sign hot out of the oven and a fresh pot of coffee."

Pearlie jumped down off the wagon and walked straight past Sally toward the door to the cabin.

Cal, climbing down more slowly, said, "You boys better make tracks toward the kitchen if you want any of Miss Sally's bear sign. If we leave Pearlie alone in there, he's liable to eat 'em all 'fore we can get through the door."

"Bear sign?" Jed asked, a puzzled smile on his face.

"I think you call them *pan dulce* down in Texas," Smoke said. "They're sweet as molasses and light as a cloud the way Sally makes them."

After the men were all seated around the kitchen table, with a platter of bear sign and mugs of steaming coffee in front of them, Smoke filled Sally in on what Monte and the two men had told him about the outlaws.

Sally's face became serious when she heard about the women being kept as hostages. "Oh, dear," she said, a hand to her mouth. "Those poor women."

"I'm going to lead Monte and the boys cross-country to see if we can intercept the train, Sally," Smoke explained. "I think you might ought to come with us, bringing your medical kit, so's you can help take care of the womenfolk if they're still alive."

She nodded. "You're right, Smoke. I'll go get my things together while you men finish your food."

She got up from the table. "Pearlie, if you and Cal can

tear yourself away from the bear sign, would you get a couple of horses out of the remuda?" she asked. "I'll need them as pack animals for the supplies we're going to need to go cross-country."

"Yes, ma'am," Pearlie grunted around a mouthful of doughnuts and coffee.

"How about that buckboard?" Jed asked. "Wouldn't it be better?"

Smoke wagged his head. "The country we're gonna be traveling over won't be suitable for a wagon," he said. "It's gonna be hard enough to get the horses through the snow in some of the passes."

"You mean, we're going up over the mountains?" Guthrie asked, a look of surprise on his face.

"If you want to make up for lost time, it's the only way to go and have any chance of catching those men."

Guthrie fingered his Army overcoat. "I'm afraid I didn't come dressed for that kind of trip."

Cal grinned. "Don't worry, Sergeant. We got plenty of cold-weather duds in the bunkhouse. Pearlie and me'll fix you up where you'll be warm as toast."

An hour later, with extra canteens filled with hot coffee and a sack of fried chicken Sally had left over from dinner the night before tied to the packhorses, the group took off toward mountain peaks in the distance.

The weather was cold, but sunny, with the temperature hovering in the midforties.

"Leastways, there don't appear to be any snow on the way," Guthrie said.

Smoke inclined his head toward the mountains, where the white, snow-covered peaks were partially obscured by roiling, black clouds.

"Not for another six or seven hours," he said, "but I expect along about nightfall, we're gonna get a storm that'll drop a couple of feet of snow by morning."

"How can you tell?" Jed asked.

Sally laughed. "Smoke spent his formative years living up in the high lonesome with an old mountain man named Preacher," she said. "He learned to read the clouds and wind like some men learn to read books."

Smoke nodded. "Living up in the mountains, if you don't learn to foretell the weather, you don't live through your first winter."

Sixteen

Ozark Jack Berlin made his way through the passenger cars until he climbed into the engine compartment. He nodded hello to Jack McGraw, who was busy shoveling small logs from the tender into the furnace of the steam engine, and stepped up next to the man at the controls of the big engine. He leaned over and yelled into the engineer's ear, "Yo, I want you to stop the train when we get about ten miles north of Pueblo."

The engineer looked over his shoulder at Berlin, fear evident in his eyes. "What you want'a stop out here for? There ain't nothin' out here but snow an' mountains."

Berlin sighed. He knew the man thought he was going to be killed when the train stopped.

He patted him on the shoulder and forced a good-humored grin on his face. "Don't worry, old-timer. Me an' my men are just gonna get off the train. You don't have nothin' to worry about."

The engineer nodded, clearly not convinced, and reached up to pull the throttle lever back a few notches, causing the train to begin to slow down.

Berlin turned his back to the engineer and said in a low voice to McGraw, "Soon's the train comes to a stop, put a bullet in him."

McGraw winked and stood up, dusting wood dust and bark off his hands as he leaned back against the wall of the compartment.

Berlin left through the rear door and made his way back toward the passenger cars.

As the train slowed more and more, he made his way from car to car, telling his men to get their gear together. They were going to make tracks as soon as the train came to a halt.

While he walked among his men, even Berlin, who was no stranger to violence or cruelty, was surprised by the condition of the women his men had been occupying their time with. Two were dead, their bodies covered with ugly black and blue marks showing they had been sorely tested before they died.

The remainder were either unconscious, or crying and moaning pitiably, most not in much better shape than those who'd been raped to death.

Just before the train came to a complete stop, Berlin heard several gunshots from the direction of the engine.

"Damn!" he muttered, drawing his pistol and running toward the front of the train. "It shouldn't've taken McGraw that many shots to kill the engineer," he said to himself as he busted through doors on his way.

When he got there, the train groaned to a stop, the engine idling loudly in the quiet mountain air.

"What the hell happened?" Berlin hollered when he found McGraw leaning out of the compartment window, his still-smoking pistol in his hand.

McGraw glanced back over his shoulder. "When I turned my head for a minute to look out the window, the engineer dove out the door and hit the ground running," he said.

Berlin shook his head. "He must've figured you was gonna shoot him," he mused.

"Yeah, I guess so," McGraw answered.

"Did you get him?"

"Nah. By the time I got my gun out and fired, he was too far away." McGraw grinned. "He run pretty fast for an old fart, though."

"Well, it can't be helped."

"Why'd you want him shot anyway?" McGraw asked. "He ain't given us no trouble nor nothin'."

" 'Cause I didn't want him taking the train into Pueblo an' tellin' the authorities 'bout us gettin' out here," Berlin said.

"Oh," McGraw said. "Well, if that's all that's bothering you, I can fix the engine where he won't be able to get it started any time soon."

"How?"

McGraw shrugged. "I'll just shut it down and drain all the water out of it. He won't be able to make any steam until another train comes along and transfers some water into the boiler."

Berlin nodded. "That's a good idea, Jack. The way we fixed those tracks back at Big Rock, another train won't be along for several days anyway."

McGraw grinned. "And without no food nor water, the engineer and the girls will probably be frozen to death by then. Won't nobody be left alive to tell 'em which way we went or when we left."

Berlin slapped McGraw on the back. "Come on, Jack," he said, "get your gear together an' let's get the hell outta here 'fore it starts to snow again."

McGraw began turning switches on the engine. "I'll be there soon's I turn this thing off and drain the water."

In less than an hour, the men had their horses off the train and saddled up and ready to go.

Blue Owl came up to Berlin, an evil glint in his eyes. "You want me to get back on the train and kill the women?" he asked.

Berlin shook his head. "No, let the bitches freeze to death," he said. "It'll be a lot slower for them that way."

Blue Owl, who had a deep and abiding hatred for all women, nodded, his lips curling up in a smile. "Yeah. Why let them off easy with a bullet or a knife when we can let them die slow and painful?"

"Exactly my thoughts," Berlin said. He jerked his mount's head around and waved his arm in the air. "Come on, men. Let's ride!"

It was heavy going for Berlin and his gang. The trails that ran between the mountain passes were clogged with snow that reached almost to their mounts' chests, and they'd only managed to travel six miles by the time the sun began to set.

Just when he thought they were going to have to make camp in the open, an unappetizing thought with temperatures plunging to well below freezing, Blue Owl called out, "Hey, Boss, look over there!"

In the distance, barely visible through the ground fog that was beginning to form as the temperature dropped, was a log cabin nestled among a grove of pine trees. The roof had several holes in it, and the mud caked between the logs was absent in places, but at least they'd be able to get out of the worst of the weather.

When Berlin kicked open the door, the smell of the animals who'd made the place a temporary home was strong and musty.

"We're in luck," Berlin said when he spied an old pot-bellied stove in a corner. "Blue Owl, send some of the men out to gather wood and bring in some of our provisions. At least we'll be able to keep warm an' fix up some coffee an' grub."

Before long, with all the men crammed into a space meant for four or five, and with the stove glowing a dull red, the cabin began to heat up to a comfortable level.

While some of the men patched the worst of the holes in the walls with pine needles and branches to keep the wind out, others used shovels they'd brought along to dig down in the snow and uncover enough grass for the horses to eat. Leaving the animals covered with blankets to keep out the worst of the cold, the men gathered inside to drink hot coffee and eat jerked beef and beans cooked on the stove.

After they'd eaten their fill, most of the men got their sleeping blankets and spread out on the floor to grab some shut-eye, lying almost shoulder to shoulder in the small cabin.

Berlin took a final mug of coffee, lit a cigar, and motioned for Blue Owl and Sam Cook to follow him outside where they could talk.

He turned an old barrel upside down and placed it against the south wall of the cabin, out of the frigid wind blowing from the north.

He pulled his coat tighter around him and sipped the coffee, letting cigar smoke trail from his nostrils as he talked.

"We got to make us some plans, men," he began. "We're gonna be goin' into areas where there's more people, an' that means more law. It's time to take stock of who we got ridin' with us to make the best use of 'em."

Blue Owl upended the small flask of whiskey and took a deep drink. "You're right, Boss. We got some good men with us, but some of 'em ain't exactly cut out for what we got in mind."

Berlin nodded. "That's why we're gonna do like the Army. We're gonna divide up into squads, with good men leadin', an' mix up the weaker ones among 'em so's each squad will be more effective. When we raid, we got to hit hard an' fast an' not give anybody a chance to get organized against us. In and out 'fore they know what hit 'em."

As Cook and Blue Owl agreed, Berlin said, "So, I need you two to let me know what you think of each of our men. I don't know all of 'em as well as you two do since I ain't been inside with 'em as long as you have."

"How many squads you want?" Cook asked, thinking.

"I figure five to begin with, with six men in each group. As time goes on an' we lose men, which we're bound to do sooner or later, we'll mix 'em together, trying to keep at least six or so men in each group."

"So, you're figuring for each of us to lead a squad, so we're gonna need two more leaders?" Blue Owl asked.

Berlin nodded.

"I think Jack McGraw an' Billy Bartlett ought'a be leaders," Cook said.

Blue Owl shook his head. "Naw, Billy's too young. He's pretty good, but I think we need somebody a mite older . . . like Wiley Gottlieb."

"I agree," Berlin said. "We'll let the men know the plan in the morning, and we'll let each squad leader pick one man at a time until everybody's been picked."

Cook looked skeptical. "That's gonna piss the ones off who're picked last," he said.

"I know," Berlin agreed. "That's why we're gonna do the picking in private, just the five squad leaders. Once the men are all chosen, the leaders will tell the men who's gonna ride with who."

Blue Owl smiled. "That'll make planning the attacks easier too, not having to discuss it with all thirty men."

"So, we're in agreement then?" Berlin asked.

When they nodded, he said, "Good. Then let's get inside where it's warm an' get some shut-eye. I have a feeling tomorrow's gonna be a busy day."

Seventeen

By four o'clock in the afternoon, Smoke and his party were well up into the mountains in an area between Big Rock and Pueblo, Colorado. They hadn't yet made it to the railroad tracks running between the towns, but Smoke figured they only had a couple of more miles until they crossed the tracks.

Jed McCulloch, riding along next to Sergeant Bob Guthrie, kept sneaking glances at Sally, who was riding just behind Smoke. She was dressed in jeans and a flannel shirt, and was wearing a leather coat made from deerskins with a fur lining. She had her .32 Smith and Wesson short-barreled pistol in a holster around her waist, tied down low on her leg in the manner of a gunfighter.

Jed, though he hailed from Texas, had never seen a woman who looked so at home wearing a pistol and riding a horse, as if she were born in the saddle, and yet who still managed to be remarkably attractive and feminine at the same time.

He leaned sideways in his saddle to speak in a low tone to Bob. "That Sally Jensen is some kind of woman."

Guthrie nodded. "At first, I didn't believe the stories Sheriff Carson told us about her, but now that I see her in the saddle, ridin' along just as good as the men, I realize he wasn't exaggeratin' a bit when he said she wouldn't have any trouble keepin' up with us."

"What do you think of Smoke?" Jed asked.

"I think he looks every bit as hard an' tough as the stories I've heard about him make him out to be."

Jed nodded. "My uncle Jake told me about some of his exploits when he was down Texas way visiting the King Ranch. I thought he was pulling my leg at first, but now that I met him in person, I'm not so sure."

"Some of the more famous gunfighters out here in the West tend to make up stories to make 'em seem bigger than life," Guthrie observed, "but this Jensen feller seems just the opposite. He don't seem to want to brag about his past like most of the gunnies I've been around."

"Well, if we ever catch up to those bandits, I guess we'll have a chance to see just how good with a gun he is."

"If he's half as good as people say, Ozark Jack Berlin won't stand a chance."

Up ahead, Smoke held up his hand and reined his horse around. He glanced up at the sky, where dark clouds were gathering and moving toward them over mountain peaks to the north.

"Looks like we got a storm brewing," he said to the group. "We don't have more'n a couple of hours of daylight left, so I guess we better get to building us a camp for the night."

Everyone nodded their agreement. The temperature had been falling steadily for the past two hours, and they were tired and chilled to the bone from being in the saddle most of the day. They were all ready to take a break and have some hot food.

"Pearlie, you and Cal remember what I taught you that time we spent up in the high lonesome?" he asked.

Cal and Pearlie nodded. "Sure, Smoke," Pearlie said.

Smoke pointed to a flat area just ahead. It was a small clearing among a stand of pine trees, with a collection of boulders on one side.

"Get your axes off the packhorse and see if you can cut us some branches off those trees to make a lean-to up against those rocks. That'll keep the worst of the wind and snow off us when the storm hits."

As the boys got down off their horses and began to unpack the tools they'd need, Smoke looked at Jed and Bob. "If you two will search around for some fallen wood for the fire, Sally can unload the provisions for supper and I'll hobble the horses over in those rocks so they'll be out of the weather."

"Why not just cut some wood off'n those trees," Jed asked, "rather than digging around in the snow for fallen wood?"

"The wood on the trees is too green to make a good fire, and it'll also give off a lot more smoke," Smoke answered. "We don't know where the outlaws may be, but it wouldn't be a good idea to send up a lot of smoke to tell 'em where we are."

"Oh," Jed said shortly, chagrined that he hadn't thought of that.

By the time Cal and Pearlie had cut enough branches to form a lean-to that would keep the wind and snow off, Sally had a large fire going and was cooking supper while water boiled for coffee.

Smoke laid out some grain for the horses, then stood in front of the fire, holding his hands palm out to get them warm.

Sally glanced up from where she squatted next to a large iron skillet full of frying meat. As she stirred a kettle full of beans, she said, "Coffee should be about ready now, dear."

The men gathered around the fire and filled their mugs with the steaming brew, glad to get something warm inside them as the air got colder and colder and snowflakes began to drift lazily down through the trees.

After they'd eaten, the men leaned back against their saddles, pulled blankets up to their necks, and either built cigarettes or lit cigars to enjoy with after-supper coffee. Sally lay down next to Smoke and pulled a blanket over the both of them as the men talked.

Jed looked around at the group and smiled. "You look like you got you a good crew here, Smoke," he said, inclining his head toward Cal and Pearlie. Cal was lying with his blanket over his head, already snoring softly, while Pearlie had a plate with his third helping of food on it, still shoveling it in as if he hadn't eaten in weeks.

Smoke looked at the boys and nodded. "They'll do to ride the river with, I suspect."

Guthrie blew on his coffee to cool it a mite, and asked, "How long they been with you?"

Smoke laughed shortly. "Seems like forever, doesn't it, Sally?"

She smiled, only her face visible above the blanket. "Yes. I can hardly remember a time when we didn't have them with us."

"Cal there looks a mite young," Jed observed. "He must've joined up with your outfit when he was just a tyke."

"That's a funny story," Smoke said, looking at Sally and grinning.

"Well, we ain't got nothin' else to do. Let's hear it," Guthrie said.

"Cal showed up on the Sugarloaf one day, wearing nothin' but rags, and tried to hold up Sally," Smoke began, then stopped. "You were there, Sally, why don't you tell it?"

"Cal was only fourteen years old that year," Sally said, sitting up a little so she could talk better as she told the story. . . .

It was during the spring branding, and Sally was on her way back from Big Rock to the Sugarloaf. The buckboard was piled high with supplies, because branding hundreds of calves made for hungry punchers.

As Sally slowed the team to make a bend in the trail, a rail-thin young man stepped from the bushes at the side of the road with a pistol in his hand.

"Hold it right there, miss."

Applying the brake with her right foot, Sally slipped her

hand under a pile of gingham cloth on the seat. She grasped the handle of her short-barreled Colt .44 and eared back the hammer, letting the sound of the horses' hooves and the squealing of the brake pad on the wheels mask the sound. "What can I do for you, young man?" she asked, her voice firm and without fear. She knew she could draw and drill the young highwayman before he could raise his pistol to fire.

"Well, uh, you can throw some of those beans and a cut of that fatback over here, and maybe a portion of that Arbuckle's coffee too."

Sally's eyebrows raised. "Don't you want my money?"

The boy frowned and shook his head. "Why, no, ma'am. I ain't no thief, I'm just hungry."

"And if I don't give you my food, are you going to shoot me with that big Navy Colt?"

He hesitated a moment, then grinned ruefully. "No, ma'am, I guess not." He twirled the pistol around his finger and slipped it into his belt, turned, and began to walk down the road toward Big Rock.

Sally watched the youngster amble off, noting his tattered shirt, dirty pants with holes in the knees and torn pockets, and boots that looked as if they had been salvaged from a garbage dump. "Young man," she called, "come back here, please."

He turned, a smirk on his face, spreading his hands, "Look lady, you don't have to worry. I don't even have any bullets." With a lightning-fast move he drew the gun from his pants, aimed away from Sally, and pulled the trigger. There was a click but no explosion as the hammer fell on an empty cylinder.

Sally smiled. "Oh, I'm not worried." In a movement every bit as fast as his, she whipped her .44 out and fired, clipping a pine cone from a branch, causing it to fall and bounce off his head.

The boy's knees buckled and he ducked, saying, "Jimminy Christmas!"

Mimicking him, Sally twirled her Colt and stuck it in the waistband of her britches. "What's your name, boy?"

The boy blushed and looked down at his feet, "Calvin, ma'am, Calvin Woods."

She leaned forward, elbows on knees, and stared into the boy's eyes. "Calvin, no one has to go hungry in this country, not if they're willing to work."

He looked up at her through narrowed eyes, as if he found life a little different than she'd described it.

"If you're willing to put in an honest day's work," she added, "I'll see that you get an honest day's pay, and all the food you can eat."

Calvin stood a little straighter, shoulders back and head held high. "Ma'am, I've got to be straight with you. I ain't no experienced cowhand. I come from a hardscrabble farm, and we only had us one milk cow and a couple of goats and chickens, and lots of dirt that weren't worth nothin' for growin' things. My ma and pa and me never had nothin', but we never begged and we never stooped to takin' handouts."

Sally thought, *I like this boy. Proud, and not willing to take charity if he can help it.* "Calvin, if you're willing to work, and don't mind getting your hands dirty and your muscles sore, I've got some hands that'll have you punching beeves like you were born to it in no time at all."

A smile lit up his face, making him seem even younger than his years. "Even if I don't have no saddle, nor a horse to put it on?"

She laughed out loud. "Yes. We've got plenty of ponies and saddles." She glanced down at his raggedy boots. "We can probably even round up some boots and spurs that'll fit you."

He walked over and jumped in the back of the buckboard. "Ma'am, I don't know who you are, but you just hired you the hardest-workin' hand you've ever seen."

Back at the Sugarloaf, she sent him in to Cookie and told him to eat his fill. When Smoke and the other punchers rode into the cabin yard at the end of the day, she introduced Calvin around. As Cal was shaking hands with the men, Smoke looked over at her and winked. He knew she could never resist a stray dog or cat, and her heart was as large as the Big Lonesome itself.

Smoke walked up to Cal and cleared his throat. "Son, I hear you drew down on my wife."

Cal gulped. "Yessir, Mr Jensen. I did." He squared his shoulders and looked Smoke in the eye, not flinching, though he was obviously frightened of the tall man with the incredibly wide shoulders standing before him.

Smoke smiled and clapped the boy on the back. "Just wanted you to know you stared death in the eye, boy. Not many galoots are still walking upright who ever pulled a gun on Sally. She's a better shot than any man I've ever seen except me, and sometimes I wonder about me."

The boy laughed with relief as Smoke turned and called out, "Pearlie, get your lazy butt over here."

A tall, lanky cowboy ambled over to Smoke and Cal, munching on a biscuit stuffed with roast beef. His face was lined with wrinkles and tanned a dark brown from hours under the sun, but his eyes were sky-blue and twinkled with good-natured humor.

"Yessir, Boss," he mumbled around a mouthful of food.

Smoke put his hand on Pearlie's shoulder. "Cal, this here is Pearlie. He eats more'n any two hands, and he's never been known to do a lick of work he could get out of, but he knows beeves and horses as well as any puncher I have. I want you to follow him around and let him teach you what you need to know."

Cal nodded. "Yes, sir, Mr. Smoke."

"Now let me see that iron you have in your pants."

Cal pulled the ancient Navy Colt and handed it to Smoke. When Smoke opened the loading gate, the rusted cylinder fell to the ground, causing Pearlie and Smoke to laugh and Cal's face to flame red. "This is the piece you pulled on Sally?"

The boy nodded, looking at the ground.

Pearlie shook his head. "Cal, you're one lucky pup. Hell,

if'n you'd tried to fire that thing, it'd of blown your hand clean off."

Smoke inclined his head toward the bunkhouse. "Pearlie, take Cal over to the tack house and get him fixed up with what he needs, including a gunbelt and a Colt that won't fall apart the first time he pulls it. You might also help him pick him out a shavetail to ride. I'll expect him to start earning his keep tomorrow."

"Yes, sir, Smoke." Pearlie put his arm around Cal's shoulders and led him off toward the bunkhouse. "Now, the first thing you gotta learn, Cal, is how to get on Cookie's good side. A puncher rides on his belly, and it 'pears to me that you need some fattin' up 'fore you can begin to punch cows."

Both Jed and Bob chuckled at the tale. "That's a hell of a way to hire on hands," Jed said. "My Uncle Jake would've just shot the boy and let him lay where he fell."

"Sally's not like that," Smoke said, putting his arm around her and hugging her closer to him. "She can almost always see the good in others, even when most of us men can't."

Pearlie glanced up as he finished the last of his food. "That don't stop her from blowin' hell outta anybody that tries to do harm to Smoke or one of her hands, though," Pearlie said.

"I can see she's wearing a pistol, though I admit I didn't think she'd had much cause to use it," Jed said, eyeing Sally with a speculative look in his eye.

"Oh, she's saddled up and gone to war with me and for me on more than one occasion," Smoke said. "Don't ever underestimate the fury of a woman who's protecting one of her own."

Jed nodded solemnly. "I won't, I promise."

"How about you, Pearlie?" Guthrie asked, flicking his cigarette butt into the dying fire.

Pearlie looked up from building his own cigarette. "I was on my way to makin' my reputation as a gunslick," he said. "I'd hired out my gun to a galoot named Tilden Franklin, who was intent on takin' over the territory, includin' Smoke's ranch."

"Oh, so you also came to work for Smoke after taking up guns against him?"

"Yeah, only when the man I hired out to began to rape and kill innocent farm folks, I found I didn't have no stomach for the gunslick work, so I changed sides . . . an' I been with Smoke ever since."

Guthrie turned to look at Monte Carson, who was lying a little off to one side, quietly smoking his pipe and drinking his coffee.

"Sheriff Carson," Guthrie began, "I been meanin' to ask you where you hail from. I know I seen your face sometime in the past, but I just can't remember where."

Monte nodded slowly. "I thought that about you too, Bob, an' it came to me a while back. I was in the Army 'bout a hundred years ago when I was knee-high to a toad. If my memory serves me correctly, you were a corporal when I was a private."

Guthrie snapped his fingers. "Now I remember. You was a lot thinner then, no bigger around than a stick, and had a lot more hair."

Monte laughed, patting his ample stomach. "Well, a lot of years with a woman who is almost as good a cook as Sally has added a few pounds."

Cal snorted, coming awake and raising his head. "You folks gonna jaw all night?" he asked, rubbing his eyes sleepily.

"Cal's right, men," Smoke said. "We need to make an early start and it figures to be a long day tomorrow. Let's call it a night."

Eighteen

The next day, Smoke's band had their breakfast eaten and the horses fed and were on their way by dawn. The air was bitterly cold and snow was still falling, though lightly. The new snow that fell during the night was making rough going for their mounts, and it took them almost two hours to find where the railroad tracks crossed their path.

As they approached the tracks, Guthrie rode ahead and got down off his horse to look at the rails.

"Which way should we go?" Cal asked. "What if they stopped the train 'fore it got this far?"

Guthrie straightened up from where he was squatted next to the rails. "Looky here, men," he said. "The snow on the tracks is only half as deep as on the bank next to 'em. The train must've come through here late yesterday or early last night. That means we ought'a head south, toward Pueblo."

Smoke stood up in his stirrups and looked to the south. "Your reasoning is impeccable, Sergeant," he said. "And from the looks of that smoke on the horizon, someone's got a large fire going down that way."

The group followed his gaze, and could see distant plumes of smoke rising in the air.

"You think it's the outlaws?" Jed asked, unconsciously fingering the butt of his pistol.

Guthrie shook his head. "I doubt they'd be that stupid, but if they was smart, they'd wouldn't've been in prison."

"Only one way to find out," Smoke said. "Let's ride."

* * *

Their going was faster since they were keeping their mounts on the railroad tracks, so it only took them three hours to come within sight of the fire they'd seen.

Smoke held up his hand when they crested a ridge over-looking the scene below. They could see the train engine and its cars sitting still, covered with a layer of snow. Off to one side was a large fire, with stacks of wood from the tender behind the engine piled high next to the flames. Figures could be seen lying on the ground close to the fire, covered with blankets, trying to keep warm.

"That don't look like the outlaws," Guthrie said, peering through his Army binoculars.

"No," Smoke agreed, shielding his eyes from the sun overhead with his palm. "I think it's the passengers."

"Let's hope they're still alive," Sally said, spurring her horse into a gallop down the hill.

The men hurriedly followed, not wanting her to get there first in case there was going to be gunplay.

When they arrived, they found the engineer of the train going from blanket to blanket, encouraging the women lying there to drink water he'd warmed in buckets next to the fire.

"Oh, thank God you've come," he called when he saw the riders. "I got some sick womenfolk here that need tending to."

Sally jumped down from her horse and ran to assist him. "Smoke, get some coffee going and see if you can make some beef soup with that steak we had left over from break-fast."

The engineer stood up, stretching his back. "That'd be right nice. We ain't had no food nor coffee for mite near twenty-four hours. I been trying to keep 'em alive with hot water, but they need something more'n that in their stomachs."

The women looked pitiful. Most had ugly black bruises and cuts on their faces, and some were missing teeth; all of them looked as though they'd been badly mistreated.

"Those bastards!" Sally muttered when she saw what had been done to the women.

The engineer walked over to Smoke and said in a low voice, "There's three of 'em that didn't make it. I got their bodies in one of the cars, covered with blankets."

"Why'd they let you live?" Guthrie asked. "That ain't like them to leave witnesses."

The engineer gave a lopsided grin. "They didn't intend to, that's for sure. One of 'em had me covered, and was just waitin' to plug me, when I surprised him and jumped off the train whilst it was still moving."

Jed glanced around at the women. "I guess they figured the women wouldn't survive the night as cold as it was, and didn't want to waste ammunition on them."

"You're probably right," the engineer agreed. "When I saw them take off, I snuck back along the tracks until I got to the train. After I did what I could for the women, I took some wood outta the tender and made us a fire to keep us warm and to melt some snow to heat up some water to drink."

"Why didn't you just start the engine and head on into Pueblo?" Guthrie asked.

"The bastards shut down the engine and drained all the water out so's it wouldn't run no more. Can't make steam for the engine without water."

Smoke turned to Cal and Pearlie. "Boys, get the shovels off the packhorse. If we can shovel enough snow into the boiler we should be able to get the engine running again."

"That's gonna take a heap of snow," the engineer said, scratching his head.

"Well, we can't leave you out here in this weather," Smoke said, "and those women look like they're going to need medical care as soon as possible."

* * *

While Sally and the engineer spooned beef soup and coffee into the women, Smoke and the rest of the men took turns shoveling snow as fast as they could into the boiler of the engine. It took until almost nightfall before the engineer said they had enough to get him to Pueblo.

While he started a fire in the engine to melt the snow and make steam, Smoke pulled Sally aside. "Sally, I want you to ride to Pueblo with the train. The doctor in town is going to need your help fixing up these poor women."

Sally nodded, her face grave. "Yes. Some of them are in pretty bad shape."

Then she turned back to Smoke, put her arms around his neck, and kissed him hard on the mouth. "Smoke, you ride with your guns loose and be careful."

He nodded, squeezing her tight. "I will."

She leaned back and stared into his eyes. "But whatever you do, plant the men who did this. They don't deserve to live another day!"

"You can bet on that," Smoke said with feeling.

Just before the train took off, Smoke asked the engineer if he saw which way the outlaws went when they rode off.

He nodded. "Yep. They took off to the southwest. That's about the only way they could go, since the passes to the north are gonna be plugged with snow until the spring melt."

Smoke glanced over his shoulder in the direction the men had taken. It was toward Big Rock and the Sugarloaf, and a lot of ranches owned by friends of his lay in the outlaws' path.

"Would you do me a favor when you get to Pueblo?" he asked.

"Sure thing, mister. Whatever you want."

"Send a telegraph to the U.S. marshal's office in Denver. Tell them to get as many men down here as fast as they can. I have a feeling there's gonna be blood all over the mountains before we're though with these sons of bitches."

The engineer nodded. "You're right about that," he said. "I've been out here a long time, and I've never seen men as hard as them."

the mountains. Berlin, she re thought with these was of his use.

Dan Gilbert nodded. "You're right about that," he said, "Let's get there along now, and I've never been mad as hell before..."

Nineteen

Ozark Jack Berlin and his men were tired, and becoming increasingly irritable from the constant cold they were enduring in the mountains. Most of the men were used to sleeping in hotels and eating at cafés and boardinghouses. None were accustomed to living outdoors, and certainly not under conditions such as they'd endured the last couple of weeks.

When the horse of one of the members of Jack McGraw's squad bumped the flank of Dan Gilbert's mount, Gilbert drew his pistol, and was on the verge of shooting the man when Berlin drew his gun and fired in the air.

"Goddamnit!" Berlin shouted, lowering the pistol until it pointed at Gilbert's face. "I'm the leader of this here gang, an' nobody draws a gun unless I tell 'em to!" he shouted, earing the hammer on his Colt back.

Gilbert, his face ashen, slowly raised his hands. "I'm sorry, Boss. I didn't mean nothin' by it."

Berlin shook his head. "Put that thing away 'fore I cram it up your ass, Dan," he said, holstering his own weapon.

After Gilbert complied, Berlin addressed his men. "I know we're all tired an' saddle-sore. We need fresh mounts an' fresh grub, an' soon as we come to a ranch, we'll get both. But until then, keep your tempers in check or I'll give you something to be mad about."

The men all nodded agreement, some pulling their coats tighter around them against the chill in the air from the north wind blowing down out of the mountains. Luckily, they were riding southward, so the wind was against their backs and not in their faces, which made it only marginally more bearable.

Berlin jerked his horse's head around and rode on down the trail, satisfied he'd kept his men in line for the present. But he knew he'd better find them fresh horses and a place to get out of the weather soon, or he was going to have a revolt on his hands, one a few harsh words and the threat of his pistol wouldn't keep quiet.

Just before noon, when Berlin was thinking about stopping for a fire and some lunch, he noticed a trail of smoke rising over the next hill.

He signaled his men to keep the noise down, and he rode ahead to scout out the situation. Just before he got to the edge of the hill, he got down off his horse and walked until he could see below.

There was a ranch house, with smoke coming from a chimney. There were no horses visible, and the corral near the house was empty, but there was a large barn fifty yards from the house, and he figured the livestock would be in there due to the recent snow. What looked to be a bunkhouse was next to the barn, with the snow undisturbed around it.

He got back up on his horse and rode back to his men. "We're in luck, boys. There's a ranch down there an' it looks ripe for the pickin'."

"How many you think we're going up against?" Blue Owl asked.

Berlin shook his head. "I don't know. The bunkhouse looks empty, an' there ain't no smoke comin' from its chimney, so I suspect the rancher has let most of his hands go for the winter."

"If that's so, shouldn't be too many to worry about,"

Jack McGraw growled, pulling his pistol from its holster and checking the loads.

"Well, we're gonna be careful anyway," Berlin said. "Jack, you and Wiley take your squads around to the east an' come at 'em from that direction. I'll take my men an' Blue Owl's and Sam's an' head straight down the hill. Wait for my signal, then we'll go in with guns blazin'."

"Yessir, Boss," Jack McGraw said as he turned his mount to lead his men off to the left along the ridge overlooking the cabin below.

Berlin built himself a cigarette, lit it with a lucifer he struck on his saddle horn, and settled down to wait for McGraw and Gottlieb to get their men in position.

By the time he'd finished his smoke, he reckoned the men were ready. He drew his pistol and eared back the hammer. "Let's go!"

He spurred his horse into as fast a gallop as the deepening snow would allow, and led his men down the hill toward the house below.

The people in the house must have heard or sensed something, because while Berlin and his men were still a hundred yards from the house, the door opened and a man with a rifle stepped out on the porch. When he saw the gang of men riding hard toward him with pistols and rifles drawn, he drew a bead and fired.

George Goodwin, a heavyset man whose particular specialty was robbing stages, was hit dead center in the chest and blown backward over his horse's rump.

Before the man could fire again, a fusillade of bullets from the gang spun him in a circle and dropped him on the porch in front of the door to the house.

Seconds later, a woman wearing an apron and a long dress crawled out onto the porch, took a quick look at the man, then picked up his rifle.

She jacked a shell into the chamber and began to fire as fast as she could work the lever. Two more of Berlin's men went down with shoulder and leg wounds before McGraw's men came riding around the corner of the house. McGraw, who carried a double-barreled twelve-gauge shotgun, let the woman have it with both barrels, catching her in the chest and somersaulting her backward to lie half inside the doorway, her guts spread all over the porch.

"Check out the house," Berlin called to McGraw, then turned to Blue Owl. "Take your men and make sure the bunkhouse is empty."

While they were doing that, Berlin took his men and rode over to the barn. He carefully pulled open the big double doors, and found fifteen horses in stalls in the enclosure, along with two mules.

"All right," he said to himself, "fresh horses."

When he got to the house, he was met by McGraw. "The house is empty, ain't nobody else around."

Berlin turned just as Blue Owl entered the door. "Same thing with the bunkhouse. Don't look like it's been used for a few weeks or more."

Berlin nodded. "We're in luck. This must be a small operation an' the rancher just hires hands for brandin' and calvin' when he needs 'em."

Blue Owl glanced at the bodies on the porch. "It's a cinch he ain't going to need them no more."

"Throw those bodies out into the snow so's we can close that door," Berlin said. "An' send a couple of men out there to see if our wounded are still kickin'."

He went over to the fireplace and put another couple of logs on the fire. "Gottlieb, you an' your men get in the kitchen an' see 'bout fixin' us some grub while I warm this place up a little."

Later, after the wounded had been taken care of and the men had all eaten, Berlin sat in front of the fireplace and stretched his legs out on an ottoman close to the fire.

"Blue Owl, figure out a schedule an' send some men out to keep watch. We don't want any surprise guests while we rest up."

"The men ain't going to like going back out in that cold, Boss," Blue Owl said.

Berlin turned hard eyes on the half-breed. "They'll like it even less if they don't do what I say. The people of Pueblo must know the train's overdue by now. If they send out search parties, or somehow manage to get in touch with one of the towns we went through, they're gonna be sending men out after us. You want'a be asleep when they come callin'?"

"No, I guess not."

"Keep the watches short so's they don't get too cold. I noticed a case of whiskey in the kitchen. That ought'a keep 'em warm enough till they can get back here under cover."

"Jack, you really think they're that close on our trail?" Blue Owl asked.

Berlin shook his head. "No. I figure we got five or six days 'fore we really have to worry about anyone on our back trail. But my momma didn't raise no fools. I don't intend to be caught nappin' if they're closer than I think."

"You're right. It don't never hurt to be careful," Blue Owl said as he turned to give the orders.

"Especially if somebody else is freezin' their butts off watchin' out for me," Berlin mumbled to himself as he took another sip of his coffee.

Twenty

Sam Cook shivered and slapped his hands against his sides while standing guard over the ranch house. He took a couple of quick sips of the whiskey he'd been given, but other than burning all the way down to his stomach, it didn't seem to help much.

This escape ain't exactly going the way I thought it would when we busted outta that prison, he thought to himself. He was more than a little pissed off that Ozark Jack Berlin had assumed he was the leader of the gang, without so much as a vote among the members, or even discussing it with anyone.

What gives that son of a bitch the right to boss me around? he asked himself for the fiftieth time. Hell, I'm just as tough as he is, maybe even more so, and I'm a damn sight smarter, thought the man who'd been arrested and sentenced to prison for beating a bartender almost to death for giving him watered-down whiskey.

He was also angry because of the squad members he'd been allotted. They were a motley crew at best, and there wasn't a one of them he'd trust to watch his back in a fight. Johnny "Four Fingers" Watson, a common footpad and burglar, had no expertise with a gun at all; Murphy Givens, in prison for shooting a man in the back, was certainly no prize when it came to courage or willingness to fight face-to-face; Josiah Breckenridge, a half-black son of a bitch, was big enough, standing over six feet tall and weighing in at over two hundred pounds, but he had the intellect of a six-year-old, hence his conviction for soliciting the services of a white woman on her way to church one Sunday morning when he was already drunker'n a skunk; Sylvester "Sly" Malone was perhaps the only man who knew which end of a gun the bullets came out of, but he had a real problem with whiskey, preferring it to water at all times, and never without one or two bottles in his saddlebags, usually more than half empty. Not exactly a man to inspire confidence in a leader, Cook thought as he tried to figure out what he should do. The other member of his squad, Phil Blackman, was laid up in the cabin with a hole in his leg from the assault on the ranch.

That damned Berlin is bringing too much attention to us, he thought as he sipped his whiskey and walked around in circles trying to stay warm. Pretty soon, we're gonna have half the lawmen in the territory on our trail, and it's just a matter of time before we're all dead or back in that rattrap of a prison, he told himself.

Finally, he made a decision. He had to break with Berlin before the fool got them all killed. His squad had been given the watch from midnight until dawn, what he'd heard cowboys call the dog watch because you had to be dumber'n a dog to take it.

He climbed on his horse and rode slowly over to round up the rest of his men to see what they thought of his idea.

Once they were all gathered together, he put it to them straight. "Men, sooner or later, Ozark's gonna get us all killed, running around shooting up the countryside like this."

"You figger on goin' up again' him?" Breckenridge asked, a doubtful look on his face. "He's meaner'n a snake, an' twice as fast with that six-killer of his," he added as he cut a chunk of tobacco off a plug and stuck it in the corner of his mouth.

Cook shook his head. "No, that wouldn't solve the problem. Riding with so many men just brings too much attention to us. I think we'd do better to go off on our own. Nobody's looking for five men . . . they're all looking for a gang of thirty."

"Berlin ain't gonna take kindly to no suggestion we split up," Four Fingers Watson said. "Matter of fact, he's liable to get downright testy about it."

"That's why we're not going to ask his permission," Cook said. He nodded at Watson. "You're an experienced burglar, so I want you to sneak down to the barn where Berlin put all the horses."

Watson looked unsure. "What if they see me?"

Cook shook his head. "They won't. By now, they're all whiskeyed up and sleeping like babies."

"What do you want me to do once I'm there?" Watson asked.

"Take one of the packhorses and load it up with as much food and ammunition as you can, then come on back up here. If we take off on our own, we're gonna need some grub to tide us over until we can get to a town."

"Where you figuring on heading to?" Malone asked.

"The closest town is Pueblo, off to the northeast. I figure if we go in one or two at a time, they won't place us as members of Berlin's gang."

"Then what're we gonna do?" Breckenridge asked.

"Stay there a day or so until things calm down, then head on off to some smaller towns, where we can rob a bank or two to get traveling money."

"What if Ozark Jack comes after us?" Givens asked, a look of fear on his face.

"He won't dare come near Pueblo. He knows they're gonna be on the lookout for his gang there, so he's bound to steer clear of that town for sure."

"I don't know," Breckenridge said. "It all sounds pretty risky to me."

"Not half as risky as riding with Berlin until every U.S. marshal and Army man in the country is after us."

After some more discussion, the men agreed with

Cook's plan, and Watson got on his horse and walked it down toward the ranch, staying on the side of the barn where he couldn't be seen by the men in the ranch house.

Less than an hour later, the five men, along with their packhorse, were headed northeast, back along the way they'd come, toward Pueblo.

"We'll ride back along our back trail so as not to leave Berlin any tracks to follow," Cook explained. "We'll stay in the tracks we made coming here until we get a few miles up in the mountains, then cut over toward Pueblo."

He laughed. "By the time they realize we're gone, it'll be too late for them to take out after us."

Smoke and his party were about a day and a half behind Berlin's men. They'd been delayed by the necessity of taking care of the women the gang had left behind, but Smoke was pushing the horses as fast as he could to make up for lost time.

Luckily, the snow was helping, for the gang had left a trail that even a blind man could follow. Thirty horses riding through snow made quite a mess, one not easily missed, and the outlaws were in too much of a hurry to try to disguise their trail. Berlin had not been smart enough to have his men ride off in different directions and join up later to confuse anyone on his trail.

Smoke suddenly held up his hand.

"What is it, Smoke?" Monte Carson asked, riding up next to him.

Smoke leaned over his saddle horn and pointed at the ground. "Look there, Monte. There's some tracks coming back in this direction along the back trail of the gang. See where they cut off and head off to the north?"

"How many you figure, Smoke?" Jed McCulloch asked from behind Monte.

"Looks like five or six, near as I can make it," Smoke answered.

"What'a you think's goin' on?" Pearlie asked. "You think they're splittin' up or somethin'?"

Smoke wagged his head. "No. This looks like a party of men came back along this way six or eight hours after the main party went south. See how the snow's covered some of the older tracks, but not the newer ones?"

"If you say so, Smoke," Jed said. "I never was much good at tracking."

"Smoke could track a field mouse in a blizzard," Cal said.

"What do you think we should do, Smoke?" Bob Guthrie asked. "Should we split up an' some of us follow these new tracks?"

Smoke shook his head. "No. There's too many of them for us to divide our forces. Since these are the most recent, we'll probably stand a better chance of catching them before the larger party, so let's see where they take us."

Two hours later, Smoke once again held up his hand. A couple of hundred yards ahead he could see a group of five men seated around a small fire under some pine trees.

"You think they're part of the bandits?" Jed asked, letting his hand fall to his pistol.

"Don't know," Smoke said. "But, there's only one way to find out," he muttered as he spurred his horse forward at a slow walk toward the group ahead.

As they got closer, Guthrie said in a low voice, "Be careful, Smoke. I think I recognize that big black man sittin' off to the side."

"You sure?" Smoke said.

Guthrie nodded. "Yeah. You don't forget somebody that big, especially when he's killin' your friends."

Smoke released the rawhide hammer-thong on his Colt and kept moving forward.

One of the men looked up and saw them coming. He

rolled to the side and grabbed for a rifle lying next to the fire.

Quicker than it takes to tell it, Smoke drew and fired in one lightning-fast movement. His slug took Johnny Four Fingers Watson in the side of his neck, blowing out his Adam's apple and almost taking his head off.

As the other four men drew pistols and began to return fire, Smoke leaned over his saddle horn and took his reins in his teeth while he steered his mount with his knees and spurred him forward at a full gallop.

Cal and Pearlie drew and followed, catching Monte Carson, Jed McCulloch, and Bob Guthrie by surprise.

Pearlie's first two shots hit Sly Malone in the stomach and chest, doubling him over to fall into the fire, sending sparks and flames scattering in all directions.

Cal and Murphy Givens fired at the same time. Givens's bullet creased Cal's neck at the shoulder muscle, spinning him sideways in the saddle just as Cal's slug hit Givens low in the stomach, in the groin area. Givens screamed, dropped his pistol, and doubled over, holding what was left of his manhood with both hands.

Smoke snapped off two quick shots at Sam Cook as he dived behind a nearby tree, pocking bark off the tree but missing the outlaw by inches.

As Cook leaned around the tree and took aim at Smoke, both Jed and Guthrie fired simultaneously, followed seconds later by Monte Carson. One shot missed, the other two did not. Twin holes appeared in Cook's forehead, snapping it back and breaking his neck as his brains exploded out of the back of his head.

The big black man, Breckenridge, jumped behind his horse and pulled a short-barreled shotgun from his rifle boot. As he leaned over the horse to fire, Monte Carson shot, knocking the horse to its knees just as Smoke put a bullet in the middle of the big man's chest.

Breckenridge stumbled backward, still on his feet, and brought the shotgun up again, blood pouring from the hole in his chest.

Pearlie, Jed, and Guthrie all snapped off shots, riddling the man's body with holes and blowing him backward to land spread-eagled in the snow, blood from seven wounds staining the snow bright scarlet.

While Jed and Monte rushed to kick Breckenridge's pistol out of his reach, Smoke jerked his horse's head around and rode over to Cal, who was sitting leaned over his saddle horn, his hand to his neck with blood running from between his fingers.

"Are you all right, Cal?" Smoke asked as he jumped out of the saddle and ran to his side.

"Hell, no, Smoke!" Cal replied, a lopsided grin on his face. "I been shot."

"Damn, Cal," Pearlie yelled as he raced over to help. "If I told you once, I told you a thousand times, duck when you hear gunshots."

Cal gave Pearlie a look, his eyes filled with pain though his lips were still curled in a smile. "If I'd ducked, Pearlie, the bullet would've hit me in the head 'stead of the neck, you dumb cowboy."

Once Pearlie saw Cal wasn't hit too bad, he grinned back. "That's what I mean, Cal. Yore head's harder'n any other part of your body. Wouldn't've hurt near as much had you taken one in the pumpkin."

"Let me see that," Smoke said, prying Cal's hand away from his wound.

There was a shallow groove, half an inch deep, running from the front of Cal's neck to the rear. Though it was bleeding fairly heavily, as neck wounds do, it wasn't life-threatening.

"Pearlie, get some fatback out of my saddlebags," Smoke said. "We'll put it on the wound and wrap it tight with a bandanna. That ought to stop the bleeding."

As Pearlie brought over a slab of pork fatback from

Smoke's saddlebags and unwrapped it, he shook his head. "It's a waste of good bacon to use it like that," he said.

"Well, Pearlie, I'll be sure an' save it for you when I'm done with it," Cal said sarcastically.

"Hey, Smoke," Monte called. "This one's still alive," he said, standing over Murphy Givens, who was rolling and writhing on the ground, moaning in pain.

Smoke, once he saw Pearlie was taking care of Cal's wound, walked over to the fire. As he passed, he used his boot to kick Sly Malone's body out of the flames. He rolled it in the snow a couple of times to put out the fire in the outlaw's shirt, but he was already dead.

Then Smoke squatted next to Givens and peeled the man's hands back from his wound. There was a large hole in his lower abdomen. Cal's bullet had torn through the man's bladder and coursed downward to take his penis and balls off. He was bleeding rapidly, and there appeared no way to staunch the flow of blood. The wound was too severe.

"How bad am I hit?" Givens moaned through clenched teeth, staring up at Smoke through terror-filled eyes, afraid to look for himself.

"You're hit about as bad as can be," Smoke said. "You better make your peace with whoever you believe in, 'cause you're sure as hell going to meet your Maker soon."

"Goddamn!" Givens cursed. "I knowed I shouldn't've listened to Cook."

"Where is the rest of the gang?" Guthrie asked, leaning over the dying man.

"Go to hell, Army," Givens said, noticing Guthrie's uniform. "I ain't no rat."

Guthrie straightened up. He took Givens's pistol and emptied out all the shells but one. Then he squatted again and put his face next to Givens's. "Tell us where they are, an' I'll let you have this pistol to put yourself outta your misery," he said calmly.

"Uh-uh," Givens said, shaking his head.

"All right then," Guthrie said. He turned his attention

to Smoke. "Smoke, you're a mountain man. What do you think will get him first, the buzzards or the wolves?"

Smoke scratched his chin. "With that much blood around, I'd bet on the wolves. Course," he added, "the buzzards'll finish up what the wolves leave."

"Damn you!" Givens said, holding out his hand. "Give me that pistol."

"Not until you talk," Guthrie said, his voice hard.

"All right, damn you. They're holed up at a ranch 'bout ten miles south of here," the man said, his voice harsh and clotted with pain.

Smoke looked up, judging the distance and direction. "That must be the Sanders ranch," he said to himself.

He leaned over and stared into Givens's eyes. "What happened to Mr. and Mrs. Sanders?" he asked.

"What'a you think?" Givens said. "Now, I played square with you. Give me that pistol."

As Guthrie started to hand the gun to the man, Smoke reached out and took it from him. He squatted next to Givens, holding the gun just out of his reach. "Joel and Bertha Sanders were sixty years old, you scum. They were worth more than all of you bastards put together."

Givens's voice took on a whining quality. "But they fired on us first," he croaked through dry lips.

Smoke pitched the pistol off to the side, where Givens couldn't get to it.

"When you get to hell, mister, tell the devil to keep the door open, 'cause your friends are gonna be coming soon."

Givens's eyes opened wide when he saw Smoke throw the gun away. "But you promised. . . ."

"So, sue me," Smoke said, and stood up. "Come on, I know a shortcut to the Sanders place. Maybe we can catch them while they're still there."

"What about these bodies?" Jed asked, looking around at the dead men scattered everywhere. "Shouldn't we bury them or something?"

"To hell with them," Smoke said. "Wolves got to eat, same as worms."

As they climbed on their horses, Guthrie said in a low voice, "They didn't bother to bury my dead, so let 'em lie here till something hungry enough to eat shit takes 'em."

Twenty-one

Blue Owl leaned over the bed where Ozark Jack Berlin was sleeping and shook his shoulder.

Berlin came instantly awake, jerking a Colt from under the covers where he was holding it.

Blue Owl held out his hands, "Whoa, Boss," he said, stepping back a step. "It's just me."

"What is it? What do you want?" Berlin asked sleepily, rubbing his eyes with the back of his hand.

"We got trouble, Boss. Sam Cook and his men took off during the night."

"What?" Berlin asked, sitting up in the bed and swinging his legs over the side.

"Yeah. They snuck into the barn and took one of the packhorses, and some of the grub and ammunition too."

"That dumb son of a bitch," Berlin growled, grabbing his hat from the table next to the bed and striding out of the room.

He found the rest of the gang crowded into the parlor of the ranch house, waiting for him.

"Any sign of anybody on our trail?" he asked.

Blue Owl shook his head. "Not yet anyway. I got a couple of men up on the hill keeping watch."

"Anything else?" he asked, walking into the kitchen and pouring himself a mug of coffee from the pot on the stove.

"Yeah. Billy Bartlett thought he heard some gunfire a little while back."

"From which direction?" Berlin asked as he blew on the coffee to cool it before taking a drink.

"Off to the northeast, he thought, though it's kind'a hard to tell with all the echoes from the mountains."

Berlin shook his head. "That idiot must've headed back toward Pueblo, right into the hands of whoever's on our back trail."

Blue Owl nodded. "That's the way I figure it," he said.

"How long ago did Billy hear the shots?"

"About half an hour."

"That means we don't have much time. Get the men saddled up an' let's make tracks outta here, 'fore they get here."

"You think they'll be coming here?" Blue Owl asked.

"Of course. Whoever fired those shots ain't ridin' around in the mountains this time of year for their health. They're on our trail, an' I don't suspect they'll give up just 'cause they killed a few of us."

"You think they got Sam and his men?"

Berlin grinned. "Yeah, an' it serves him right too. He always was dumber'n a snake. Now, let's get movin'. We're burnin' daylight."

U.S. Marshal Ace Wilkins was having lunch at the Lucky Lady Saloon in Pueblo when a young boy came running up to his table.

"Marshal," the boy cried, breathless from his run, "Jake over at the ticket office told me to tell you the train's finally coming in."

"The one that was due three days ago?" Wilkins asked around a mouthful of steak.

"Yes, sir."

"Tell him I'll be right over," the marshal said, flipping the boy a shiny coin for his trouble.

"Thank you!" the boy said, stuffing the coin in his back pocket and running out the door.

* * *

By the time Marshal Wilkins finished his lunch and walked the two blocks to the train station, the train was already in. He noticed there was quite a crowd around the passenger car, and some men were loading what looked like people into several buckboards standing nearby.

He pulled his hat down tight on his forehead against strong north winds and walked up to one of the buckboards. A pretty woman with long dark hair and hazel eyes seemed to be in charge, giving orders for the men to be gentle with the women they were hauling out of the passenger car and loading onto the buckboards.

"Miss," Wilkins said, tipping his hat.

Sally Jensen turned around, pushed a stray lock of hair out of her eyes, and said, "Yes?"

"I'm U.S. Marshal Ace Wilkins," he said. "Would you mind telling me what's going on here?"

"Not at all, Marshal. My name is Sally Jensen, and these women were taken captive by a band of escaped prisoners from the Utah Territorial Prison while on the way here. During their trip, they were repeatedly raped and beaten within an inch of their lives, and three women were killed by the outlaws."

Wilkins's expression grew hard. "How many men we talking about, Miss Jensen?" he asked, glancing at the women in the buckboards, then turning quickly away at the sight of their bruised and battered faces.

"It's Mrs. Jensen, Marshal, and I'm told there were about thirty or so."

"That many?" Wilkins said, as if to himself. He focused his attention back on Sally. "How is it you escaped similar treatment, Mrs. Jensen?"

"I wasn't on the train, Marshal. I was with my husband and some others in a party that was tracking the criminals.

I left the party to accompany the women here for medical care, while the others went on."

"And just who is in this tracking party?"

"My husband, Smoke Jensen; two of our ranch hands; the sheriff of Big Rock, Monte Carson; a Sergeant Bob Guthrie from the Army; and another man named Jed McCulloch from Texas."

"Smoke Jensen? *The* Smoke Jensen?" he asked, eyes wide.

Sally smiled. "I'm only aware of the one, Marshal. Now if you'll excuse me, I need to get these women to the doctor's office where they can be properly cared for."

"Before you go, Mrs. Jensen, do you know which way the outlaws headed when they left the train?"

"South, I believe," she said over her shoulder as she tucked a blanket tighter around one of the injured women. "Oh, Marshal," she added, turning back around. "Smoke asked if once I got here I could notify the U.S. marshal's office and the Army about the outlaws."

Wilkins tipped his hat again. "Consider us notified, ma'am," he said.

After Sally and the buckboards headed toward the doctor's office, Wilkins walked as fast as he could toward the telegraph office. With only two deputies in town, he was badly outnumbered, and he intended to telegraph the nearest Army post to ask for help. He knew he would have little chance of getting any men from Pueblo to join a posse, as they were too intent on digging in the ground for gold to go traipsing off on a chase for outlaws.

Once the telegraph was sent, Wilkins rushed back to his office to round up his deputies. Being a U.S. marshal often meant going up against impossible odds, and Wilkins didn't intend to let the number of outlaws he was chasing keep him from doing his duty. But just to be sure, he would hold off telling his deputies just how many men they were going to be up against until they were well out of town. No need to give them the bad news until it was absolutely necessary.

Twenty-two

Smoke and his men cut cross-country toward the Sanders ranch. He paced the horses, knowing there was no need to hurry. The Sanderses were beyond help, and he didn't want to arrive at the ranch with worn-out mounts in case the outlaws were still there.

As they rode, Jed leaned over in the saddle to talk in a low voice to Sergeant Bob Guthrie. "Bob," he said, glancing forward at Smoke's back as he talked, "did you see how fast Smoke was on the draw back there?"

Bob nodded. "Yep. I blinked an' he already had his gun out an' was ridin' hell-bent for leather at the outlaws."

"Not only that, but he fired at full gallop and hit that first man in the neck at more'n twenty yards." Jed shook his head. "I ain't never seen shooting like that before, and I've ridden with some pretty bad hombres with a six-shooter."

Smoke, who had heard every word of the conversation, twisted in his saddle, a grin on his face. "Now, don't put too high a mark on it, boys," he said. "You're right, I hit my target in the neck, but I was aiming at his chest."

"Oh," Jed said, his face burning red at being overheard. "I guess it was a lousy shot then, Smoke. You were only off twelve inches while firing from the back of a running horse at better'n twenty yards."

"And as far as the speed of my draw is concerned," Smoke continued, ignoring Jed's sarcastic compliment, "I've always found it's more important to be accurate than fast. It doesn't do much good to be first on the draw if you miss and your opponent doesn't. It's the end result that counts in a gunfight."

Cal laughed at the exchange. "That's right. Smoke always says the man who ends up forked-end-up loses, no matter who cleared leather first."

Bob glanced at Cal and Pearlie, riding behind Smoke. "Speakin' of that, that was some pretty fancy shootin' by you boys too," he said with admiration.

Pearlie blushed. "Well, Smoke's a pretty good teacher. He's worked with us a lot over the years to make sure we hit what we aim at."

Pearlie hesitated, then grinned. "Course, with Cal bein' such a magnet for lead, he usually gets nicked a place or two in most every gunfight we been in."

"That's not true, Pearlie," Cal protested. "Why, only last year we had a shootout an' I wasn't touched."

"What's that, one out of five or six?" Pearlie asked. "Why, Cal, you got more scars from bullets on you than that old target we got out behind the bunkhouse at the Sugarloaf."

"That's just 'cause you miss the target more'n you hit it when we're practicin'," Cal retorted, smiling.

"I been shot a few times myself, Cal," Bob said, enjoying the easy camaraderie of the group. "It's no shame to be hit, 'specially if you live to fight another day."

Jed shook his head. "I ain't never been shot," he said. "Does it hurt much?"

Smoke looked over at him. "Not much, at least at first. Early on, the shock of the bullet hitting you deadens the pain. Often, you don't know how bad it is until later. Then it begins to burn like you've been branded."

Bob glanced at Jed. "Let's hope you never find out what it's like. For me, if I never get shot again, it'll be too soon."

Smoke raised up in his stirrups. "There's the ranch house up ahead."

Bob pulled his Army binoculars out of his saddlebags and rode up next to Smoke to get a look.

After peering through them for a few minutes, he said, "I don't see no horses in the corral, but the barn door's shut an' they could be in there."

Smoke pointed to the south end of the house. "Look over there. It looks like plenty of horses took off that way."

"You're right, Smoke," Bob said, lowering the glasses. "How can you see that without binoculars?"

"Smoke can tell the sex of an ant at fifty paces," Pearlie observed proudly. "He don't hardly ever need them glasses you use."

"It comes from lots of years living with mountain men in the high lonesome," Smoke said. "You get used to looking at things from far off. I guess the talent stays with you."

"How do you want to approach the ranch?" Jed asked.

"Let's separate and come at it from different directions," Smoke said. "That way, if it's a trap, they won't be able to get more than one of us in their sights at a time."

The men agreed and rode off in four different directions, to approach the ranch house from all sides.

Cal broke off and rode to the barn, keeping the building between him and the ranch house. He drew his pistol, eased the big double doors open, and slipped inside. In a few moments he was back outside, waving to Smoke that the barn was empty.

Smoke realized there was probably no one inside the house, so he rode up to the front, guns drawn, and kicked the door open.

Quickly searching the premises, he soon found the cabin to be completely empty. He stepped out on the porch and waved the others in from their positions on all sides of the house.

Monte Carson climbed the steps. "Any sign of the Sanders couple?" he asked.

Smoke shook his head. "No, but look there," he said, pointing to the porch.

Dried bloodstains could be seen on the wooden planks of the porch, along with blood and pieces of dried meat on the wall next to the door.

"That don't look good, Smoke," Cal said, glancing around.

"No, it doesn't."

"Uh-oh," Pearlie said in a low voice from the front of the porch.

"What is it?" Smoke asked, walking over to him.

Pearlie didn't say anything, but pointed off to one side of the house, where two lumps could be seen under the snow that had accumulated in the front yard of the house.

Smoke jumped down off the porch and went to the two forms under the snow. He squatted and gently brushed the snow aside, to find Mr. Sanders's face staring up at him through dead eyes.

"Damn!" Smoke muttered. "They didn't even have the decency to cover them up or bury them."

"What'd you expect, Smoke?" Guthrie asked from behind him. "They killed dozens of my men an' left 'em for the buzzards and wolves. I've told you before, these men are little better than animals."

Smoke turned angry eyes up at Guthrie. "Then that's how we'll treat them. We'll hunt them and kill them like the animals they are."

"When do you want to start?" Guthrie asked, a half-crazy gleam in his eyes.

Smoke stood up and brushed snow off his trousers. "First, we have to bury Mr. and Mrs. Sanders. Then we need to get some rest for us and the horses."

"And some hot food wouldn't hurt none neither," Pearlie said, glancing toward the cabin, as if anxious to see what was left in the kitchen.

Smoke smiled. "Yeah, you're right, Pearlie. Like they say, an army travels on its stomach."

"If the soldiers were all like Pearlie, they'd never get anywhere 'cause they'd be stoppin' to eat every thirty minutes," Cal said derisively.

"Well, Mr. Smart Mouth, since you're not hungry, I'll just eat your share of the grub," Pearlie said, striding up the stairs and into the cabin.

"Like hell you will!" Cal said, following close behind him.

Twenty-three

U.S. Marshal Ace Wilkins rode slowly down a mountain trail that led south from Pueblo, keeping his eyes peeled for any sign of a campfire or other evidence of the presence of the outlaw band he was hunting.

Behind him rode his two deputies, Louis McCarthy and Samuel Bogart, men who were barely out of their teens but who felt it was exciting to be deputy marshals, a thought that Marshal Wilkins knew would soon sour as they found that the job usually meant long hours on a lonesome trail doing work that was ninety percent boring and ten percent terrifying.

The three lawmen had with them five privates in the U.S. Army, all that the commanding officer of the post nearest Pueblo had said he could spare. He gave as a reason continuing troubles with renegade Pawnee Indians, who'd been raiding some mining camps in the mountains north of Pueblo.

From the looks of the men sent to ride with him, Wilkins was fairly certain the captain in charge had sent his most useless troops, men who would probably be more trouble than they were worth if push came to shove.

After hearing the report from Sally Jensen, Wilkins had decided to make a wide sweep to the south, in hopes of getting ahead of the outlaws and catching up to them before they had time to get to any nearby ranches or mines and cause more deaths.

He'd twice had to twist in his saddle to warn the soldiers

against making so much noise. They were talking and laughing about their good luck in going on a hunting expedition with the marshal and his deputies, instead of the boring assignments of searching frozen mountain passes for whiskeyed-up redskins.

Just as he was getting ready to call a halt to the search for the day and make camp, Wilkins's nose twitched. He thought he'd caught a whiff of smoke on the air.

It didn't smell like campfire smoke, more like a cigarette burning. The sun was almost down, and the air was gloomy with presundown semidarkness and the persistent ground fog that rose every evening as temperatures fell.

Off to their right, Wilkins saw the rosy glow of a lit cigarette among bushes next to the trail. With a start, he realized they were riding into an ambush.

He simultaneously drew his pistol and jerked his horse's head around while yelling, "Look out! It's a trap!"

Men stepped out of the forest and underbrush on either side of the trail and opened fire as Wilkins spurred his horse off the trail and over a ledge to a steep, precipitous incline.

The deputies managed to get their pistols out and fire a few shots before they were hit.

Louis McCarthy took a slug in his right shoulder, twisting him half around in the saddle so that the next bullet hit him dead center in the middle of his back, between his shoulder blades, pitching him over his horse's rump to land facedown in the snow.

Samuel Bogart wasn't so lucky. He was hit twice in the stomach, doubling him over his saddle horn and making his horse rear up and charge straight into the outlaws' guns. Bogart was hit four more times before he fell off his horse almost at the feet of the outlaws who were standing in the trail drawing down on the men.

Two of the soldiers, who were riding in front, were both

wounded by multiple gunshots before they could clear leather. Both died in their saddles before they hit the ground.

The three soldiers riding in the rear never hesitated. As one, they whirled their mounts around and skedaddled back up the trail, leaning over their horses' heads and whipping them with their reins as fast as they could. The last man in line took a slug in his left buttock, but he kept riding, never even feeling the blow in his terror.

Marshal Wilkins's horse ran and jumped, trying to keep its balance as it half-stumbled down the steep hill next to the trail. Bullets whined around Wilkins's head, buzzing like a swarm of angry bees, as he did all he could to stay in the saddle. He knew if he was thrown off, he was a dead man.

Fifty yards down the hill, his mount's left hoof hit a hole, covered by deep snow, and snapped his leg like a stick.

The horse swallowed his head and sent Wilkins flying ass over elbows out of the saddle. A small Norfolk pine broke his fall, and he landed in a snowbank covering some bushes.

He lay still behind the bush as bullets pocked the snow around him, two of which hit and killed his horse. Wilkins ducked his head and cursed silently when the bronc screamed in pain in its death agony.

Two of the outlaws started down the hill to see if the marshal was dead, but stopped when one of the men sprained his ankle badly on the steep slope.

"Come on, men," that outlaw said as he clambered painfully back up the hill, limping on his injured foot. "If he's not dead, he'll freeze to death up here without no horse."

As they disappeared out of sight over the edge of the slope, Wilkins moved on hands and knees off to one side to get behind a large pine tree. He'd lost his pistol in his mad rush down the hill, and was trying to decide if he should make a run for his horse to get his long gun out of his rifle boot when he heard a scream from above that chilled his blood.

A voice drifted down out of the darkness. "Well, looky here, boys. One of those star-packers is still alive."

A raspy, hoarse voice cried, "No!" followed shortly by the single report of a gunshot.

"Damn!" Wilkins whispered to himself. He shook his head, knowing both his deputies must've been killed in the attack. So much for the glory and excitement of being a marshal, he thought bitterly as he eased over to his horse and slipped his rifle out of its scabbard. He grabbed his saddlebags, threw them over one shoulder, put the rifle over the other one, and started walking away from the trail.

If it was the last thing he ever did, he was going to make those outlaws pay for what they'd done today, he vowed as he trudged through knee-deep snow down the mountain.

Smoke was taking his watch, sitting on the porch of the Sanders cabin, smoking a cigarette and drinking a cup of coffee to keep awake while the other men slept.

The moon was almost full and cast a ghostly glow over the snow and trees of the mountainside. On any other occasion, Smoke would've been thinking about how beautiful the high lonesome is in winter. But this night, his heart was outraged at the fate of the Sanders couple, two people who'd never done any harm to anyone and who'd just wanted to live out their lives together in the beauty of the mountains around their ranch.

His jaw muscles were bunched and tight as he sipped his coffee and smoked, thinking of how sweet it would be when he finally caught up with the bandits.

Suddenly, his eyes caught movement in the trees above the cabin. He was on his feet in an instant, his Henry rifle in his hands as he stared at the trail leading down to the cabin from the mountain.

He saw three figures on horseback riding as rapidly as the scant light would allow, all leaning forward as if their lives depended on getting wherever they were going in a helluva hurry.

Smoke reached behind him and banged once on the door to alert the others they had company coming, then knelt down behind the rail running around the porch and placed his rifle on it for steady aim. He eared back the hammer and waited to see what would happen.

When the men got within a hundred yards, the one in front yelled, "Yo! The cabin!"

Smoke stood up, holding his rifle in plain sight, letting the moonlight sparkle off the barrel.

"Hold it right there, gents!" he hollered back.

"Don't shoot, mister," one of the men on horseback screamed as they all jerked their mounts to a halt in front of the house. "We're soldiers!"

"Get down off your horses and approach the cabin with your hands held high," Smoke commanded just as Monte and the others came out of the front door of the house with guns in their hands.

The three men, one of them limping badly, walked slowly toward the house with their hands up.

"Monte," Smoke said, "get some lights on, would you?"

"Sure, Smoke," Monte said, and turned back into the house to light some lanterns in the parlor.

When the men got to the porch, the leader said, "We were ambushed a couple of hours ago by some escaped convicts." He inclined his head at the man standing next to him. "My friend here took a bullet in the ass an' he needs some help."

Smoke took in their Army uniforms and saw that their saddles also had Army insignia on them, so he lowered his rifle and said, "Come on in, boys. We'll get you some hot coffee and food and see what we can do about your friend's wound."

* * *

The men were given hot coffee and some reheated biscuits and beans, and while they ate, Pearlie worked on the wound in the injured man's butt. The bullet had gone through the fleshy part of his hip muscle and posed no real problem.

"What's your name?" Smoke asked the one who seemed to be the leader of the men, though all were privates.

"I'm Marcus Giles," the heavyset man growled around a mouthful of beans and biscuit. "That there is Johnny Wyatt an' Carlos Balboa," he added, inclining his head toward his compatriots across the room.

"Tell us what happened," Smoke said.

"Well, our capt'n sent us out to ride the mountain with this U.S. marshal named Wilkins. Seems Wilkins had been in Pueblo when this woman came in on the southbound train with a load of other women who'd been beaten up an' raped by these men who escaped from the territorial prison over in Utah."

When he mentioned Sally, Smoke breathed a silent sigh of relief. Evidently she'd made it to Pueblo without any trouble.

"Go on," he said when the man paused to drink more coffee and take in another spoonful of beans.

"Marshal Wilkins an' his two deputies an' us began to move south along the trails from Pueblo. He said he was hopin' to flank around the outlaws an' catch 'em 'fore they could do any more harm."

"And you did catch up to them?" Monte Carson asked.

"More like they caught us," the man named Balboa interjected.

Giles gave him a look that shut him up, then continued his story.

"Yeah. We was goin' down this trail just 'fore dark, an' all of a sudden, from outta nowhere, these men jumped outta the bushes an' commenced to fire on us."

"The marshal led you into a trap?" Guthrie asked, a look of disbelief on his face.

"It weren't his fault exactly," Giles said defensively. "The outlaws gave us no warnin' at all, just sorta appeared."

"What happened to the marshal and the two deputies?" Smoke asked.

Giles shrugged his shoulders. "I don't know 'bout the marshal. He yelled to look out just before the outlaws opened fire, an' jumped his horse off'n the trail into the brush." Giles hesitated, a look of sadness on his face. "The two deputies an' two soldier friends of ours were blown outta their saddles 'fore you could spit."

"So, at least four men are dead, but you don't know if the marshal survived or not?" Smoke asked.

"That's right."

"And you didn't bother to go back and check on him to see if he was wounded or lying out in the snow somewhere?" Sergeant Guthrie asked, a look of extreme distaste on his face.

"No," Giles replied belligerently. "They was a whole lot of men out there takin' potshots at us. We weren't about to go back just to see if anybody was left alive. There weren't hardly no way a man could'a survived that shootin'."

"Where did this shooting take place?" Smoke asked.

" 'Bout five or six miles northeast of here."

"Isn't your post up near Pueblo? To the north?" Guthrie asked, an edge in his voice.

Giles's eyes glanced at the sergeant's stripes on Guthrie's uniform and he sullenly nodded his head.

"Then why were you traveling south?" Guthrie continued.

Giles's face burned red. "Uh, we didn't rightly know which way to go to get away from the outlaws. We was plannin' on turnin' back toward the post in the mornin'."

Guthrie nodded, but it was clear from his face he didn't believe a word the man was saying. He stood up and walked out the front door onto the porch, where he slowly built himself a cigarette and stood there smoking, looking at the stars.

Smoke said, "Finish your food, Private Giles."

He walked out onto the porch to join Guthrie.

"You think they were planning on deserting, don't you?" he asked Guthrie.

Guthrie nodded. "It's plain to see they're the bottom of the barrel. That's probably why their captain sent them with the marshal. He was probably glad to get rid of them."

"You think there's any chance this Marshal Wilkins is still alive?" Smoke asked.

Guthrie shrugged. "Most likely not, but I've known a lot of marshals in my day, an' most of 'em are damned hard to kill."

Smoke nodded his agreement. "We'd better ride on out to where the attack took place and see what we find. If nothing else, we can bury the deputies and soldiers who were killed and see which way the outlaws headed after the attack."

Guthrie looked at Smoke. "You think we should wait until daylight? I don't rightly relish the idea of ridin' into an ambush like the marshal did."

Smoke shook his head. "No, we can't afford to wait. If by some chance the marshal, or one of the other men, is still alive, they'll freeze before morning if we leave them out there. Besides, as cold as it is, the outlaws are going to be sitting around a fire somewhere, not hiding in the bushes waiting to see if anyone returns to the scene of the ambush."

"I hope you know what you're talkin' about, Smoke," Guthrie said, pitching his cigarette butt over the porch rail into the snow in the front yard.

"Well, if I'm wrong and the outlaws ambush and kill us all, I'll apologize, Bob," Smoke said with a grin.

Guthrie returned the smile as he walked into the house. "I'm gonna hold you to that, Smoke."

Twenty-four

After the ambush, Ozark Jack Berlin led his men away from the area in case someone else was following the men he'd killed.

As they rode, Blue Owl pulled up next to him. "Say, Boss. You notice two of them men were wearing Army uniforms."

Berlin nodded. "I noticed."

"I thought by going south we'd get away from the Army," Blue Owl said, scowling.

"Me too," Berlin said. "At least they didn't send a whole company after us. I'm not too concerned 'bout five or six men."

"Yeah, but the Army's got telegraphs," Blue Owl observed. "They're bound to notify their posts farther south to be on the lookout for us, 'specially after all the bluecoats we've killed lately."

"I know," Berlin said. "That's why I've decided not to go any farther south just yet."

"No?"

"No. I think we'll turn an' head back up into the mountains. Long as these winter storms keep comin', it's gonna keep the Army from comin' after us in force."

"It's gonna be slim pickin's up in the mountains, Boss," Blue Owl observed, frowning. "The men are expecting to get rich robbing banks and trains and such. They aren't gonna take kindly to being told we're going back up into the high country."

Berlin glanced at him. "Don't be too sure 'bout there bein' slim pickin's in the mountains. Remember, there're more mines than you can shake a stick at, there's ranchers with no banks to keep their money in, and best of all, there ain't a whole lot of law up here to bother us."

"I hadn't thought of it that way."

Berlin nodded. "That's why I'm leadin' this here gang an' not anybody else, Blue Owl. You tell the men it won't do no good to rob a bunch of banks an' get a bunch of money an' then not be able to spend it 'cause the Army's got us danglin' from the end of a rope."

"You're right, Boss. It won't do no harm to winter over in the mountains, pick off a few mines and ranches, and then head down south next year when the heat's off and everybody's forgotten all about us."

"My thoughts exactly, Blue Owl. I'm gonna leave it up to you to convince the men to stick with us through this. The more of us there are, the less chance anybody'll be able to stand against us when we come calling."

"You leave the men to me, Boss," Blue Owl said, a hard look on his face. "Anybody don't like the way things are being handled can argue about it with my pistol," he said, patting the handle of his Colt.

"That's what I like about you, Blue Owl," Berlin said with a grin. "You have such a way with words."

Once the three soldiers had eaten and gotten their fill of coffee, and Carlos Balboa's butt wound was properly bandaged, Smoke's group saddled up their mounts and had the men lead them back toward where the ambush had taken place.

The soldiers were understandably reluctant to return to the area, but Smoke finally convinced them it would be safe, that the outlaws had undoubtedly left by now.

When they rounded a turn in the trail, Private Giles

reined his horse to a halt, pointing down the path. "I think it was just up there, Smoke," he said.

Smoke got down off his horse. "You men stay here," he said. "I'll go on ahead on foot and see what I can tell from the tracks."

Smoke walked down the trail, his head down, reading tracks as easily as if they'd been a book telling him what had happened earlier that night. The moon was still up, so he had sufficient light to make out the marks in the snow.

He found where the outlaws had been camped, and saw how they'd spread out into the brush alongside the trail. Something must have alerted them to the arrival of the marshal and his men, he thought. Evidently the marshal's party had made enough noise so that the gang knew they were coming and had time to arrange an ambush. Either that, or the outlaw leader was smart enough to have men stationed along his back trail to warn him of anyone tracking them.

Smoke walked around the scene, seeing just how it'd come down. He found the dead bodies sprawled just where they'd fallen. One of the men had a bullet wound to the head surrounded by powder burns, indicating he'd been still alive after the assault and someone had put a bullet in his head at close range.

Twenty yards farther up the trail, he found disturbed snow alongside the road where the marshal had jumped his horse down the slope. There was no blood alongside the marshal's horse's tracks, so perhaps he hadn't been hit.

Smoke pursed his lips and gave a shrill whistle, indicating for his men to come on up.

When they arrived, he pointed down the slope. "Here's where Marshal Wilkins took off," he said.

Pearlie leaned over his saddle horn. "That's a mighty steep slope, Smoke. I don't see how his horse could'a stayed on his feet, 'specially in the dark."

"Speaking of horses," Smoke said. "Why don't you and

Cal ride around and see if you can round up the dead men's mounts. We're going to need them to carry the bodies when we're done."

Pearlie nodded, and motioned for Cal to follow as he rode off up the trail.

"What're you gonna do, Smoke?" Guthrie asked.

"I'm going down that slope and see if the marshal is still alive," Smoke answered.

"That's a helluva drop-off," Jed said, shaking his head doubtfully at the idea of riding a horse down the slope.

Smoke swung up into the saddle. "Don't worry, boys," he said. "This is a mountain pony I'm riding. He's used to much worse."

With that, Smoke spurred the horse forward over the hill and down the slope, taking it slow and easy and letting his mount pick the best way down.

At the bottom of the hill, Smoke found the marshal's horse, lying dead, its legs twisted under it and several bullet holes in it.

Smoke eyed the tracks around the horse, and noted the saddlebags were missing and the rifle boot was empty.

"Well, well, well," he said to himself. "It looks like the marshal survived the trip down. Now let's see if he's survived the cold."

Smoke got down off his horse and led it by its reins as he followed the marshal's tracks in the snow. He saw no other tracks, so he knew the outlaws hadn't bothered to track the marshal, which meant he had a good chance of still being alive.

After he'd gone two hundred yards, Smoke saw the tracks heading out of the clear and into the brush. The marshal was looking for cover to hole up until dawn, Smoke thought.

He didn't want to walk up on the man and perhaps get shot for an outlaw, so Smoke cupped his hands around his mouth and hollered, "Marshal Wilkins!" several times as loud as he could.

From twenty yards off to the right, Smoke heard the unmistakable sound of the lever action of a rifle.

"Marshal, we've come to help you," Smoke called. "We're friends . . . don't shoot."

A weak voice called back from the darkness of the undergrowth, "How do I know you're friends?"

"How else would I know your name, Marshal?" Smoke called back. "Some of your men escaped and brought us back here. Come on out and I'll keep my hands in the air."

"I can't," the voice said, becoming weaker by the moment. "My damn feet are near frozen."

"I'm coming in," Smoke said, and walked into the bushes.

He found the marshal burrowed down in the snow, pine boughs and limbs pulled over him to keep the cold out, his rifle barrel pointing out through the cover at Smoke.

"If you'll point that rifle somewhere else, I'll help you outta there," Smoke said.

"Come on, mister," the marshal replied, lowering the rifle. "I'm in no shape to fight back if you're not who you say you are anyway."

Thirty minutes later, Smoke had the marshal back up the slope, having put him on his horse and led the horse back the way they'd come.

"Pearlie, Cal, build a fire, quick," Smoke said as he clambered over the crest of the hill.

While Cal and Pearlie got a fire going, the other men helped the marshal off the horse and laid him on a ground blanket next to the flames.

"Thank God you came," he rasped through swollen, chapped lips. "I managed to get my saddlebags off my horse, but my matches were wet and I didn't have no way to start a fire."

"Another couple of hours an' you'd've froze to death,"

Guthrie said as he pulled the marshal's boots off and began to rub his feet.

"Oh, shit! That hurts," the marshal cried.

"You got the beginnings of frostbite here, Marshal. You're gonna be lucky if you don't lose some toes."

"Better my toes than the whole foot," the marshal grunted through gritted teeth.

Smoke grinned. He liked this man. Not one to whine and complain about his hard luck.

"What about the other bodies?" Smoke asked Jed, who was busy fixing a pot of coffee to boil on the fire.

"They looked like they'd been stripped. Their boots and most of their belongings were gone, including their guns and ammunition."

Smoke looked around and noted three new horses tied up next to his men's. "I see you found some mounts," he said to Pearlie.

"Only three, Smoke. The other one either ran off or was taken by the outlaws."

"Would you see about getting the dead men on two of them? We're gonna need one for the marshal here."

"You mean we're not going to bury them here?" Jed asked.

Smoke shook his head. "No. Seeing as how we're going to have to take the marshal back to Pueblo, might as well save time by sending the bodies back too."

"But I thought we were going after the outlaws," Guthrie protested.

Smoke glanced at the outlaws' tracks. "They've turned and headed back up into the mountains," Smoke said. "There's no hurry."

"But Smoke, what if we lose their tracks under new snow?" Guthrie said.

"We won't. Cal and Pearlie and I will go on tracking them. You and Jed can take the marshal and bodies and other soldiers back to Pueblo," Smoke said, accepting a cup of coffee from Jed.

"No! I want to go with you," Guthrie said, anger in his voice. "Those bastards killed my men!"

"Bob, be reasonable," Smoke said in a low voice. "I don't trust those other soldiers to go back to Pueblo. The marshal is in no shape to travel by himself, and Jed would only be one against three if the soldiers decided to hightail it south instead of north." Smoke put his hand on Guthrie's shoulder. "I think it'd be safer all around if you went back with them and explained things to the Army captain up there."

"But . . ."

"With any luck, you'll be able to convince him of the need to send another squad up into the mountains to go after the outlaws. Remember, there are lots of miners and ranchers up there who are going to need our protection."

"Damn it, Smoke," Guthrie argued with feeling, "I want revenge for what they did to my men."

"You'll get it, Bob. Just be mighty convincing when you talk to that Army captain."

Monte Carson stepped forward. "You want me to help you track these bastards, Smoke?"

Smoke shook his head. "No, Monte. This figures to be a long campaign . . . hell, it might take weeks before we manage to catch up to them. Your place is back at Big Rock."

"But, hellfire, Smoke," the sheriff protested. "It'll just be the three of you goin' up against more'n thirty of those outlaws."

"Like I said, Monte, that's liable to be weeks from now. The people of Big Rock elected you to take care of the town, not traipse all over the mountains looking for escaped convicts. Besides, what if the outlaws turn south again and decide to hit Big Rock? You need to be there to make sure the town's ready . . . just in case."

Monte ducked his head, turning his hat over in his hands. "I guess you're right, Smoke, but that don't mean I like it."

"I don't particularly like it either, Monte, but sometimes, we have to do things we don't want to do."

Monte turned to his horse and climbed in the saddle. "Remember, Smoke. I'll be in Big Rock if you need me."

Smoke nodded. "I know, Monte. You take care on the ride back to town, you hear?"

Monte grinned fiercely. "I just hope those sons of bitches do try to tree Big Rock. They'll be in for the surprise of their lives."

Twenty-five

Ozark Jack Berlin led his men in a wide circle back to the west, edging upward into the mountain range just above Big Rock, Colorado.

"Why're we going this way?" Blue Owl asked. "Aren't we heading back toward the men who're trailing us?"

"Yeah," Berlin replied, grinning. "It's something they'll never suspect."

"There someplace special you're heading to?" Blue Owl asked as he unfolded the map Berlin had been following and laid it across his saddle horn. "I don't see nothing but mountains on this here map. No towns or nothing."

"That's just it, Blue Owl. There's nothin' up here to make them suspect we'd head this way, so they're not likely to look for us up here."

"But they'll know we're here soon's we hit some ranches or mines," Blue Owl protested.

"Who's gonna tell anybody?" Berlin asked, looking sideways at the Indian. "I don't plan to leave nobody alive to tell anybody what we done."

"But we gotta have someplace to hide out," Blue Owl said, glancing at the sky as snow began to fall again. "The men are getting kind'a tired of camping out in this weather, and it figures to be a mite colder the higher we go up into the mountains."

"Look on the map, where I made an X," Berlin said.

Blue Owl held the map closer to his eyes. "I see the X,

but I don't see nothing near it 'cept the words 'Hot Springs.' "

"When we were in Lode, I asked the assayer if there were any caves up here. He said there were some old Indian caves near the hot springs area. I figure we can hole up there and make our raids from that place. It'll get us outta the weather, an' there'll be hot water to use if we need it."

Blue Owl looked at him. "Hot water? You think any of these men are planning on taking a bath?"

"You never know, Blue Owl. A few weeks stuck in a cave together may make them want to get some of the stink of the trail off."

Blue Owl laughed. "That'll be the day."

"One good thing," Berlin said.

"What's that?"

Berlin held out his hand, and it was quickly covered with snow. "This snow's gonna make trackin' us almost impossible."

"Yeah, but if it keeps falling like this, it's also gonna make it rough going for our mounts."

Berlin shrugged. "From the looks of the map, we don't have that much farther to go anyhow."

Smoke, along with Cal and Pearlie, followed the tracks left by Berlin's gang. As the snow continued to fall and the wind picked up out of the north, the tracks were becoming increasingly more difficult to see.

"Smoke," Pearlie said, pulling his hat down tight on his head and tying a bandanna around his face, "if this keeps up, we ain't gonna be able to track squat by afternoon."

Smoke, who had the collar of his buckskin coat pulled up over his ears, nodded. "I know."

He reined in, fished a compass out of his pocket, and held it out, glancing from it to the tracks for several minutes.

"What're you doin'?" Cal asked from Smoke's other side. He was hunched over with his hands in the pockets of his coat, steering his horse with his knees.

"Since we aren't going to be able to see the tracks much longer, I'm trying to get a fix on the direction they're taking right now. Once the tracks are covered up, we'll just keep going in that direction until we catch up with them."

"What if'n they change course?" Pearlie asked.

"Then we're out of luck," Smoke said, "and we'll just have to wait until we hear some news of where they hit next. One thing's for sure. They're not going to stay under cover for long without causing some trouble somewhere."

"What's that compass tell you?" Cal asked, shaking snow off the brim of his hat.

Smoke's eyes grew thoughtful. "Looks like they're making a wide circle back to the northwest."

"The northwest?" Pearlie said. "But that's back toward Big Rock, ain't it?"

"Yes," Smoke replied shortly. "It looks to me like they're headed up into the mountains north of town."

"But, there ain't nothin' up there but some mines an' ranches," Cal said.

"Yeah," Smoke replied, "mines and ranches run by friends of ours."

Two hours later, with all evidence of the outlaws' tracks completely covered, and the snow falling so thick they couldn't see the trail in front of them, Smoke decided to make camp.

"We've got to get these mounts under cover, before we get stranded out in the open," he said, almost having to yell to be heard over the howling of the wind.

"I don't see no cover handy," Pearlie yelled back.

"Let's head straight up the mountain," Smoke replied.

Within twenty minutes, they came to a thick grove of pine trees nestled up against a cliff.

"Perfect," Smoke said, getting down off his horse. "You and Cal get some branches and tree limbs for a lean-to.

I'll hobble the horses and get them some grain out of the packs."

"How about getting a fire started first?" Cal asked.

Smoke shook his head. "Nope. You're forgetting what I taught you, Cal. The horses get taken care of first, 'cause without them, we're as good as dead."

Within half an hour, the lean-to shelter was keeping the worst of the wind and snow off the men and horses, and Smoke had a roaring fire going up against the side of the cliff.

"Why'd you build the fire next to the cliff?" Pearlie asked. "Looks like it'd be better out in the open so's we could get around it on all sides."

"No, it's just the opposite," Smoke said. "Building it up against the stone cliff keeps the flames out of the wind and heats up the rock. Once we go to sleep and the fire dies down, the rock wall will continue to put off heat for several hours. That way, no one has to stay awake to tend the fire and the wind won't scatter our coals all over the place."

Pearlie reached down, picked up the pot of coffee, and poured mugs for everyone. "It's shore nice campin' with an old mountain man," he said, grinning. "You learn all sorts of things."

Smoke stared at him through narrowed eyes. "The first thing you gotta learn, Pearlie, is not to call the mountain man who's teaching you things *old*."

"Yeah," said Cal from the other side of the fire. "If you make Smoke mad, Pearlie, he's liable not to let you have seconds on the grub."

"Old? Did I say old?" Pearlie asked, smiling over his mug of steaming coffee. "I meant to say *experienced* mountain man."

Smoke laughed. "That's better, Pearlie. Now, why don't you take that skillet of bacon and eggs off the fire before all we have to eat is charcoal."

* * *

The next morning, Smoke awoke to find two feet of snow covering the ground as far as they could see. Though snow was still falling, the wind had died down and the temperatures had moderated to tolerable levels.

Smoke climbed out of his sleeping blankets, stirred the coals into life, and added some wood from the pile they'd gathered the night before. While coffee and biscuits were heating, he stepped out of the lean-to and surveyed the mountain range around them.

Soon, Cal and Pearlie stirred and squatted next to the fire, holding their hands out to the flames to warm them as they drank coffee and munched on warm biscuits with pieces of jerked beef in them.

"What's the plan, Smoke?" Pearlie asked.

"Well, it's obvious we're not going to be able to track the outlaws through this layer of snow," Smoke said, holding his mug with both hands and sipping the steaming brew.

He built himself a cigarette and lit it off a twig from the fire. "I think it's time to head for home."

"You mean the Sugarloaf?" Cal asked, a hopeful look in his eyes.

"Yeah," Smoke replied. "We need to let the horses get some rest, and if we're going to go up into the mountains and take this gang on by ourselves, I want to get some extra provisions and equipment."

"You plannin' on gettin' some of the hands to go up there with us an' help us out?" Pearlie asked.

"No. Tracking these men in the high lonesome is a job for as few men as possible. We're going to need to travel light and fast, and be able to hit and run." He shook his head. "Can't do that with a whole passel of flatlanders along to slow us down."

"That why you got Jed and Bob to head back to Pueblo?" Cal asked.

Smoke nodded. "Yes, in part. They're both good men, but neither are experienced in high-mountain tracking.

I'd hate to see them get killed because they didn't know what to expect."

"Speakin' of knowin' the high-mountain country, Smoke," Cal said, "you think we'll run into any of your mountain-man friends up there?"

Smoke nodded. "I hope so," he said, glancing up the mountainside as if he could see them in his mind's eye. "The mountain men know just about everything that's going on in their neighborhoods. If the outlaws are hiding out up there, some of the old beavers will know where."

"You think we'll see Bear Tooth, or Long John Dupree, or Bull Durham?" Cal asked.

Smoke smiled. "I take it you remember ol' Bear Tooth, huh?"

Both Cal and Pearlie nodded, smiling. They'd met Bear Tooth a couple of years back when Monte Carson's wife, Mary, had been kidnapped by Big Jim Slaughter and they had gone with Smoke to help rescue her.*

"Well, if he's still alive and kicking, which I suspect he is, we'll certainly try to find him. Nobody in the high lonesome knows more about what's going on up there than Bear Tooth. He's a natural-born gossip and likes to keep track of who's coming and going in his neck of the woods."

"He'd be a big help if we go up against them outlaws too," Pearlie said. "He's right handy with that Sharps Big Fifty he carries."

Smoke grinned. "There is that to consider too. The way I figure it, there's way too many of them for us to try and attack them head-on."

"That mean we're gonna do like them *ninjas* you an' Sally are always tellin' us about?"

Smoke laughed. "Yeah, sort'a like we did up in Jackson Hole against Big Jim Slaughter with Muskrat."

Cal laughed. The old mountain man named Muskrat

* *Heart of the Mountain Man*

Calhoon, because he smelled like a muskrat, had been an instant friend of both Cal and Pearlie.

"You mean, hit and run, terrorize them so they don't know who or what is after 'em, and keep doggin' 'em till they go crazy with fear?" Pearlie asked.

"That's about the size of it," Smoke replied.

"Ol' Bear Tooth would love that," Cal said. "I think he was kind'a miffed to miss out on the excitement we had up in Jackson Hole."

"If we manage to find him, and he agrees to help us," Smoke said, "I have a feeling he'll get his fill of excitement this go-around."

Twenty-six

After some roaming back and forth, and checking the map again and again, Ozark Jack Berlin finally managed to find the area marked as hot springs in the mountains.

He crested a small rise in the trail and looked down into a shallow valley to find a seven-foot-wide stream winding through it with steam rising from the pool in the middle of the valley like ground fog on a humid morning. In the walls of the cliffs surrounding the valley could be seen dark openings of caves scattered around the periphery of the area. Out in the middle of the valley floor, near the steaming pools of hot mineral water, there were three clapboard and log cabins that looked to be in moderately good repair.

"Well, men," Berlin said, sitting back against the cantle of his saddle, "here's our new home for the next few months."

"I didn't know there was cabins here," Blue Owl said. "I thought you said we'd be living in caves."

Berlin shrugged. "The assayer I talked to didn't mention nothin' 'bout no cabins. Guess they been built since he was up here."

He glanced at Blue Owl. "Course, if you want, you can stay in the caves instead."

Blue Owl shook his head. "No. I had my fill of caves back in California."

Berlin raised his eyebrows. "I didn't know the Modoc lived in caves."

Blue Owl gave a sly smile. "We didn't, usually. But once, after the Battle of Lost River, the Army chased us across some lava fields near Thule Lake. We hid in some caves and they decided not to try and get us out."

He showed his teeth. "It was a smart decision on their part. They would've lost a lot of men trying."

Berlin looked thoughtful. "You know, Blue Owl, you make a good point. Those caves would be a whole lot easier to defend if by chance somebody comes callin' on us here."

"Yeah. Those cabins are kind'a out in the open. It'd be too easy to surround them if we came under attack."

"Well, I guess what we'll do is fix up the caves with supplies an' provisions an' ammunition in case that happens. We can stay in the cabins, with guards posted on all sides to warn of any upcomin' attack, an' at the first sign of it, we'll get on into those caves, where we can stand off an army if we need to."

"Sounds good to me," Blue Owl agreed. He pointed. "See the way the caves are backed right up against the cliffs overhanging them? If we put men in caves on both sides of the valley, there ain't no way anybody could get at us without getting in a cross fire between the two sides. It's a natural fort that'd be hard to attack."

"That's what we'll do then," Berlin said, spurring his horse down the trail to the valley below.

By the end of the day, his men had the caves on either side of the valley fitted out with enough supplies and ammunition to last them several weeks in the event of a siege by the Army or anyone else. The men then spread out with minimal belongings in the cabins, which were easier to heat and keep warm, where they would stay unless they were attacked.

While several men began to cook supper and heat coffee, the other men used the time to wash out stinking, soiled clothing in the hot water of the springs. A few of the more fastidious even waded out and applied soap to bathe, to the hoots and hollers of those less concerned with personal hygiene.

Berlin and Blue Owl strolled around the camp, checking out the preparations the men had made in the caves.

"You notice the temperature down here near the water?" Berlin asked.

Blue Owl nodded. "Yeah. It's about twenty degrees warmer than up on the ridge."

Berlin grinned. "So, if we do get attacked, we'll be warm down here while our attackers will be freezin' their asses off up on the ridge."

Blue Owl walked into one of the caves, lighting a torch he'd made by twisting a pine bough around a stick of wood. As he got toward the back of the cave, the ground began to rise and the ceiling got lower. Soon, he was crawling on hands and knees.

"What the hell are you doin'?" Berlin asked, following the Indian.

"See how the smoke from the torch blows toward the entrance to the cave?"

"Yeah. So what?"

"That means there's an opening back here somewhere. I want to see if it's big enough for a man to get out of."

"Why would you want'a do that?" Berlin asked.

Blue Owl stopped his crawling and turned around. "Just suppose we get trapped down here in this valley, Boss. Wouldn't you like a back door to use to escape, just in case?"

Berlin pursed his lips, then grinned. "You got a point, Blue Owl. Lead on."

After another fifty yards, and having to get almost down on their stomachs, they came to a hole in the roof wide enough for a man to squeeze through, if he sucked in his gut.

They exited the hole to find themselves in a small area between two tall cliff walls, no more than fifteen feet across and narrowed at both ends by bushes and small trees so that it was invisible from more than fifty yards away.

"This is perfect," Blue Owl said, looking around.

Berlin nodded thoughtfully. "Yeah. The only problem is, once we get out of the cave, we'd be on foot up here in this godforsaken wilderness. I'd almost rather be shot than escape only to starve to death on foot."

Blue Owl thought for a minute, then snapped his fingers. "I'll tell you what, Boss. Later on, when nobody's looking, I'll take a couple of the extra horses and bring them here, with enough grain and water to keep them happy. Ever so often, I'll bring more so's they don't starve to death. That way, if push comes to shove, you and I'll have a way out if need be."

"That's a good idea," Berlin said. "Why don't you pack enough grub for a couple of days and leave it here too?"

Blue Owl nodded. "It never hurts to have a backup plan, does it?"

Berlin smiled. "And enough men to keep our enemies busy while we make our getaway."

It took Smoke and Cal and Pearlie a day and a half to get back down to the Sugarloaf from where they'd left the outlaws' tracks.

By the time they arrived, having ridden all through the last night, they were cold, hungry, and almost asleep in their saddles.

As they approached the cabin, Smoke called out, "Yo, the cabin!" to let Sally know they were coming so as not to surprise her.

She burst out of the cabin door and ran to his horse, taking him in her arms as soon as he stepped out of the saddle.

"Oh, Smoke! I'm so happy to see you."

"Me too, darling," he replied, stifling a huge yawn with the back of his hand.

She leaned back, looking from him to Cal and Pearlie. "You men look exhausted," she said.

"Cold, tired, an' most of all, hungry!" Pearlie said.

"Come on in the house," Sally said. "The fire's going and I've got a roast I can heat up and some leftover biscuits from breakfast that are probably hard as a rock."

"I could eat a rock," Pearlie said, starting toward the house.

While the men thawed out by the fire and ate roast, boiled carrots, and biscuits, Smoke told Sally of their exploits on the trail of the bandits.

After he finished, he asked her what had happened to her.

"Once we got the women seen by the doctor and taken care of, I got on the next train headed for Big Rock. By then, the tracks had been repaired and it was an uneventful trip."

"How'd you get out to the Sugarloaf?" Smoke asked.

"Louis Longmont loaned me a wagon," she answered. "He offered to ride with me, but since it was the middle of the day, I told him I'd be all right. Before I left, I wired Pueblo and told the man there to let me know of any news about the men hunting the outlaws. I knew you'd wire me if you got to a town with a telegraph, but I wanted to make sure I heard anything as soon as it happened."

She stopped talking when she noticed Cal and Pearlie were almost asleep in their chairs.

"Cal, you and Pearlie go on over to the bunkhouse and get some rest," she ordered, standing up.

"Yes, ma'am," they both said sleepily, and filed out of the door.

Sally turned to the pump at the sink and began to fill a large bucket with water.

Smoke glanced over at her. "What are you doing?" he asked.

She put the bucket on the stove and began to fill another.

"In case you don't realize it, Smoke Jensen, you smell like you've been holed up for the winter with a bear. I'm fixing you a hot bath to take before you go to bed."

"Aw, Sally," Smoke protested. "I'm dead tired. We've been in the saddle for two days straight."

She put her hands on her hips. "And you smell like you've been in those clothes for a month. You're not getting in my bed smelling like that, mister." She gave a shy smile. "Now, if you want to sleep out in the bunkhouse with Cal and Pearlie, you go right ahead."

Smoke let his eyes roam up and down her supple body. Then he grinned. "No, I think I can stay awake long enough for a bath," he said.

She grinned back. "Only long enough for a bath?" she asked, her voice husky.

"Oh, maybe a little longer than that, if I have a good enough reason to stay awake."

"We'll just have to see if I can come up with a good reason then," Sally said, a blush creeping up her neck to light up her cheeks.

When Sally went into the bathroom with her fourth bucket of hot water to pour into the bathtub, Smoke was leaning back with his eyes closed, asleep in the tub.

She added the water, then got down on her knees next to the tub. She leaned him gently forward, took a washcloth, and began to scrub his back.

As he moaned in pleasure, she lightly ran her fingers over the many scars from old gunshot and knife wounds that crisscrossed his back like a road map.

"Smoke," she said quietly.

"Yes, dear?"

"You know when I asked you to hang up your guns and not go on any more . . . hunting trips?"

"Yes."

"Well, after seeing what those . . . men did to those women, I've changed my mind."

"Oh?"

"Yes. Monsters like that need to be stopped before they kill again. If you want to go back up into the mountains and make sure they never hurt anyone again, I'm all for it."

Smoke looked over his shoulder at her. "I'm glad to hear you say that, Sally," he said. " 'Cause the outlaws are up in the mountains north of Big Rock, and it figures that they don't intend to just sit up there enjoying the winter in the high lonesome. If no one stops them, some of our friends and neighbors are bound to get killed sooner or later."

"Are you planning to go up there after them?"

"If it's all right with you, Sally. I figure if Cal and Pearlie and I go up there alone, we'll have a much better chance to take them out than if the Army goes up there with a lot of men who don't know how to survive in the mountains, especially in the winter. I could never live with myself if those bastards aren't stopped before they kill again."

"Well, Smoke, I'm sure you and the boys will have something to say about that, won't you?"

"Yes, dear," Smoke said sleepily, leaning back so she could do his chest and stomach.

When she was done, she handed him a towel. "Now you're clean as a newborn baby. Go get into bed and I'll join you in a few minutes."

Smoke climbed out of the bath and dried off, then walked slowly into the bedroom.

Sally changed out of her dress into a nightgown she wore for special occasions, brushed her hair, and cleaned her teeth. Then she sprayed on some perfume she'd bought while on a trip to the East to see her parents a few years back.

She went into the bedroom and stood in the doorway. Smoke was lying on his back, dead asleep, snoring softly.

Sally shook her head, smiled, and crawled into the bed, cradling Smoke in her arms while she too fell asleep.

Twenty-seven

The next morning, Smoke awoke to find Sally in his arms. He inhaled deeply. She smelled like lilacs in June. Good enough to eat, he thought.

He leaned over and kissed her awake.

"Good morning, darling," she mumbled, coming awake. "Are you ready for breakfast?"

He shook his head, pulling her to him.

"Me neither," she said with a moan as he kissed her.

Later, after Smoke was dressed, Sally stood at the stove in the kitchen. "Go wake up Cal and Pearlie, would you, dear?" she said. "I wouldn't want them to sleep through breakfast."

"Fat chance," Smoke said with a laugh. "Pearlie's never slept through a meal in his life. I'll bet he's already smelled that bacon cooking and is on his way here right now."

A knock came at the door, and Cal and Pearlie walked in. "Did I hear my name?" Pearlie asked, not waiting for an answer, but heading for the counter where a platter of bear sign was cooling.

As he reached for one, Sally tapped his hand with her spatula. "Uh-uh, Pearlie," she said, "not until after you have some real food first."

"But Miss Sally," the cowboy protested, looking pained. "Bear sign is real food."

"Come on and sit down, Pearlie," Smoke said from the

table. "You know you've never won an argument with Sally."

He shook his head and walked to the table. "That's right, Smoke, an' if she wasn't the best cook in the territory, I wouldn't put up with it neither."

Cal laughed. "You ought not talk like that, Pearlie," he said. "Ever'body knows you think Miss Sally hung the moon."

"Yeah," Pearlie whispered back, "but don't tell her, it'll just go to her head."

Sally brought heaping plates of scrambled hens' eggs, bacon, sliced tomatoes, and fried potatoes to the table. "Cal, if you'll pour the coffee, I'll get the biscuits out of the oven."

"Yes, ma'am."

While they ate, Smoke discussed his plans for the hunt for the outlaws, with Sally every now and then offering suggestions.

"The real problem is going to be figuring out where they've holed up," Smoke said.

"They could be almost anywheres up there," Pearlie said.

Cal shook his head. "That's not true, Pearlie. With all the snow that's fallen, we can eliminate some of the places where they'd have to go through deep passes to get to."

"That's a right smart idea, Cal," Smoke said, pointing a fork at him. "I'll get one of the maps out that Preacher and I worked on in our years up there, and see if I can figure out which areas are still accessible to flatlanders. They are for sure not going too high this time of year, not without ponies that are experienced mountain climbers."

"I'll bet they don't have none of those special shoes you and Preacher used to go through heavy snow neither," Pearlie said. "That means they're gonna have to stick pretty much to the trails up there. They won't be able to go cross-country at all."

Sally nodded. "That does narrow it down some, Smoke. And since they are, as you say, flatlanders, they won't be comfortable camping out. That means they'll probably try and find some old line shacks or miners' cabins to stay in. There can't be too many of those suitable for thirty men."

"You're right, Sally. They're gonna need at least three or four cabins to get out of the weather in. Most of the mining camps like that are marked on my map. It'll just be a matter of going to the ones easiest to get to. Sooner or later, we're bound to run across them."

She looked at him, her eyes serious. "Just make sure you see them before they see you, Smoke. I told you before, I'm getting tired of patching up bullet holes in your hide."

Smoke gave her a look, then smiled. "Sally, if I can't sneak up on a bunch of men who've never been up in the high lonesome before, I wouldn't be much of a mountain man, would I?"

"But don't forget, dear," she replied, "these men have all been on the run before, and anyone who's been riding the owlhoot trail for any length of time soon learns how to watch their back trail. I'm afraid they won't be as easy to surprise as you think they will."

"You're right again as usual, Sally. Any animal that's been hunted does develop an instinct for survival sooner or later." He looked at Cal and Pearlie. "We'd do well to keep that in mind, boys."

After they'd finished eating, Smoke told Sally he was going to take a ride into Big Rock. He wanted to see if Monte had gotten back all right and he wanted to pick up some supplies from town they were going to need for their expedition into the mountains.

"You want us to go with you, Smoke?" Cal asked.

Smoke shook his head. "No, not this time. I want you boys to curry the horses and give them plenty of grain. They're gonna need all their strength for the trip." He smiled. "Then I want you boys to get some extra shut-eye.

We've been pushing it pretty hard the last week or two, and I want you fit as fiddles when we take off tomorrow."

Pearlie yawned. "I can go for that, Smoke."

Cal laughed. "You don't have to tell Pearlie to hit the hay twice, Smoke," he said. "The only thing I know of Pearlie likes almost as much as eatin' is sleepin'."

"I'll go with you, Smoke," Sally said. "I need to pick up some supplies for the ranch. The hands have been complaining they're getting short of nails and wire for the fence repairs they've been doing."

"Good. I'll enjoy the company," Smoke said, putting his arm around her shoulders. "It'll be a nice quiet trip before I head for the mountains."

Ozark Jack Berlin stood in the cabin where the outlaws had stored their provisions, his hands on his hips. He shook his head.

Blue Owl, standing at his side as usual, glanced at his leader. "What are you thinking, Boss?" he asked.

"We're gettin' kind'a low on provisions, Blue Owl." He turned and walked to the door to the cabin and stood there, looking out over the mountains that surrounded them. "Maybe it's time we made a little foray into a nearby town to resupply ourselves."

"The nearest town is Big Rock, Jack," Blue Owl said.

Berlin looked at him. "How big is this Big Rock?" he asked, stroking his chin.

"Not much bigger than a gnat's ass. Why?"

"I'm just wonderin' how much risk we'd run by goin' in there an' buyin' some supplies with the gold we stole."

"Buying? You mean taking, don't you?"

Berlin shook his head. "No. Since it's the closest town to us, I'd rather not bring any attention to ourselves by stirrin' up any trouble. I think it'd be better if you took just a few men in there, not too many so as not to cause any talk, an' just bought what we need."

Blue Owl grinned. "That's a right good idea, Boss. I've been hankering for some female companionship ever since we left those women on the train."

Berlin glared at him. "No, you don't! I said I don't want any attention to be drawn to you. Leavin' a woman all cut up ain't exactly the way to sneak in and out of town, Blue Owl."

Blue Owl looked pained. "Aw, Boss. It just won't seem right to go all the way to town and not get close to any womenfolk."

"That's the way it has to be, Blue Owl," Berlin said sternly. "Otherwise, I'll send somebody else."

Blue Owl nodded, a resigned look on his face. "All right. You're the boss."

"And make sure while you're in Big Rock, you don't forget it neither."

Fat chance of that, Blue Owl thought as he left the cabin to find some men to go to town with him. He was getting tired of the way Ozark Jack Berlin was ordering him around, but he wasn't quite ready to call him on it . . . yet.

After picking up Monte Carson at his office, Smoke and Sally went to Louis Longmont's saloon to have an early lunch.

As they waited for Louis's French chef Andre to prepare their food, Monte told them about his trip down from the mountains.

He shook his head, letting smoke from his pipe trickle from his nostrils as he talked. "I'll tell you the truth, Smoke. A couple of times I thought I wasn't gonna make it. Snow up to my mount's withers, the air blowin' cold as a well-digger's . . . uh"—he hesitated and glanced at Sally, his face turning red—"well, you know."

Sally grinned, not at all offended by the earthy language men in the West often used. "I know what you mean, Monte," she said. "Why, last week when I tried to cook some of the hens' eggs from the chicken coop, they were frozen solid. It's been a really cold winter, and it's just begun."

Monte nodded, glancing at Smoke. "Like I said, I'm lucky I didn't get frostbite on that trip. I was sure glad to see Big Rock when I finally got here." He laughed. "Hell, first thing I did was go to my house and hug the big Franklin stove Mary uses to keep the house warm."

Smoke smiled. "This has been just about the coldest winter I can remember for a long time, all right."

Louis Longmont, sitting at the table with them, leaned forward. "How do you think that's affecting those hombres you're looking for, Smoke?"

"For one thing," Smoke said, finishing his coffee, "they've got to be mighty uncomfortable up in the high lonesome as cold as it is. From what I can gather, most of them are flatlanders, not used to the weather we're having up here in the high country."

"What about supplies?" Sally asked. "How are they getting them?"

"The marshal over in Pueblo said he had reports they'd been stealin' them," said Smoke, "along with extra guns, ammunition, and even dynamite and blastin' powder.

"Course, with the weather so cold, and thirty or so men to feed, they're gonna be going through lots of grub and supplies," Smoke added, thoughtfully. "That means it won't be long before they have to hit another ranch or town to resupply themselves."

Conversation ceased when Andre and a young black waiter brought platters of food to the table, and the four friends set to eating the best food west of the Mississippi.

Sally glanced up from her plate of roast duck à l'orange, served with mint jelly and freshly steamed vegetables from Andre's private garden.

"I swear, Andre," she told the beaming chef, "if Louis wasn't such a good friend, I'd try to hire you away from him to cook for us at the Sugarloaf."

Smoke shook his head. "Can't do that, Sally," he said.

"Because before long, we'd all be so fat we'd have to ride a buckboard instead of horses."

Sally took a bite of duck, licked her lips, and sighed. "Yes, dear, but it would be worth it."

Twenty-eight

Blue Owl and six other men from the outlaw gang reined in their mounts in front of the general store in Big Rock. They had two extra horses to be used to pack the supplies they came for.

As they dismounted, he reminded the men, "The boss don't want no trouble, so keep your mouths shut and behave yourselves just like ordinary citizens."

Moses Johnson, the huge black man, grinned and rubbed his stomach. "If'n it means we get some more food to eat, I'll be quiet as a mouse in church. I been 'bout to starve to death on those meager rations Ozark Jack's been handin' out at the camp."

Blake Whitney, a skinny, rail-thin man with pale skin pockmarked with old smallpox scars, laughed. "Yeah, Moses," he said, looking up at the man who towered almost a foot taller than he, "you look like you're just wastin' away."

The seven men entered the general store, laughing as if they had nothing to worry about.

Ed Jackson, who owned the store along with his wife, Peg, looked up from behind the counter where he was arranging some tinned peaches and canned milk.

"Howdy, gents," he called, smiling. "Welcome to my store."

Blue Owl nodded and didn't reply as he and his men spread out and began to fill flour sacks with groceries and staples.

The small bell over the door rang as a gangly boy of about eleven years old entered.

"Hello, Jerry," Ed said, opening a jar of peppermint sticks on the counter.

The boy said hi, and dug deep in his pockets and brought out a shiny new penny. He placed it on the counter and then reached into the jar and pulled out a stick of candy.

Ed winked at him. "Go on, Jerry, take another."

"But I only gots the one penny, Mr. Jackson," the boy said.

"That's all right. You need two to ward off the chill outside," Ed said, tilting the jar so he could get another stick.

"Gee, thanks, Mr. Jackson," Jerry said. He took the extra stick of peppermint and put it in his pants pocket. The other one he stuck in his mouth, and ran out the door.

As the men piled their goods on the counter, Moses Johnson reached into the jar and took out a handful of the sticks. "That candy sure do smell good," he said.

Ed glanced at the large pile of goods the men were stacking up. "You gents look like you're getting enough food to feed an army," he said as he began to total up the bill on a scrap of paper.

"We figure on doing a little mining up in the high country during the winter," Blue Owl said, scowling. "Don't want to have to stop to come back for supplies any more than we have to."

Ed grinned, shaking his head. "Well, boys, this ought'a last you at least till next spring."

Jerry sucked contentedly on his peppermint as he skipped and ran down the boardwalk toward the center of town. When he got to Sheriff Carson's office, he stopped, seeing a new poster tacked to the wall. As he read what was on it, his eyes got wide and the peppermint dropped out of his mouth.

He pushed the door to the office open and ran inside. Monte's deputy, Jim, was sitting at Monte's desk, his feet up on the desk, snoring softly.

"Mr. Jim," Jerry said, excitement in his voice. "Where's the sheriff?"

Jim started awake, dropping his feet off the desk guiltily.

"Why do you need him, Jerry?" Jim asked, rubbing his eyes and laughing. "Somebody robbin' the bank?"

"No, sir!" Jerry replied. He pointed out the door. "But I think I seen some of the men on that poster outside."

Jim got suddenly serious. He jumped up and grabbed a shotgun off the rack on the wall. "Where'd you see 'em, Jerry?" he asked, filling his pockets with shotgun shells.

"Down at Mr. Jackson's store. They was buyin' all kinds of things."

Jim knelt down, his hands on Jerry's shoulders. "How many of 'em were there, boy?"

Jerry shrugged. "I don't know. Five or six, I guess."

"You run on home now, and stay off the street. You hear me?" Jim said sternly.

"There gonna be gunplay, Deputy?" the boy asked, his eyes wide.

"If you're right about this, there damn sure will be!"

Smoke and the others were just finishing their lunch when Deputy Jim rushed into Longmont's.

"Uh-oh," Monte said when he saw the look on his deputy's face and noticed he was carrying two shotguns cradled in his arms.

Jim stopped inside the batwings, looked around until he saw where Monte was sitting, then rushed over.

Monte held up his hands. "Catch your breath, Jim, then tell me what's got you all riled up."

"There's some men over to the general store, Sheriff," Jim gasped between breaths.

"There generally is, Jim," Monte said calmly.

"Yeah, but Sheriff, little Jerry says the men fit the description of that poster you put up 'bout them outlaws you been lookin' for."

"What?" Monte said, jumping to his feet.

Smoke stood up too. "Sally, you stay here while we check it out," he said, unfastening the rawhide hammer thongs on his Colts.

Louis did the same, and got to his feet along with Smoke and Monte. "Andre," he called.

When the chef stuck his head out of the kitchen, Louis said, "I'm going to be down the street. Shut and lock the front door, just in case there's trouble."

"Oui, monsieur," Andre said, wiping his hands on his apron and following them to the door.

Sally reached in her handbag, pulled out her snub-nosed .38-caliber Smith and Wesson revolver, and started walking out with the men.

"Sally, I don't want you involved in this," Smoke said.

Her face got that look on it that told him not to push it. "I don't particularly want you involved either, Smoke Jensen, but I don't have any more choice in the matter than you do."

With that, the four men and Sally walked out of the door. Monte and Jim ran across the street and began to walk up the boardwalk toward the general store, while Louis and Smoke did the same on their side of the street. Sally positioned herself in a doorway next to Longmont's Saloon, and eared back the hammer of her .38 while she waited to see what was going to happen.

Blue Owl and Moses Johnson were out in the street in front of the store, tying down the supplies on their packhorses while the five men with them stood next to their horses.

Marcus Weatherby and Slim Bartholomew were building

cigarettes when Marcus glanced up and saw the men headed down the boardwalks toward them.

He dropped his paper and tobacco and grabbed for his gun. "Uh-oh, looks like trouble comin', Blue Owl," he said in a low voice, moving around to get behind his horse.

Blue Owl glanced over the back of the packhorse and cursed. "Goddamnit!" he said, knowing they'd been recognized.

"Get on your mounts and shag tail, boys!" he yelled, whirling around and jumping for his horse.

Moses Johnson grabbed the short-barreled shotgun out of his saddle boot and aimed over the back of the packhorse.

"They're goin' for their guns!" Monte yelled, pushing Jim to the side out of the line of fire just as Moses let go with both barrels.

Monte dove behind a water trough in the street just as several of the shotgun pellets tore into his right arm just below the shoulder.

The outlaws swung into their saddles and jerked their mounts' heads around, trying to get out of town.

Smoke and Louis, in one coordinated movement, crouched, drew, and began to fire their pistols.

As they shot, Marcus Weatherby and Blake Whitney were blown out of their saddles, bullets in their chests.

Blue Owl and Moses Johnson spurred their horses down the street, leaning over their saddle horns and firing as they rode.

Jim stepped back out of the doorway Monte had pushed him into and let go with his shotgun, knocking Slim Bartholomew backward off his horse, a load of buckshot in his gut.

Blue Owl fired across his saddle, his bullet hitting Jim in the thigh and knocking him to the ground, his shotgun empty on the ground next to him.

George Carver and John Ashby fired at Smoke and Louis, their bullets pocking the buildings next to where they crouched, making them dive to the ground.

Smoke rolled to the side, aimed, and fired, hitting Carver between the shoulder blades. He flopped forward, but somehow managed to stay in the saddle as his horse galloped down the street.

Louis lay on his back, firing between his boots, but his shots went wide as the men jigged their mounts back and forth as they rode.

Sally stepped out of her doorway, spread her legs, and starting firing her .38, unmindful of the bullets whizzing past her head.

Her first two shots missed; her third hit Carver for the second time. As the bullet entered his right temple, his head jerked to the side and he catapulted out of the saddle, to be trampled by John Ashby's horse as it thundered past.

Her gun empty, she stood helpless as Blue Owl aimed his pistol at her as he rode past.

With a grunt, Monte Carson scrambled to his knees and raised his shotgun with his left hand, his right arm hanging useless at his side.

He pulled both triggers, and his load tore into Blue Owl's hand, knocking his pistol to the ground before he could fire at Sally.

Blue Owl, John Ashby, and Moses Johnson continued their mad dash out of town as Smoke and Louis ran to Monte's and Jim's aid.

"You all right?" Smoke asked Monte, while Louis checked on Jim's leg, taking a bandanna from around the deputy's neck and tying it around the leg to slow the bleeding.

"Yeah, damn it!" Monte exclaimed, cradling his wounded arm in his left hand. "But three of the bastards got away."

Satisfied his friend was going to live, Smoke glanced over his shoulder at Sally, relieved to see she was unharmed.

"Sally," he yelled, "go get Doc Spalding!"

Sally nodded once, quickly, and ran up the street toward the doctor's office.

Monte turned to look at Jim. "Is he going to be all right?" he asked Louis.

"Yes. It appears you saved his life by knocking him out of the way when that big black let go with his shotgun."

"Thanks, Sheriff," Jim groaned from where he lay on the boardwalk.

"Damn fool," Monte replied, a smile on his face. "You should'a stayed there an' you wouldn't be bleedin' all over the street."

Jim nodded, returning the smile. "Yeah, but then there'd be four of 'em ridin' off 'stead of three."

Louis, satisfied Jim's bleeding was under control, pulled his pistol and stood up. "I'd better see if any of them are still alive," he said, walking toward the bodies lying in the street in front of the store.

"I'll help you," Smoke said, standing. "Maybe we can get one of them to tell us where their camp is."

As it turned out, all of the men were dead, so no information could be gotten as to the whereabouts of their camp.

After Monte and Jim were taken to Doc Spalding's office, Louis and Smoke and Sally went back to Louis's place for some coffee and dessert.

Over a magnificent flan, Louis asked Smoke, "What are you going to do now?"

Smoke finished his flan, built a cigarette, and leaned back with a cup of coffee in his hand. "Well, they didn't get the supplies they came to town for, so that means they're going to have to hit a ranch or mining camp soon."

"Uh-huh," Louis agreed, tilting smoke from his nostrils toward the ceiling.

"I'm going to get the supplies I came for, then take Cal

and Pearlie up into the high lonesome to see if we can get to them before they hurt anyone else."

Louis's eyes lit up and he leaned forward. "You want some company?"

Smoke slowly shook his head. "No, old friend. As much as I'd like that, with Monte and his deputy both injured, the town's going to need someone who knows how to use a gun to be on guard in case those outlaws make another try here."

"They wouldn't dare," Louis said.

"Don't be too sure, Louis. If they're as short of food as I think, you never know what they're liable to do."

"Jimminy," Cal said, shaking his head. "I knowed we should'a gone to Big Rock with you."

Pearlie nodded gravely. "See, you were right, Miss Sally. Ever time Smoke goes anywhere without Cal an' me to cover his back, he gets into trouble."

She laughed. "Well, we won't let that happen again, boys. I'm counting on you to make sure nothing happens to him up in the mountains."

"You can bet on that, Miss Sally," Cal said. "Pearlie and me'll make sure he don't take no chances with them galoots."

Sally shook her head. "Cal, what are we going to do about your language? When you get back, we need to spend some serious time with one of my English grammar books."

Cal dipped his head and concentrated on his food. "I'd rather go up against an outlaw any day than fight them schoolbooks," he mumbled.

Pearlie, trying to change the subject, interjected, "Smoke, why'd you buy all them new clothes?"

"We're going to be going up against a group of men with superior numbers, Pearlie. That means we're going to have to use stealth instead of brute force. Since we'll be doing a lot of our work at night, I wanted us to wear dark clothing so as not to be able to be seen in the dark."

"What about those tins of bootblack?" Cal asked. "You think the outlaws are gonna care if our boots are shiny?"

Smoke laughed. "The bootblack is for our faces, Cal. It's about time for a full moon, and nothing shows up in moonlight like a white face."

"You mean we got to put that stuff on our faces?" Pearlie asked.

"Not only our faces, but on our hands and arms as well," Smoke said.

Ozark Jack Berlin stepped out of the cabin when he heard hoofbeats approaching the camp.

His eyebrows raised when only three men rode in, with no packhorses.

Blue Owl, his right hand wrapped in a blood-soaked bandanna, reined to a stop in front of Berlin.

"What the hell happened?" Berlin asked, grabbing Blue Owl's reins.

He swung down out of the saddle. "We were ambushed before we could get out of town with the supplies," Blue Owl replied, shaking his head.

"What about the other men?"

"Whitney, Weatherby, Bartholomew, and Carver all got hit. They didn't make it."

"Damn!" Berlin exclaimed. "You think any of 'em will be able to talk about where we're camped?"

Blue Owl shook his head. "No. They were all hit real hard. I don't think any of them will be talking to anybody ever again, leastways, not in this life."

Berlin glanced up at John Ashby and Moses Johnson. "Either of you boys hurt?" he asked.

They shook their heads.

"Come on into the cabin an' we'll see about gettin' that hand fixed up," he said to Blue Owl. "You boys go on over to the other cabin an' get yourselves some grub," he said to Ashby and Johnson.

After Blue Owl's hand was cleansed and bandaged, Berlin lit a cigar and poured himself and Blue Owl a glass of whiskey.

"We really needed those supplies," he said, his eyes staring out the window of the cabin.

"I know, Boss," Blue Owl replied after taking a large swallow of his whiskey. "We did all we could, but it was as if they was waiting for us."

Berlin nodded. "I suspect the word has got out to all the towns around this area by now."

Blue Owl nodded his agreement.

"Well, there's nothin' else we can do. The men gotta eat, an' pretty soon we're gonna need more ammunition."

"Guess we're gonna have to find some ranches or mines nearby to replenish our stock," Blue Owl said.

"Yep. After you get some hot food into your gullet an' a good night's sleep, why don't you and me take a little ride around the area first thing in the morning an' see what we can find?"

"Sounds good to me," Blue Owl agreed, finishing off his glass of whiskey and getting to his feet.

After a good night's sleep and a hearty breakfast fixed by Sally, Smoke and Cal and Pearlie saddled up their horses for the trip into the high lonesome.

Smoke decided to take their best horses this time, so he told Cal and Pearlie to bring out Joker, Silver, and Cold, the crosses from Smoke's Palouse mares and Joey Wells's big strawberry roan stud Red. The legendary gunman, Joey Wells, and his wife had bought the old Rocking C ranch in Pueblo, Colorado, after killing Murdock, the man who'd owned it. Sally, as a gift to Joey's wife, had given them some Palouse mares to breed with Red and start their remuda.*

The offspring Joey had sent to the Sugarloaf were all beautiful animals that had inherited their father's big size and strength and the Palouses' speed and endurance.

Smoke's stud was a blanket-hipped Palouse, red or roan-colored in front with hips of snow white, without the usual spots of a Palouse. Smoke had named him Joker because of his funny coloring.

Pearlie's descendant of Red was a gray and white Palouse he'd named Cold. When Smoke asked him why he'd named him that, Pearlie said it was because the horse was

* *Honor of the Mountain Man*

cold-backed in the morning and bucked for the first ten minutes every day when Pearlie saddled him up.

Cal's mount was a quicksilver gray, and was actually almost pure white, differing from a true albino by having gray in front with snow-white hips, also without the usual Palouse spots. Cal had named him Silver, and the two seemed to have a bond that was as close as any Smoke had seen between animal and man.

As they saddled the animals, Cal looked over at Smoke. "Saddlin' these broncs reminds me, Smoke," he said. "Why didn't you look up Joey an' see if he'd help us while we were over near Pueblo?"

Smoke shook his head. "I thought of that, Cal, but Joey's settled down with a wife and family now. He's been a rancher a long time, and the last word Sally got from his wife said he'd hung up his guns for good. I respect the wishes of a man who wants to change his way of life, and I certainly wouldn't want to be the one to ask him to strap his guns back on after all these years."

Pearlie grinned. "Plus, if you asked him to ride with us an' somethin' happened to him, Sally'd have your ears," he said.

Smoke laughed. "I won't say that thought didn't cross my mind too, Pearlie."

Once the horses and pack animals were saddled and ready to go, Smoke stepped into the house. He found Sally busily washing dishes from breakfast.

When he turned her around, he saw tears in her eyes.

"What's the matter, darling?" he asked.

She threw her arms around his neck. "I'm just being a silly wife, Smoke. I'm worried that this may be the last time I ever see you."

He leaned back and stared into her eyes. "Now, don't you fret, Sally. I promise to be careful, and I promise to have Cal and Pearlie watch my back at all times."

She put a finger on his nose. "I'm telling you right now, Smoke Jensen," she said sternly. "If you're not back here inside of a month, or I don't hear from you, I'm going to ride up into the mountains and find out why."

"We'll be back before then, Sally," Smoke said, taking her finger off his nose and kissing it gently. "If this thing can't be done in a month, then it can't be done at all."

"You sure you don't need more men?" she asked.

He shook his head. "No, this is a job best done by as few men as possible. The more men I have along, the more chance the outlaws will know we're coming. This thing is best done by stealth, as I told Cal and Pearlie, not by brute strength."

"So, you plan to pick them off one at a time?"

"If everything goes as planned," he answered.

"When was the last time everything went as you planned?"

He laughed. "Never, now that you mention it."

"I'll keep the bed warm for you, mountain man."

"You do that, lady," he said, bending and giving her a long, serious kiss. " 'Cause just the thought of that will make me be sure to come back."

Sally and Smoke walked out onto the porch, her arm around his back.

"Cal, Pearlie," she said to the boys sitting in their saddles in front of the house.

"Yes, ma'am," they answered.

"I'm counting on you two to make sure this big galoot doesn't get anything vital shot off, you hear me?"

Both Cal and Pearlie blushed and smiled. Sometimes, even as well as they knew Sally, her plainspoken ways shocked their Western ideas of women.

"Yes, ma'am," Pearlie said, touching the brim of his new black Stetson. "I'll make sure he don't take no unnecessary chances."

"That'll be the day," Cal murmured, causing both Smoke and Pearlie to give him hard looks.

Sally laughed. "If you can manage that, Pearlie, it'll be the first time in his life Smoke Jensen has ever played it safe."

Thirty

Fully rested after a good sleep, Ozark Jack Berlin and Blue Owl headed out searching for a nearby ranch or mining camp to raid for food and supplies.

As they rode out of the outlaws' camp, Berlin glanced at Blue Owl's right hand. "How's the hand this mornin'?" he asked, noticing the way the Modoc was favoring it.

Blue Owl held his hand up and looked at the blood-soaked bandage. "It hurts and the fingers are so swollen I don't think they'll fit in my trigger guard."

"Can you still use that scattergun in your rifle boot?" Berlin asked.

"Yeah. If I need to, I can fire it left-handed."

"Good, 'cause I'd hate to think you wouldn't be any good to me in a fight."

"Don't worry about that," Blue Owl growled. "If need be, I'll hold up my end if we get in a fracas."

Berlin nodded, and led the way down a snow-covered trail out of the valley of their camp.

After a while, Blue Owl spoke again. "You know something, Jack?"

"What?"

"I think one of those men who attacked us back in Big Rock was Smoke Jensen."

"Smoke Jensen? The gunslick? Are you sure?"

"Yeah, I'm sure. I saw him once in a gunfight over near

Tucson. He went up against three men who all slapped leather before he did."

"Yeah?" Berlin asked.

"That's right, and not one of the men managed to clear leather before he'd planted 'em all forked-end-up."

"Why in hell would a man like Smoke Jensen take up arms against you? He wasn't wearin' a badge or anything, was he?"

Blue Owl shook his head. "No, but he was sure as hell standing there on the boardwalk next to a fancy-lookin' gent and they both drew down on the boys."

"That's interesting," Berlin said, his lips pursed in thought.

"I heard a while back that Jensen hung up his guns and settled in some hick town in the mountains. Maybe he considers Big Rock his home."

Berlin scowled. "Well, if he gets in our way again, his home's gonna be six feet under Boot Hill."

Blue Owl chuckled. "There was also this lady involved."

"A lady?"

"Yeah, a right pretty little thing with long black hair. She stepped out of a doorway with this little bitty old pistol in her hand and blew half of George Carver's head off while he was riding by at a full gallop."

"That's pretty good shootin' for a lady," Berlin mused, shaking his head.

"Hell, that's damn good shooting for anybody, man, woman, or child."

"Did you take her out?" Berlin asked, glancing at Blue Owl, his eyes narrowed.

"I was fixing to when somebody shot the gun right outta my hand with an express gun." He paused a moment, thinking back on the event. "It's funny too. She was out of bullets and saw me aiming right at her gullet, and she never ducked nor flinched at all . . . just stood there staring at me with those big eyes."

"Probably too scared to move," Berlin said.

Blue Owl shook his head. "Nope. Far as I could tell, this woman wasn't afraid of nothing nor nobody."

Berlin laughed. "Well, Blue Owl, I wouldn't go repeatin' that story to the men. We don't want them thinkin' women an' children are gettin' the best of us."

Blue Owl nodded, then pointed up ahead over a small rise in the trail. "Hey, look there, Jack. A ranch."

Berlin reined his horse to a stop on the crest of the hill overlooking a small valley below. Smack in the middle was a large ranch house, corral, barn, and what looked like a smaller bunkhouse off to one side.

As they sat there staring down at the ranch, a voice came from off to one side. "Howdy, gents."

Both men whirled in their saddles, hands going to pistol butts.

An older man, who looked to be in his midfifties, held up his hands. "Whoa, hold on there," he said with a smile. "Didn't mean to startle you. My name's Jim Morrow, and that's my spread down there."

Berlin let his hand relax and forced a smile on his face. "Howdy, Mr. Morrow. My friend and I were just headin' cross-country from Pueblo toward Big Rock. We seem to have gotten lost in the snowstorm yesterday."

Morrow grinned. "You certainly are. Big Rock's off in that direction, 'bout ten miles or so."

He looked at them, his face curious. "I don't see no supplies on your mounts. You trying to get to Big Rock without any food along?"

Berlin grinned sheepishly. "No, sir. Our packhorse slipped his lines and ran off during that storm. Truth of the matter is, we're 'bout starved to death."

"Well, come on down. I'll have my wife fix you up some vittles to eat right now, an' I'll pack you some to take along. It's doubtful you'll make Big Rock in less than two days, as deep as the snow is."

"We're much obliged, Mr. Morrow," Berlin said, winking at Blue Owl when the rancher couldn't see.

While Bess Morrow, Jim's wife, fixed the men some breakfast, Jim took them out to the barn. He opened a door to a large storeroom.

Stacked inside were stacks of canned goods, several sides of beef and pork hanging from hooks in the ceiling, and many large sacks of flour, beans, and other sundry dry goods.

Berlin whistled softly. "Looks like you got near enough food here to feed an army, Mr. Morrow," he said, glancing out of the corner of his eye at Blue Owl, who was similarly impressed with the amount of food before them.

Morrow laughed. "Yeah, you're right, Mr. Jones," he said, using the fake name Berlin had given him.

"You see, we're quite a ways from the nearest general store. It's a good three-day trip to Big Rock by buckboard. Not an easy journey in the winter, so we stock up with all we think we'll need to get through the winter while the weather's still good," Morrow explained.

"You need this much to feed your hands?" Blue Owl asked, trying to figure out how many men they might have to kill to get the food.

"Not during the winter," Morrow said. "We let most of the hands go this time of year. There just ain't enough work to keep 'em on year-round. Spring comes, I go down to Big Rock and hire however many I need for the spring calving and branding. Otherwise, there's just me, the missus, and Hank, our foreman."

Berlin nodded while Morrow began to pack an empty burlap sack with enough food to last two men the two days it would take to get them to Big Rock.

While he was working, Berlin and Blue Owl wandered out of the barn to light up cigarettes.

"You think we ought'a take them now?" Blue Owl asked.

Berlin shook his head. "No. We're gonna need several of the men to help us carry off all this stuff, so it'd be better to come back later in force an' take what we need then."

Morrow came out of the barn, the gunnysack over his shoulder. "This ought'a get you to Big Rock, all right. Once we've eaten, you can be on your way," he said, handing the sack to Blue Owl.

Smoke and Cal and Pearlie swung to the east on their way up the mountain. Smoke wanted to go by Johnny and Belle North's spread on the way and let them know about the outlaws being in the area.

As they approached the North ranch house, Belle came out on the porch, wiping her hands on an apron around her waist.

"Howdy, men," she said. "Come on in out of the cold and have some coffee."

"Is Johnny around, Belle?" Smoke asked as he stepped up on the porch.

"Yes," she replied, looking over her shoulder at the barn out behind the house. "He's out in the barn." She grinned. "Probably smoking one of those big black cigars I won't let him light up in the house."

"Cal, you and Pearlie go on in," Smoke said. "I want to talk to Johnny for a spell."

Johnny North was sitting behind the barn on a bale of hay, a cup of coffee in one hand and a long, black cheroot in the other.

His face broke out in a wide grin when he saw Smoke walking around the corner of the barn.

"Howdy, Smoke," he said. "Long time no see."

Smoke smiled and shook Johnny's hand. "It has been

a while, Johnny," he said. "Sally's always after me to invite you and Belle up for a meal, but . . ."

"I know," Johnny said. "Seems there's always something to do around a ranch that keeps you from visiting your friends."

Smoke laughed. "You miss the owlhoot trail, Johnny?" he asked. He was referring to Johnny's past, when he was a notorious gunfighter who hired his gun out to the highest bidder. He'd been hired years ago by a man who went up against Smoke and the town of Big Rock, but Johnny couldn't tolerate the methods of the man, and he'd switched sides. Soon thereafter, he'd met and fallen in love with the Widow Colby, Belle, and they'd been peaceful ranchers ever since.

Johnny shook his head. "Not for a minute, Smoke. How about you?"

Smoke shook his head. "No. Same as you, Johnny, a good woman saved me from that life forever."

"Ain't that the truth," Johnny agreed.

"The reason I'm here, Johnny, is to warn you."

"Warn me? About what?"

Smoke went on to tell Johnny about the outlaws' escape and that they'd been sighted in the mountains just above Big Rock and the North ranch.

"How many we talking about?" Johnny asked, his eyes worried.

"Between twenty and thirty," Smoke said. "They tried to get supplies in Big Rock the other day and we managed to kill four of them, but there's plenty more up in the hills."

"So, you figure they'll be raiding some ranches looking for supplies and such?"

"That'd be my guess," Smoke said. "I just wanted you and Belle to be on the lookout for anyone you don't know."

Johnny nodded. "Will do, Smoke. I'll get my guns all loaded and board up the windows of the house until they're caught, or move on."

"You think you and Belle will be safe out here all by yourselves?" Smoke asked. "You're welcome to head on over to the Sugarloaf and stay with Sally. I've kept most of my hands on, so there'll be some extra guns in case they're needed."

Johnny shook his head. "No, thanks, Smoke. Belle is right handy with a Winchester, and I haven't lost all of my abilities. We'll do just fine now that you've warned us to be on the lookout for strangers."

"Anybody else you can think of needs warning?" Smoke asked.

Johnny scratched his face for a moment, thinking. "Yeah, you might swing on by the Morrow place. Jim and Bess only keep the one hand on during the winter, and their place is a mite closer to the mountain than mine."

Smoke thought for a moment. "Their place is over by Slaughter Creek, isn't it?"

"Yeah, in that little valley just before you start up the steep slope to the peak over yonder," Johnny said, pointing at a snow-covered peak in the distance.

"Soon's you finish that wolf-turd you're smoking, come on in the house," Smoke said, grinning. "Belle's making fresh coffee."

Johnny stubbed the cigar out on his boot heel, then put it in his shirt pocket. "I'll just save it for later," he said.

"Times getting that tough you got to save your old cigar stubs, Johnny?" Smoke asked, only half-kidding.

Johnny grinned. "No, but come winter, with all the snow and storms and such, being married to a woman who won't let you smoke in the house is kind'a tough. After a while, a man gets cabin fever stuck in the house. Sometimes, you just need a good excuse to get away from one another for a while. Otherwise, you get to griping and fighting and life gets hard."

"I can't imagine you and Belle fighting," Smoke said, thinking the Norths' marriage was one of the best he'd ever seen, outside of his and Sally's.

Johnny's face became serious for a moment. "Oh, I ain't

saying it's Belle's fault, Smoke. A finer woman never lived. But, even after all these years as a rancher, I'm still an ornery old cuss, and sometimes the meanness just comes out if I'm cooped up too long."

Smoke nodded, understanding completely. "I know, Johnny. After all the years we spent on the owlhoot trail, sometimes you get to feeling trapped when you stay in one place too long."

"That's it, exactly, Smoke."

Thirty-one

When Ozark Jack Berlin and Blue Owl arrived back at the camp, the men wanted to know what they'd found.

"An old codger an' his wife have a ranch 'bout five or six miles off to the east," Berlin told them as he unpacked the supplies Jim Morrow had given them.

"They got enough food to last us the rest of the winter stashed in their barn up there," Blue Owl added.

Moses Johnson grinned and rubbed his stomach. "That's good, Boss, 'cause we been on such short rations lately, my stomach thinks my throat's been cut."

"Well," Berlin said with an evil laugh, "we'll have plenty to eat after tomorrow."

"Why not go an' get it now?" Dan Gilbert asked.

Berlin glanced at the sky, where dark clouds roiled over the peaks to the north. " 'Cause it's gonna be dark soon, an' it looks like there's another storm on the way. I wouldn't want you men to get lost if a blizzard hits," he said.

Jesus Santiago shivered and flapped his arms around his chest. "Me, I'm getting very tired of this cold," he complained, glancing at the sky.

"I tell you what, Jesus," Berlin said roughly. "If you're tired of the weather, we can send you back to Utah. I'm sure the warden still has your old cell kept nice and warm for you."

Santiago grinned, showing a gleaming gold tooth in his

Smoke jumped down off his horse and pulled his Sharps fifty-caliber rifle out of his saddle boot in one swift motion.

Pearlie grabbed his binoculars out of his saddlebag and put them to his eyes. "Looks like they got the drop on the Morrows, Smoke," he said.

He could see five men with guns drawn, covering a man and a woman on the porch, who stood with their hands in the air. Lying flat on his face on the porch was another man, who looked like he'd been shot.

Smoke eared back the hammer on the Sharps and flopped down on his stomach in the snow.

He took careful aim, remembering what Preacher had taught him about shooting at a distance when the targets were downhill.

He raised the vernier sight on top of the rifle and adjusted the range to a thousand yards, raising his head to feel which way the wind was blowing before sighting in on the man in the front of the group.

While he was doing that, Cal and Pearlie, who'd remained in their saddles, pulled Winchester rifles out of their saddle boots and jacked shells into the chambers.

"I'm going to take out the lead man," Smoke said. "As soon as I fire, you two hightail it down toward the ranch house. I may be able to get another one or two before you get in range. As soon as you start firing, I'll get up on Joker and join you."

"You think you can get them 'fore they kill the Morrows?" Pearlie asked.

"I don't know," Smoke said, "but it's their only chance, so here goes. . . ."

He gently squeezed the trigger. The big fifty-caliber rifle exploded, kicking back and turning Smoke halfway around as flame and smoke erupted from the barrel.

As soon as he fired, Cal and Pearlie leaned over their saddle horns and kicked their mounts forward. They rode as Smoke had taught them, reins in their mouths, steering their horses with their knees as they brought their rifles up to their shoulders.

With Smoke's shot, the man in the front of the group was knocked off his horse as if he'd been hit by a cannonball, arms flailing, hat flying.

The other men on horseback looked wildly around to see where the shot had come from as Smoke, without waiting, jacked another shell into the Sharps and took aim again.

When the outlaw was blown off his horse, Jim Morrow whirled around and shoved his wife through the door of their cabin, diving after her as fast as he could.

One of the outlaws snapped a shot at him, hitting him in the back of his left shoulder and driving him to the floor just inside the door.

Bess Morrow reached down and grabbed him by the shirt, dragging him inside and slamming the door just as more bullets pocked the wood of the door frame.

Smoke's second shot was low, missing the man he aimed at but hitting his horse in the chest, knocking it to its knees as blood spurted from its hide.

By then, Cal and Pearlie were in range, and began to fire and load and fire again as fast as they could, peppering the group of outlaws with .44-caliber slugs.

Two more men were hit, flying off their mounts to lie dying in the snow.

In the barn, Blue Owl was busily loading sacks of supplies and sides of beef on the back of a packhorse when he heard the booming explosion of the Sharps.

"Goddamnit!" he exclaimed. "What now?"

He ran to the door of the barn and saw three of his men down, the others trying to stay in their saddles as their mounts crow-hopped and jumped around, frightened by the gunfire.

"Shit!" Blue Owl said, running back into the barn and jumping into his saddle, grabbing the dally rope of the packhorse and galloping off toward the mountain, trying to keep the barn between him and the attackers as he raced for their camp.

Smoke swung onto Joker's back, stuffing the Sharps into his saddle boot as he urged the big stud down the hill.

The lone remaining outlaw on horseback leaned over his saddle horn and made tracks away from the cabin, while the man on the downed horse struggled to his feet and began to fire his pistol at Cal and Pearlie as they rode toward him.

The cabin door opened and Bess Morrow stepped out on the porch, a long-barreled shotgun cradled in her arms.

She leveled the scattergun at the outlaw's back and let go with both barrels.

He was thrown facedown in the snow, cut almost in two by the buckshot in her loads, dead in his boots.

Pearlie slowed Cold to a stop, took careful aim with his Winchester, and fired.

The man on horseback straightened, flung his arms out to the side, and toppled off his mount onto the ground, a hole in the middle of his back.

By the time Smoke got to the house, it was all over. Five men lay dead or dying in the snow in front of the ranch house.

He looked up in time to see a distant figure, trailing a packhorse, disappear into the pine trees on the mountain slope north of the house.

Cal whirled around, breathing heavily from his ride. "You want me to go after him, Smoke?" he asked, inclining his head toward the man riding off.

Smoke shook his head. "No, he's got too big a lead, Cal. Besides, we can use his tracks to lead us to the gang's hideout."

Bess Morrow, seeing all the outlaws down, turned and went back inside the house.

Smoke and Cal and Pearlie followed her in. On the way, Pearlie knelt by the man on the porch to check him.

He glanced up as Smoke walked by. "He's had it, Smoke."

Smoke nodded and opened the door. Bess was kneeling

next to her husband, wrapping her apron around his bleeding shoulder.

She glanced up. "Smoke Jensen," she said, "you're a sight for sore eyes!"

"Howdy, Mrs. Morrow," he said, stepping to her side. "Is Jim going to be all right?"

Jim Morrow groaned and rolled on his side, sticking his right hand out toward Smoke. "I want to thank you for what you did, Smoke," he said. "If you and your men hadn't showed up, we'd've been goners for sure."

Smoke tilted his head toward the front porch. "I'm sorry about your man. He's dead," Smoke said.

Bess shook her head, tears in her eyes. "Good ol' Hank," she said. "He tried to draw on them men, never mind the odds."

Smoke bent and examined the wound on Jim's shoulder. "You're lucky, Jim. Looks like the bullet passed through clean without hitting the bone.

"Cal, Pearlie, help me get him onto the bed," Smoke said.

Once Jim Morrow was situated on the bed, his head propped up by pillows, Bess wiped her hands on her skirt.

"You boys gonna go after that galoot?" she asked.

"Not tonight," Smoke said. "It'd be too easy for him to ambush us in the dark by the time we got up onto the mountain. I'd rather give him time to get to the outlaws' camp and think he's safe."

He glanced out the window. "Besides, we need to help you bury Hank, and clean up that mess in your front yard."

She nodded. "I'd appreciate the help with Hank," she said. Then her voice got hard. "As far as that other trash, you can just haul their bodies up the hill a ways and let the wolves and coyotes have 'em."

Thirty-two

After Dan Gilbert and Blue Owl took their men and left the camp to go and get Jim Morrow's supplies, Ozark Jack Berlin joined his men around the campfire for some coffee mixed with whiskey to ward off the chill.

Berlin glanced around the group sitting or standing near the fire. There were fourteen, counting himself, left in camp. "Damn," he muttered to himself, thinking the loss of Sam Cook and his men and the four Blue Owl lost in Big Rock was whittling down his gang from more than thirty to less than twenty.

He smiled to himself grimly. If this keeps up, he thought, we won't need near so much grub to get through the winter, and the gold we steal will go a lot further.

Wiley Gottlieb walked over to stand next to Berlin. "Jack," he said, glancing over his shoulder at a group of men huddled near the fire.

"Yeah?"

"The men are gettin' kind'a restless, just sitting around here trying to keep their fingers from freezing off. What say we make a little run around the area today and see if we can find something to do?"

Berlin looked up at him. "Something to do? You mean, somebody to rob an' kill?"

Gottlieb grinned slyly. "The men need a little excitement, Jack. Otherwise, 'fore too long, they're gonna be at each other's throats."

Berlin thought about it for a few minutes. Gottlieb was

right. These were not the sort of men to stay idle too long before their natural aggressiveness began to cause trouble in the camp.

"You're right, Wiley," Berlin said, getting to his feet and dusting the seat of his pants off. "Tell the men to saddle up. We're goin' huntin'."

Three hours later, after following winding mountain trails that cut back and forth across the side of the mountain, Berlin raised his hand to bring his band to a halt.

Down the trail in front of them were three small cabins made of logs and chalked with mud in the chinks between the logs.

The cabins were by the side of a small, bubbling stream that ran down the side of the mountain. About a quarter mile up the slope, a hole could be seen cut in the rock of the mountain, with some wooden steps arranged on the steepest part of the slope.

Berlin pointed at the cabins, then at the hole in the rock. "Looks like we found us a mine, boys." He grinned as he looked from one to the other. "Let's hope these miners have had a good run of luck this year . . . 'cause their luck is gonna take a sudden turn for the worse.

"Get down off your mounts an' spread out. We'll go in on foot. These miners have been known to not take kindly to somebody takin' their gold," Berlin ordered as he stepped out of his saddle.

Berlin took a Henry rifle from his saddle boot and levered a shell into the chamber, then, crouching, began to walk down the trail toward the cabins.

Behind him, his men spread out and filtered into the piney woods on either side of the trail, guns drawn, grinning at the prospect of both action and gold.

When Berlin was fifty yards from the first cabin, the door opened and a man with a bushy, black beard walked out and moved toward the stream, a coffeepot in his hands.

He was dressed in the canvas pants favored by miners who spend a lot of time on their knees, and when he got to the stream, he squatted next to the water. As he bent over and began to fill the coffeepot, Tony Cassidy stepped from behind a pine tree and shot him in the face.

When Cassidy's gun exploded, four more men ran from the cabins, and three came out of the mine on the mountainside.

The outlaws opened fire, dropping the men before they had time to get off more than a couple of wild shots.

As the smoke, which hung in the air like ground fog, began to clear, Berlin reloaded his Henry and walked toward the cabins.

"Get their guns an' ammunition, men. Then we'll check out the cabins to see where they hid their gold."

An hour later, Berlin and his men stepped from the cabins. They'd found six pounds of gold dust and nuggets hidden beneath the bunk beds in the houses. Another ten ounces was still in the mine where it'd just been dug up.

Berlin bounced a canvas sack of dust in his hand, grinning. "Not a bad mornin's work, huh, boys?" he asked, looking around at his men.

As he looked, he noticed a figure sitting on a horse on top of a ridge above the mine, several hundred yards away.

Berlin quickly shielded his eyes and glared up the slope at the man. The man appeared to be dressed in buckskins, and was sitting on a paint pony, a long rifle cradled in his arms. He had some sort of fur hat on his head, and he was glaring down at the outlaws.

Berlin pointed at the man and hollered, "Hey, you!"

As the outlaw gang all turned to look, the man shook his head and slowly rode out of sight without looking back.

"What the hell?" Moses Johnson asked, his eyes wide. "You think that was a spook, Boss?"

Berlin shook his head, a curious look on his face. "Naw.

Probably an old mountain man. I've heard there are still some of 'em up in these parts."

"You think we ought'a go after him?" Billy Bartlett asked, his hand dropping to the butt of his pistol.

Berlin shook his head. "No. From what I hear, those old coots tend to mind their own business. It's a wonder we even seen him."

Spotted Dog looked worried. "If we saw him, Jack, it is because he wanted us to see him. My people say the mountain men can become invisible if they wish."

"What?" Moses asked, his mouth open.

"It is true," Spotted Dog persisted. "I have been in camp with my people when a mountain man walked right past our fires without anyone seeing him. We only knew he'd been there by his tracks the next morning."

"That's bullshit, Dog," Berlin said. "He's just an old man who's outlived his usefulness. He won't give us any trouble."

Spotted Dog shook his head, his face a mask of fear. "I hope not, Jack. The sort of trouble a mountain man gives you is usually fatal."

"Come on, boys," Berlin said, trying to lighten the mood. "Let's get on back to camp with our gold. Blue Owl and the others ought to be there soon, so we can put on the feed bag and have ourselves a little party tonight."

The men walked back up the trail to their horses. As they climbed in the saddle, Spotted Dog looked over his shoulder up the mountain where the strange man had been seen. He shivered as he thought he saw a shadow moving among the trees and bushes there, as if it were following them.

Thirty-three

Once Hank was buried, the outlaws' bodies were moved away from the Morrows' ranch house, and Jim's wound was treated, Bess Morrow insisted on fixing some fresh food for Smoke and the boys to take on their quest after the gang.

She handed a large sack of fresh-fried chicken to Pearlie with a wink. "I've seen the way you eat, son, so I know you'll take good care of this little snack."

Pearlie opened the sack, took a deep sniff, and rolled his eyes as if he were in heaven. "Yes, ma'am, you can be sure of that," Pearlie said, carefully rolling the top of the sack over to keep the chicken fresh and putting it reverently in his saddlebags.

Cal looked at Pearlie, "You know, Pearlie, that there chicken is for *all* of us, not just for you."

Pearlie gave him a look. "Of course, Cal, an' if you're a good lad, I may share the neck and wings with you."

Smoke took Bess's hand. "Are you sure you and Jim will be all right if we leave?"

"Smoke, you don't live on a ranch twenty miles from nowhere without learning how to care for a little old bullet wound. We'll be fine." She narrowed her eyes. "You just find those . . . outlaws and give them what they got coming for what they did to Hank. I know he'll rest easier knowing they ain't gonna get away with what they done."

"You can count on that, Bess," Smoke said, climbing

up on Joker. He tipped his hat. "Give my best to Jim. We'll check back in on you on our way back to the Sugarloaf."

"Good luck, boys," Bess said, waving as they rode off up the slope of the mountainside, following the tracks Blue Owl had left when he'd hightailed it away from the ranch the day before.

Four hours later, when they were well within the thick pine and maple forest of the mountain, Smoke slowed Joker and said, "I guess it's about time we took our nooning."

"I thought you'd never say that," Pearlie said. "That chicken's been callin' to me for the past five miles."

Smoke ground-reined the horses and walked over into a small copse of maple trees, where the branches had kept the snowfall to a minimum.

"Gather up some wood for the fire, Pearlie. No need to eat a cold lunch when we've got plenty of time."

After the fire was going, using dry wood at Smoke's suggestion so it wouldn't smoke so much as to give their position away, Smoke melted some snow for the coffee and heated up some beans in a skillet to go with the chicken. Cal found a sack of day-old biscuits and put them in a pan to steam them soft.

Once the water was boiling for the coffee, Smoke added a couple of handfuls of coffee grounds to the mixture, causing a wonderful aroma to percolate into the air.

He raised his head and said in a loud voice, "If the smell of that coffee doesn't bring you into camp, nothing will, Bear Tooth."

Pearlie and Cal looked up from where they squatted next to the fire.

"Bear Tooth?" Cal asked. "Is he out there?"

Smoke grinned. "He's been dogging our trail for the past two hours. Didn't you notice?"

Thirty-four

Ozark Jack Berlin was in the main cabin at the hot springs camp, counting out and weighing the gold they'd stolen from the miners. He was grinning, and the men surrounding him were laughing with delight at the fortune they'd managed to accumulate since their escape from prison.

"Boys," he said, a wide smile on his face as he glanced around at the men in the cabin, "we're gonna live like kings in Mexico on this loot."

Jack McGraw, who was standing near the window to the cabin, uttered an oath. "Uh-oh, Boss," he said in his gravely voice. "You ain't gonna like this."

"What is it, Jack?" Berlin said, frowning. "I'm busy countin' our money here."

"Looks like Blue Owl's back," McGraw said. "An' he's all by himself."

"What?" Berlin said, jumping to his feet and hurrying out the door.

"Where the hell are the rest of the boys?" he asked, anger deep in his voice at the sight of Blue Owl sitting on his horse alone.

Blue Owl swung down out of the saddle and handed the reins of the packhorse carrying the supplies from the Morrow ranch to Billy Bartlett.

"I suspect they're coyote food by now," Blue Owl said, his face grim.

"What the hell happened?" Berlin asked, striding over

to stand next to the Indian. "You and five men couldn't handle a couple of old farts an' a woman?"

"I need a drink," Blue Owl said, walking over to the campfire and pouring some coffee into a mug, to which he added a generous supply of whiskey from a bottle in his vest pocket.

"Goddamnit! Tell me what happened," Berlin shouted.

"We was doing all right," Blue Owl began after taking a deep swallow of the whiskey and coffee. "Had the hired hand down and had the old man and his wife covered, when all of a sudden, out of the blue, somebody started shooting the men right out of their saddles."

"Who?" Berlin asked. "There wasn't but the three of them at the ranch."

Blue Owl shrugged. "Don't know for certain," he said, "but it sure looked like that gunslick Smoke Jensen to me."

"You let one man shoot up the lot of you?"

Blue Owl shook his head. "Not one man. He had two other gents with him, and they was right handy with their rifles. Jensen must've been six hundred yards or more away when he shot the first two, then those other boys rode down on us hell-bent for leather, shooting as they rode. They took out the rest."

"How'd you manage to get away during all this?" Wiley Gottlieb asked suspiciously.

"I was back in the barn, loading up the pack animal with the supplies we went there for. When I saw the boys dropping like flies, I lit out and never looked back."

"And they didn't come after you?" Berlin asked, his face thoughtful.

Blue Owl shook his head. "They were too busy with the Morrows, I guess. Like I said, we killed the hired hand and wounded the ranch man. They must've stayed behind to take care of them."

"And all of the others were killed?" McGraw asked, shaking his head.

"They sure looked dead to me, unless you can live with a hole in your chest and your head blown off."

Berlin took a deep breath, trying to calm himself. "Well, at least you got the supplies."

"Yeah, but it cost us five men to do it," Gottlieb observed drily.

Berlin tried to make the best of it. "Course, that means the gold we got will go further."

"What gold?" Blue Owl asked.

Berlin threw his arm around Blue Owl's shoulders. "Come on in the cabin and rest up while I tell you about it."

"Uh, Jack," Wiley Gottlieb said, "maybe we ought'a post some guards around the camp, just in case those shooters decide to follow Blue Owl here."

"That's a good idea, Wiley. Why don't you take care of it while I show Blue Owl our gold?"

Smoke and Cal and Pearlie followed Bear Tooth in single file up the side of the mountain, taking trails that were almost invisible to the naked eye, trails that only a man who lived on the mountain would know about.

"I'm gonna take you up the back way to the springs," Bear Tooth called over his shoulder. "That way, if'n they're smart enough to post lookouts, they won't see us comin'."

"There's no need to hurry," Smoke replied. "I don't plan to do anything until after dark anyway."

"Moon won't set till midnight or so," Bear Tooth said, glancing at the sky, "an' it appears there's another storm on the way."

Cal and Pearlie looked up, and seeing no clouds in the sky, they looked at Smoke. "How's he know that?" Pearlie asked. "I don't see no storm clouds."

Smoke smiled. "He can smell it, and so can I. When snow's on the way, the air has a different smell to it, kind'a damp and stingy to the nose."

Cal and Pearlie both sniffed loudly through their noses. "I don't smell nothin'," Cal said.

"You spend enough time up here, you will," Bear Tooth replied without looking back.

Just after sunset, Bear Tooth reined in his pony. "Whoa, Buck. This looks like a good enough place to make camp."

"How much farther?" Cal asked.

Bear Tooth shook his head. "Not too far, little beaver, but we want to camp on this side of the slope so's we can make a fire without bein' seen by those men. That is, unless you wanna make a cold camp?"

Cal shook his head. "No, sir," he said. "I'm 'bout frozen clear through. I need some hot coffee."

"Don't call me sir nor mister, young'un. Name's Bear Tooth, or just Bear."

"Yes, sir . . . uh, I mean, all right, Bear," Cal said, hurrying off his horse and beginning to gather wood for the fire.

Bear Tooth grinned and winked at Smoke. "They know 'bout not gettin' no green wood?"

Smoke nodded. "Yes, they've learned that much at least."

"Good. Now, I'll show 'em how to build a fire 'tween some rocks so the smoke don't go straight up an' signal our enemies where we are."

"While you do that, I'll get the grub ready," Smoke said, smiling to himself at the valuable lessons the boys were going to learn from the old mountain man.

Soon, Bear Tooth had a fire going up next to several boulders where the smoke was funneled in several different directions and couldn't be seen from more than a dozen yards away.

"Now, young'uns," he said, dumping a double handful of coffee grounds into the pot, "as far as makin' good coffee goes, if it's not thick enough to float a horseshoe, it's too weak."

"Hell," Pearlie said, "we won't need cups for that. We can just spoon it outta the pot."

Smoke flipped Bear Tooth something. "Here, Bear Tooth," he said.

"What's that, Smoke?" Cal asked.

"I saved some egg shells from this morning's breakfast."

"You put 'em in the pot to settle the grounds, boy," Bear Tooth said to Cal. "What are you, a pilgrim?"

"Miss Sally says cold water does just as good," Pearlie observed.

"Yeah, but that waters down the brew, boys, an' up here you need coffee strong enough to keep the winter chill off."

"You have any secrets for beans?" Cal asked as he stirred the skillet.

"Only that you can't cook 'em too long," Bear Tooth said. "That, an' a couple'a pieces of fatback, helps give 'em a right nice flavor."

"All right," Cal said, and reached into the saddlebags to get some bacon out. He sliced off a generous chunk and placed it in the skillet with the beans.

"We're gonna have you boys eatin' like mountain men 'fore this trip is over, ain't we, Smoke?"

Smoke laughed. "If we do that, it'll spoil them for any other food," he said.

After they finished supper, the men sat around the fire. Cal and Pearlie and Smoke made cigarettes while Bear Tooth enjoyed one of the cigars Smoke had brought him.

"Do you remember the springs well enough to draw us a map of the area?" Smoke asked Bear Tooth.

The mountain man nodded, took a stick, and began to draw in the snow next to him. "It's a circular valley," he said, "surrounded on three sides by sheer cliffs goin' straight up. There's an' openin' on the south where the trail enters it, an' a smaller one on the north where the stream enters that feeds the springs," he said, making the appropriate marks in the snow.

He made three X's near the line for the stream. "Right here's the three cabins the miners built."

"What about the caves?" Smoke asked.

Bear Tooth nodded, and made two more marks next to the cliffs. "They're right here, but I don't know nothin' much 'bout 'em, how deep they is an' such."

Cal glanced at the mountain man. "Didn't you ever use the caves as shelter?" he asked.

Bear Tooth shook his head. "Never cared much fer caves. If'n I can't see the stars, I get to feelin' trapped an' hemmed in."

Cal nodded as the mountain man continued. " 'Cept for the winter of sixty-six, I believe it was."

"What happened then?" Pearlie asked, leaning forward to pitch his cigarette butt in the fire.

" 'Twas the coldest winter I recollect," Bear Tooth said, leaning back and looking at the sky. "It was so cold, when you took a piss, you had to break it off 'cause it froze 'fore it hit the ground."

Smoke smiled, knowing another mountain-man tall tale was coming.

"Yep, that winter I decided to take refuge in a cave over on the north side of the mountain. Trouble is, an ol' bear had the same idee."

"Did you have to kill it?" Pearlie asked, wide-eyed.

"Hell, no," Bear Tooth replied. "It was so cold, we was both glad of the company. I just snuggled down to that old critter, and it wrapped its arms around me like an ol' squaw, an' we slept the winter through."

"Gosh," Cal said, "don't bears stink somethin' awful?"

Bear Tooth nodded. "Well, I must say, he was a mite gamy, but I'll tell you the truth, little beaver. I didn't think he'd take to kindly to me suggestin' he take a bath, so we both put up with the smell best we could."

Smoke and Pearlie laughed out loud; then Cal joined in when he realized the old man was having fun with him.

"Bear Tooth," Smoke said, "I haven't heard such a tall tale since Puma Buck was alive."

Bear Tooth looked offended. "You mean you don't believe me?" he asked.

"Is that the same year Puma talked about?" Smoke asked. "When it was so cold you had to thaw your words out in a skillet so's you could hear what the other men were saying?"

Bear Tooth smiled and shook his head. "No, now that sounds like somethin' Puma would've said. That man never told the truth a day in his life." He hesitated. "But it was the year I had a campfire freeze on me one night. Damn thing didn't start burnin' again till the next day when the sun came out an' the temperature rose to fifty below."

"On that note, I think I'll get some shut-eye," Smoke said, chuckling. "We've got to get up around midnight and ride over and take a look at the springs when the moon goes down."

"How're you gonna wake up when it's time?" Cal asked.

Bear Tooth looked at Cal as if he couldn't believe what he'd asked.

"You mean you haven't learned to wake up whenever you want yet?"

"Uh, no, sir . . . I mean, no, Bear."

"Why, you just set your mind to the time an' pretty soon, you'll just naturally get up when you're supposed to."

"Is that the truth, Smoke?" Cal asked.

"Maybe for Bear Tooth," Smoke replied, "but as for me, I'm gonna set this pocket watch Sally gave me. It'll ring a bell when midnight comes."

"Oh," Cal said.

"Cal, I swear you're dumber'n a rock," Pearlie said.

Bear Tooth shook his head. "Now you just wait an' see, boys. When that little trinket of Smoke's goes off, I'll be up an' waitin' for you."

Thirty-five

In spite of what he'd told Cal, Smoke woke up just before midnight, before the tiny alarm in his pocket watch had a chance to go off.

Like most mountain men, he came fully awake in seconds. One minute, he was sound asleep; the next, his eyes were open and checking his surroundings for danger before his body moved at all.

He turned his head and saw Bear Tooth, squatted next to a small, hat-sized fire among the boulders next to their camp. He had a pot of coffee warming on the coals of the fire, which was giving off no smoke whatsoever.

"Mornin', Smoke," the old man whispered, pouring an additional mug of coffee and handing it to Smoke when he crawled out of his sleeping blanket.

Smoke glanced at Cal and Pearlie, still snoring softly across the clearing.

"Time to wake the young'uns up," Bear Tooth said, inclining his head toward the sleeping men.

Smoke fished a couple of pine cones out of the snow and pitched them onto the sleeping bodies.

Cal and Pearlie snorted awake, both men instinctively going for their guns.

"Easy, boys," Bear Tooth growled with a smile. "Breakfast time."

Pearlie yawned and stretched. "Them's music to my ears, Bear," he said, his voice still husky with sleep.

Cal just groaned and rubbed his eyes as Smoke handed them both steaming mugs of coffee.

Pearlie glanced around at the fire. "I don't see no breakfast cookin'," he said.

"You're drinkin' it, beaver," Bear Tooth said.

Smoke finished his coffee and walked over to Joker. He took several pair of moccasins out of his saddlebags and threw them over to Cal and Pearlie. "Here, put these on," he said.

"Moccasins?" Cal asked.

"Yes, we're gonna be going right up to the outlaw camp," Smoke said. "I don't want any spurs or sounds of leather on wood or stone to alert them to our presence."

He took one of the tins of bootblack out of his saddlebag and smeared some on his face before passing the tin to the boys.

"How 'bout Bear Tooth?" Pearlie asked. "Doesn't he need some of this?"

Smoke shook his head. "No, that beard of his is black enough to keep his face hidden in the dark."

"What's the plan, Smoke?" Bear Tooth asked. "I mean, are we gonna show these dogs any mercy?"

Smoke shook his head. "No quarter, no mercy. There'll be no prisoners taken by us this trip. These bastards have already escaped from one prison, and it cost a lot of good people their lives." He patted the butt of his revolver. "I think we'll rely on Mr. Colt for all the justice these sons of bitches deserve."

Bear Tooth nodded, a grim smile on his face. "Good. I never was one for tellin' a man to put his hands up."

"If you can get us up on the cliffs overlooking the outlaws' camp," said Smoke, "the first thing we'll have to do is take out any sentries they have posted."

"Won't they hear the gunshots?" Cal asked.

Smoke shook his head and pulled out his Bowie knife. "No, 'cause we're not going to shoot them." He passed the blade next to his throat in explanation.

Pearlie began to build a cigarette, but Bear Tooth shook

his head. "Uh-uh, son," he said gently, "not 'fore battle
We don't want the smell of tabaccy on us when we're
sneakin' up on a man."

Pearlie glanced at the mountain man, wondering if he
was going to go without his smelly bearskin coat, but de
cided not to say anything.

Smoke squatted next to the fire, addressing his men
"Now, when we get to the camp, we're gonna have to spli
up and each take a different side of the valley. In case
things go to hell and there's a commotion, we'll each make
our way back to this camp, so be sure and pay attention
on the way up so's you can find your way back down here
in the dark."

"What if one of us gets in trouble?" Cal asked.

Smoke stared into Cal's eyes. "This is war, Cal, and we're
all on our own. We could all get killed rushing in to try
and save another and the outlaws would win."

Bear Tooth nodded. "So, be careful an' get the job done
right the first time. Don't go gettin' softhearted an' ever
think of givin' the man you're after an even break, 'cause
thinkin' like that'll get you killed."

"Now, after the sentries are all taken out, I'm going to
pay the camp itself a little visit," said Smoke.

"You're goin' down there alone?" Pearlie asked
"Why?"

"Because there's nothing that makes a man more ner
vous than waking up and finding his friend lying next to
him with his throat cut and his scalp gone." Smoke
grinned through bared teeth. "Makes sleeping the nex
night awfully hard, and sleepy, tired men don't think of
fight too well."

They left their horses behind and made their way up
the mountain toward the outlaws' camp on foot, to mini
mize any sound they might make. Smoke carried on his
back a large burlap bag of surprises for the outlaws.

The storm Bear Tooth had predicted began with a light snowfall, but thankfully, the wind stayed down and the temperature didn't drop too much.

"This is good," Bear Tooth whispered over his shoulder to the men following him. "The new snowfall will cushion our feet an' keep the noise down."

Once they got to the top of the trail, he squatted and pointed across the mountainside.

"The valley of the springs is right over there, past that clump of trees."

"You make out any of the sentries?" Smoke whispered.

Bear Tooth nodded, pointing again.

A bright orange speck of light could be seen off to one side where one of the sentries was smoking a cigarette.

Bear Tooth shifted his weight and pointed off in another direction, where a dark figure could be seen outlined against the lighter darkness of the sky.

"I'll take the one on the left," Smoke said. "Pearlie, you take the one on the right."

"What about me?" Cal asked.

"You go with Bear Tooth and circle around to the other side of the valley. There'll probably be a couple more over there."

Walking on the soles of his feet in a low crouch, Smoke moved as silently as the wind toward the sentry, who had finished his cigarette and was leaning back against the bole of a tree, trying to stay out of the falling snow.

Smoke slipped his knife out of its scabbard and eased up to the far side of the tree. When he heard the man yawn, he moved quickly in front of him, slashing backhanded with the Bowie knife.

The razor-sharp blade severed throat, trachea, and carotid arteries as easily as if they were made of soft butter.

The only sound the man made was a soft gurgle as he strangled on his own blood. Smoke caught him when he toppled, and laid his dead body gently in the snow. After looking at it for a moment, he grinned as a thought occurred to him. He bent and quickly arranged the body so it was sitting with its back against the tree. He put the man's hat on his head and lowered the brim so it looked like he was sleeping.

"Someone's gonna get a big surprise when they try and wake him up," Smoke said to himself.

Pearlie's job wasn't so easy. His man was standing out in the open, with no nearby cover for Pearlie to use in his approach.

Pearlie considered throwing his knife, but decided not to because if he didn't get a clean kill, the man might be able to shout a warning or get a shot off.

Finally, an idea occurred to him. He searched until he found a fist-sized rock, and heaved it over the man's head. When it landed on the side of the sentry away from Pearlie, the man grabbed his rifle and turned in that direction.

Pearlie took several running steps and was on the man before he had time to react. Pearlie's knife entered the man's back just below the ribs on the left, at an upward angle as Smoke had taught him. The point went through spleen and diaphragm on its way to savage the man's heart. Pearlie's left arm was around his neck so he couldn't cry out as he died.

The only sound was the slight noise the man's rifle made when it fell to the ground. Pearlie dragged his body into the bushes and covered it with fallen tree limbs and snow. Then he made his way to the edge of the cliff overlooking the camp to see what was going to happen next.

Bear Tooth and Cal found only one sentry on their side of the valley. Once Cal had pointed the man out, Bear Tooth nodded at Cal to go get him.

Cal, surprised and delighted that the mountain man trusted him, pulled his skinning knife from its scabbard and moved quietly toward the man, who was bent over building a cigarette.

Cal was shorter than the sentry, even bent over, as he slipped up behind him and tapped him on the shoulder.

When the man grunted in surprise and whirled around, Cal swung his hand in an uppercut with the point of his knife pointed at the sky. The knife entered the man's throat just under his jaw and drove upward to lodge in his hard palatte, pinning his tongue so he couldn't make a sound.

When the man struggled, both hands at his throat, Cal grunted and pushed harder, driving the knife blade upward into the man's brain, killing him instantly.

Cal had to put his foot on the man's head to get his knife out of the man's skull.

When Bear Tooth walked up, Cal asked him, "Why'd you let me do that?"

Bear Tooth grinned and whispered, "Since the rheumatiz has hit my legs, my knees pop somethin' fierce when I walk. I didn't want the sound to give us away."

"Oh," Cal said, wiping his blade on the dead man's shirt.

Bear Tooth squatted, and sure enough, the sound of his knees cracking was like a twig breaking. He pulled out a knife that was so long it was almost a machete, and proceeded to scalp the dead man.

The sight made Cal's stomach roll, so he turned away and looked down into the camp while the mountain man finished his grisly work.

Smoke had no trouble following his sentry's tracks back down the trail leading to the camp in the valley. The outlaws' campfire had burned itself down to just coals, so there was very little light to give him away as he scurried across the open space toward the cabins.

All of the outlaws were sleeping in the cabins, and none were outside where Smoke could get to them. He stood there a moment, undecided if he should take the chance of going into one of the cabins, when his eyes fell on several empty whiskey bottles lying next to the fire.

He smiled to himself, knowing if they'd been drinking that much, sooner or later one would have to come outside to relieve himself.

He walked to the back of one of the cabins and found what he was looking for, a small outhouse twenty yards from the cabin.

He stepped behind it and settled down to wait.

Fifteen minutes later, the door to the cabin opened and a man stumbled toward the outhouse, coughing and trying to clear phlegm out of his throat.

Smoke waited for him to get inside and get his pants down. Then he jerked the door open and drove his knife in the man's heart where he sat.

Then Smoke made a quick slice around the man's skull and yanked his scalp off, leaving his bloody skull bone exposed.

Once that was done, Smoke took a bundle of four sticks of dynamite he'd tied together and walked back to the fire. Brushing aside the snow a few feet away, he buried the dynamite, leaving a four-foot length of fuse. He put the end of the fuse near a half-burned log on the fire and covered it with snow mixed with mud. When the outlaws built up the fire the next morning, they were going to be in for a surprise.

Smoke then walked to where the outlaws' horses were grouped in a makeshift corral in the corner of the valley. He opened the gates and walked among them, shooing them out so they'd wander off during the night. He knew some would stay put, but others would walk off in search of grass to graze on, leaving many of the outlaws afoot.

Figuring he'd done enough for one night, he climbed back up the trail and headed back to their camp.

He'd heard no outcries, so he knew Cal and Pearlie and Bear Tooth had done their jobs to perfection.

Thirty-six

Once they'd all made it back to their camp, Smoke told them, "We've got time for about three hours sleep. Then we need to be on the cliffs overlooking the camp when they wake up."

Just before dawn, Bear Tooth filled eight canteens with fresh coffee and handed two to each of the men. "You're gonna need this *cafecito* to keep you alert," he said. "It figgers to be a long day."

Smoke handed each of the men a sack filled with bundles of dynamite sticks with short fuses. He then handed them each a cigar. "Light these when you see the outlaws stirring," he said. "Use them for the fuses, but be careful. You'll only have about fifteen seconds after the fuse is lit before it goes off."

"Try for the cabins first," Bear Tooth advised. "That way they won't have no cover to hide behind once the shootin' starts."

"And remember, you'll be shooting downhill," Smoke said, "so aim a little low; otherwise, you'll overshoot your targets."

He nodded at Bear Tooth. "Bear, you take Pearlie with you. I'll take Cal with me. That way, we'll have them surrounded."

"Smoke," Pearlie said, "make sure you tell Cal to keep

his damn head down. I'm gettin' tired of pickin' lead outta his carcass."

"You do the same, Pearlie," Cal advised. "I'd hate to have to eat all those bear sign Miss Sally makes by myself. I'd get big as a horse."

Bear Tooth laughed. "I'll say one thing 'bout these young beavers of your'n, Smoke. They don't scare easy."

"They've been to the river and back a few times, Bear. They'll handle themselves all right, take my word for it."

By the time the sun began to lighten the sky to the east, Smoke and his band were ensconced on all sides of the valley.

Smoke showed Cal how to lay his ammunition out in a line on one side next to where he lay, so as to be able to grab it and reload in a minimum of time. The bundles of dynamite were similarly laid out on the other side within easy reach. The cigar was to be lit at the first sign of movement below.

Ozark Jack Berlin came out of his cabin and stretched, checking the sky to see what the weather was going to be.

The storm of the night before had passed, and the sky was orange and purple with the first light of day.

"Good, no snow," he muttered to himself, thinking how glad he was going to be to get to Mexico, where the sun was as hot as the *señoritas,* and where the tequila flowed like water.

He walked over to the fire, which was down to a few smoldering coals. He threw some fresh wood on the coals, placed a pot of water next to them, and walked toward the outhouse.

As he walked, he glanced up at the cliffs overlooking the valley, wondering where the sentries were. They usually were the first in line for coffee after a night standing guard.

"Lazy bastards probably sleepin'," he muttered as he opened the door to the outhouse.

"Goddamn!" he almost shouted, seeing the bloody mess of one of his men sitting on the board over the shit-pit.

He whirled, reaching for his pistol, realizing something was terribly wrong. As he ran toward his cabin, he looked to the side, and saw only three horses standing near the open corral gate. The others were all gone.

"Son of a bitch," he yelled, pulling his pistol and firing once in the air to wake up his men.

Within minutes the cabin doors opened and men boiled out into the early morning sun, some still in long underwear with their pants around their knees as they tried to get dressed on the run.

"What the hell's going on?" Blue Owl shouted, running toward Berlin with his rifle in his hands.

Just as Berlin got next to the now-roaring fire, he saw a trail of fire burning away from the coals toward the snow.

"What the hell?" he thought, then realized it was a fuse.

"Hit the dirt!" he shouted, and dove facedown in the snow twenty feet from the fire.

The dynamite went off with a loud explosion, sending logs and burning wood in all directions.

Billy Bartlett, nearest to the fire, was blown fifteen feet in the air, a piece of burning pine log protruding from his chest and his face blown off down to the bone.

Jack McGraw's left arm was shredded by wooden splinters, spinning him around and throwing him against the cabin wall.

A loud, booming explosion from Smoke's Sharps sounded from above. Wiley Gottlieb was knocked to his knees, a hole the size of a bucket in his chest from front to back. He had time to glance down at it before his eyes clouded over and he toppled over onto his face.

Another explosion from Bear Tooth's Big Fifty sounded, and Jesus Santiago's right leg was blown completely off just above the knee, causing the Mexican to begin to scream in Spanish as he thrashed around on the ground trying to staunch the spurting stream of crimson from his stump.

Berlin rolled to the side just as the snow where he'd been was pocked by several shots from Cal's Winchester. Berlin scrambled to his feet, firing wildly upward without aiming as he ran full out toward one of the caves.

Tony Cassidy ran in a low crouch toward one of the horses near the corral, firing as he ran. He vaulted up on the bronc's back and kicked its flanks, trying to get to the head of the valley.

Pearlie calmly aimed and fired, his bullet taking the outlaw square between his shoulder blades, throwing him over the horse's head to tumble and roll several times. He died from a broken neck before he bled to death from the bullet hole.

Joe Wyatt aimed his rifle at the cliff tops and fired as fast as he could lever shells into the chamber, spinning on his heels trying to get a clear shot.

Cal ended his life by shooting him in the face, tearing his jaw off and ripping a hole in his throat. He fell into what was left of the fire and began to burn.

The rest of the men ran back into the cabins, trying to get under cover, except for Blue Owl. He saw Berlin headed for the caves, and followed as fast as he could, running almost bent double to make a smaller target.

Bear Tooth took a shot at him with the Sharps, but the bullet missed by inches and tore a hole in the wall of the outhouse, hitting the dead man inside and decapitating him.

Smoke stood up where Bear and Pearlie could see him, and held a bundle of dynamite up for a second. Then he lit it from his cigar and made a long toss toward one of the cabins.

Cal followed suit, as did Bear Tooth and Pearlie.

Four bundles of dynamite hit at almost the same time. Bear Tooth's fell short, and did little damage other than blowing snow and mud and dirt into the air.

any luck, he'll last a couple of days before the wolves find him."

Bear Tooth put his arms around Cal and Pearlie's shoulders again as they turned to go.

"Let that be a lesson to you, boys. Don't never make a mountain man mad."

"Uh, Bear," Pearlie said, "about that coat . . ."